THREE OF THE BANDITS FANNED OUT BEFORE ETHAN, THE FOURTH STOOD TOWARD THE REAR. ETHAN AIMED CAREFULLY.

The first bullet cut a hole in the leader's temple, splattering scarlet blotches across the wall. Sagging to the floor, his left hand clutched the money in a deadly grip. His second shot struck the robber standing to the left of the teller's window. The thief's pistol fell as the bullet dug between his shoulder blades.

The third bandit, standing underneath the clock, turned and raised his head. Ethan's cold gray eyes met his.

Ethan's slug pierced the robber's chest, a muscle jerked and shoved his hand upward but not high enough. His lung split in half, he died as he dropped to the floor. He'd spent four seconds of the bank's time, earning his pay.

BULLETS DON'T CRY

WILLIAM BOYD

TOR

A TOM DOHERTY ASSOCIATES BOOK
NEW YORK

BULLETS DON'T CRY

Cover art by Carl Cassler

A Tor Book
Published by Tom Doherty Associates, Inc.
175 Fifth Avenue
New York, N.Y. 10010

Tor® is a registered trademark of Tom Doherty Associates, Inc.

ISBN: 0-812-52453-5

First edition: March 1994

Printed in the United States of America

0 9 8 7 6 5 4 3 2 1

To My Loving Partner, Nikki,
For Her Understanding

<u>Part 1</u>

It Was Like Old Times, Bad Old Times!

• 1 •

THREATENING THUNDERCLOUDS GATHERED
over the southern horizon. Flashes of pale green lightning brightened the ominous sky; surely Topeka's in-
habitants thought the imperishable morning sun had
changed its course.

Inside the First National Bank, Ethan Sands pressed
against the glass. Through the fine gray mist, his eyes
followed two pairs of riders. In yellow slickers, hats
pulled low, the strangers rode two abreast through
town, one pair from Main Street's north end, the other
from the south. The first pair tethered their mounts near
the bank's front door, while the second dismounted
across the street.

Ethan's eyes were distracted by a young woman, who
carried an umbrella in one hand and with the other
gathered up her skirt. A heavy beer wagon bounced in
a chuckhole and splashed mud over her face.

"Sands?" Ethan turned from the window toward Mr. Briggs's drawn face. "This morning I've got a lot of cash to deliver and I don't want it to stray into wrong hands, understand?"

"Yes, Mr. Briggs."

Briggs was worried, and the miserable weather didn't help. The bank's money had been safe and its continued welfare was naturally the owner's utmost concern.

Briggs walked to the door that separated the office from the main room. "Dammit, Sands, if you must, shoot to kill, and don't worry about it because I'll handle the law."

Aware of Ethan's peculiar qualifications, Marshal Dillman had given him the job of protecting the bank. After the Civil War, Ethan, young and bitter, had served his apprenticeship both as a lawman and riding with Lefty Bowman, Henry Starr's friend, until his publicized death in Dodge City when he was blasted by a shotgun in the face. Lefty had shortened his life by robbing a bank where the sheriff and two deputies doubled as tellers. The cold day he dug Lefty's grave, Ethan appraised a new career. The idea of earning a living by protecting money, with benefits of longevity and decency, weighed easily upon his mind. Later, enjoying a passable life, Ethan became renowned. Including the raw days with Lefty, he counted as his contribution a dozen graves scattered through Kansas, Oklahoma, and northern Texas.

Ethan pulled a gold watch from his vest. He saw the clerk pulling on his key chain while heading for the front door. Hot coffee in hand, Ethan, the bank's protector, climbed the balcony's stairs, slid back a chair from a pine desk, and seated himself. He drew his .45, checked the load, and placed it beside the cup.

From the balcony, he commanded a view of the bank's floor including the front door and the teller's windows. The bank clerk stood to one side as three customers entered the bank followed by four men in slickers.

Ethan spotted a member of Dirk Largo's gang. When the leader nodded to the others, they took positions to cover him. Ethan tabled the coffee and grabbed the .45. A strange thought raced through his mind: Mr. Briggs must have been tipped off.

•2•

THE LEADER APPROACHED the open window and smiled at the freckle-faced teller.

"Sonny, if'n ya don't want blood splashing your boots, fill the bag with cash and don't make me wait," he said in a falsetto twang. "Forget the drawer. I want the payroll money that's stacked in the vault, and son, don't open your mouth."

Responding to the robber's unusual voice, the teller, eyes fastened on the bandit's pistol, pointed at the vault's open door. Two customers stood at the counter filling out deposit slips, while a third waited for a teller to open another window. Dirk's gang had figured this job correctly except for one thing.

On the balcony above the floor, Ethan Sands aimed his Colt .45 directly at the leader's head. As the teller handed over a full sack, the leader turned.

Three of the bandits stood in an equal arc, the fourth

stood toward the rear. Ethan aimed carefully and squeezed the feathered trigger.

The first bullet cut a hole in the leader's temple, splattering scarlet blotches across the wall. Sagging to the floor, he clutched the money in a deadly grip. Ethan's second shot struck the robber standing to the left of the teller's window. The thief's pistol fell as the bullet dug between the shoulder blades.

The third bandit, standing underneath the clock, turned and raised his head. Ethan's cold gray eyes met his.

Ethan's slug pierced the robber's chest, a muscle jerked and shoved his hand upward but not high enough. His lung split in half, he died as he dropped to the floor. He'd spent four seconds of the bank's time, earning his pay.

The smell of gunpowder spread over the room as the fourth bandit, Dirk's son, Mace, realized the costly calculation and bolted for the door.

Ethan took a long stride across the balcony to the building's front, threw open the window, and saw Mace hurrying to his horse.

Mace rammed into an old lady standing beneath the roof's overhang. Petrified, the woman dropped her parcel, splattering eggs across the boardwalk and up her black high-button shoes.

Mace grabbed his reins and leaped into the saddle while above him, Ethan steadied the Colt in both hands and fired.

The .45's slug punctured Mace's esophagus. He dropped the reins and grasped his throat. Blood flowed down his neck onto his yellow slicker.

He slid backward over the left saddle skirt, landing on his back. Mace tried to focus on the mean Kansas sky, but his eyes rolled. Mace Largo lay still.

Inside the bank, the owner, George Briggs, rushed from

his office and grabbed the money sack from the leader's hand. Slowly rising, he eyed the white-faced teller.

"Fred, is that stink you?" Briggs asked.

The teller had his hand over his crotch. "Yes, sir. I got so scared I loaded ma pants!"

Briggs stood, fascinated by the dead man's face. His skin was so fair, Briggs thought, he must have shaved twice. The hat was pulled over the bandit's ears. Briggs pulled it off. He gasped when long black hair fell to the floor.

"Ma God," Briggs shouted, *"it's a woman!"*

With ten cents' worth of lead, the professional, Ethan Sands, had sent one female and three males to hell.

Briggs, stunned, looked up at Ethan who sat calmly drinking cold coffee. Ethan slid the .45 into its holster, tapped the butt, and headed down the stairs.

"Mr. Briggs, if you expect to do any business today, I'd get these stiffs out of here. Send someone for the undertaker. And out front there's a young fella hanging from his horse."

The tall, square-shouldered shooter drew his pistol, flipped open the chamber, and replaced four shells.

"Hold on a minute," Briggs said. "You know this woman?"

Ethan leaned over the body. "Face is familiar, but I'll be damned if I . . . wait a minute." He knelt beside the body. "That half-moon birthmark on the left cheek I've seen before but not on her. Somehow she's tied into Dirk's clan, but I'll be damned if I can remember how. Trouble is"—he paused and made a circling gesture with his hand—"her friends can't help us."

Briggs reached down and closed her eyes. "Maybe someone at the funeral parlor will recognize her. I'd like to have them buried right away."

•3•

FIFTEEN MINUTES LATER, the excitement had calmed. New customers arrived and gasped at the bodies until the undertakers collected the dead and carried them outside.

Ethan walked through the front door and leaned against the brick wall. He pulled the makings from his shirt pocket and rolled a cigarette. Striking a light on the wall, he held the burning match until it burnt his finger. The dead woman's face bothered him; he had a name on the tip of his tongue but it wouldn't come.

From where he stood, he could see that a crowd had gathered a block away from the bank in front of the undertaker's. Ethan strolled over. Stacked against the undertaker's wall, four coffins open from the waist displayed four reasons why Mr. Briggs paid Ethan Maxwell Sands so handsomely.

Decency said don't look, but for bystanders, morbid curiosity won. Four ghostly faces, a woman and three men, stared blankly back. Ethan hadn't come to brag or have people slap his back; praise wasn't his style. He was a just professional in a mortal trade.

Fingers tapped his shoulder. Swinging around, he stared into Nora's frightened face.

"Honey," he said, removing his hat, "what'n hell are you doing here?" He reached over and took her hand.

Nora pulled her cheek away when he tried to kiss her.

"What's wrong with you?"

"Take a look. There, that's what's wrong. Among others you've killed a *woman*!"

Nora flinched as a photographer's powder went off behind her.

"Ethan Sands, one of those dead faces could have been you. Had I married you, I'd be a widow, and that's not my idea of a lasting marriage."

He eased her aside. "C'mon, Nora, you know that's why the bank hired me. It's my job." He forced a smile.

"Job, my foot! What's sinful is it doesn't bother you. Easily as other men wash their hands, you kill! Lord knows you've buried enough. God, I've tried to understand you. Good Lord Ethan, why didn't you just arrest them? I heard you shot one of them in the back."

Ethan nestled her chin in his hand. "Nora, if I'd tried to reason with them, you're right, I'd be on a cooling board myself. When a man's paid to protect valuable goods, fighting fair—be it with fist, gun, knife, or teeth—is poppycock. And from a dead friend, I learned if you shoot a man in the back, he rarely returns fire."

She removed a small handkerchief from her purse

and wiped her eyes. "*Ethan, our marriage is off!* I'm leaving for Chicago to marry a man who wants to live. One who'll stay alive to love me."

"Nora, you don't mean what you're saying." Ethan tried to smile.

"You're wrong, I do!"

Leaving, she bumped the man who had just aimed his camera at Ethan's blank expression.

"Photographer, get a good picture, it may be his last."

The undertaker came outside and placed a poorly lettered sign in front of the coffins: Bank Robbers / Shot Dead! He faced the crowd.

"Folks, y'all know me, Happy Zed, your servant in time of need of any kind! By the way, if anyone knows the female, I'd appreciate getting her name. The other three, I know."

Nora's words churning his gut, Ethan shoved his way out of the crowd and hurried over the boardwalk. Looking straight ahead, he didn't respond to those who called out or slapped his back. He felt as if a target was on his back for any gunslinger who wanted to try. He came to the office of Wells Fargo.

Ethan opened the door, went in, and kicked it closed. The cowbell above it clanged, startling an old man who dropped his earhorn and stared.

Matt Turner, the Wells Fargo agent, rose from the desk, arched his eyebrows, and eyed the caller over metal glasses that pinched his nose.

"Matt, if it's still available, I'll take that shotgun duty on the west-bound train."

Matt opened a book, ran his finger down the page, and stopped.

Ethan leaned over, watching him. "I'm not smoking

you, I *want* the job on the San Francisco train, and I'll be ready in two days."

"But Ethan, I—"

"Matt, when you close shop, walk down the street. Next to the corner, have a good look. *You'll understand.*"

•4•

THE 5:50, BOUND for San Francisco, pulled into Topeka's depot blowing steam over passengers waiting to board. With a padlocked bag in hand, Ethan took a last look at Topeka, grabbed the handrail, and climbed the iron step.

His job protecting documents for Wells Fargo would be a definite change from guarding banks. Entering the dining car, he found a seat next to the window.

He felt rich watching the Kansas prairie pass by. He fondled heavy silverware on the white linen cloth. The ice, in a tulip-shaped water glass, jingled as heavy wheels clicked over steel tracks. Sage, his horse, rode up front in a car near the engine.

The guard enjoyed dining first class. A tender, blood-rare steak, and mushrooms decorated with parsley, equaled any depot food he had ever tried. Sweet butter flavored with horseradish melted over corn on the cob so tasty that he asked for another. The inviting aroma of coffee drifted over a silver dish full of vanilla ice cream, an ideal ending to a perfect meal. The colored waiter smiled as he pocketed Ethan's tip.

On the second morning, waiting for breakfast, Ethan found a newspaper on the seat next to his. Turning to the inside page, he took a deep breath and read the editorial.

Ethan Sands, after yesterday's shooting, pistol in hand, facing an adversary toe to toe, is probably the most dangerous man living in the state of Kansas, perhaps in the entire West. Topeka Sands is a man who will become known as the fastest draw alive. Yesterday, Sands killed members of Dirk Largo's gang, including an unknown woman, who attempted to rob the First National Bank. Dirk's brother, Billy, served five years for riding with Jesse James. Billy was out of town.

—*The Topeka Capital,* April 1880

The conductor handed Ethan an envelope. "Mr. Sands, before we left Topeka a woman slipped this in my hand and said not to deliver it until we'd reached Salina. She tipped me two dollars."

His name, in a woman's hand, appeared on the clean white envelope.

Mr. Sands:

Dirk Largo's brother, Billy, has been released from prison on parole. I've heard he's sworn to get the man that cut his family in half. You killed his older brother, his nephew Mace, and a woman I don't know. Billy Largo is mean, clever, and a man of many faces. I know, I married him. Wherever you are

you'd better have eyes in the back of your head, because when you least expect it, Billy might be there.
I wish you well.

        Signed: A woman, afraid of Billy Largo.

Years ago, Ethan had exchanged shots with Billy, but
since then, they hadn't met. Ethan stepped onto the
open walkway between the cars. He tossed the newspaper and the crumbled letter over the low gate and
watched them fly backward away from the direction of
his new life. His reputation wouldn't flutter away so
easily.

Neither could he toss away the memory of Nora's
face.

That night, lying in his upper berth, he felt foolish. The
padlocked canvas satchel so close—annoyed him. He
struggled to sleep. Nora's words rang in his head: *"You're
a paid killer, even women!"*

•5•

THE TRAIN ARRIVED on schedule in San Francisco where Ethan deposited the canvas bag with Wells Fargo, and picked up another bag marked Los Angeles. Having time to kill, he headed for Market Street. San Francisco astonished Ethan; he marveled at the sights before him. Steeper streets than he'd ever seen, and on top of one he saw what San Franciscans called the Golden Gate. He'd seen river boats, but none equaled the ships sailing through the entrance separating the inland bay from the Pacific Ocean.

Well-dressed people hustled over the streets in every direction. Opportunity flowered in San Francisco; he felt the heat of money, and smelled energy, as he passed banks. Enjoying the cool, damp air, Ethan breathed deeply.

Two days was not enough for him to absorb San Francisco. She's like a lusty inamorata dancing to guitars inside softly lit bistros rumbling with good times, he thought. San Franciscans pursued gaiety, while the faint and unrighteous, bedamned, lingered behind. It was a unique and sinful life in a city where the devil smiled upon those who enjoyed its satanic charm. Ethan swore that he'd return.

On the train to Los Angeles, his charge consisted of escorting financial documents stuffed inside another canvas bag. The Southern Pacific tracks ran south for miles through the San Joaquin Valley. The conductor saw Ethan, who seemed rapt with the view and leaned down.

"Mister, some believe that what you're looking at someday will be the finest agricultural land in the state. The soil is rich and there's ample water. From Sacramento south, the American, the San Joaquin, and the Stanislaus rivers carry water from the High Sierra. That's the mountain range that protects Californians from Death Valley's steaming hell."

Ethan stared at tumbleweeds blowing before the wind over the wide desert valley.

"You see, after the gold rush slowed, miners came from the Sierra to the valley and planted crops. Today, there are hundreds of acres planted in wheat. In the future, irrigation'll develop the valley; then, mister, everything'll grow." He paused. "If you can, buy land in the San Joaquin, and when you're my age, you'll be rich."

He went about his business. To Ethan, buying desert land didn't make sense.

The whistle announced Bakersfield, where before the town was founded in the early 1860s Colonel Thomas Baker owned a field and corral. Ethan, bag in hand, got off to stretch his legs. Except for the Sierra Nevada Mountains to the east, it reminded him of a Kansas farm town. At the depot, he asked a wiry cowboy for a match.

Holding the light, the cowboy said: "Mister, not far from this depot the largest beef herds in California pass through Bakersfield, and besides beef the town has a reputation that's less than holy. Along L Street we've got Chinese tongs, josh houses, and a string of whores to match anything Virginia City, Tombstone, or Bodie ever had. And we've got a bad man with a legend that'll go up against any of the shooters in Abilene or Dodge—a handsome gent called Jim McKinney. Don't mix with him, especially if he's been drinkin'. He's mean and he's fast."

On the train, Ethan had read of Jim McKinney in Bakersfield's *Californian*, and like Billy Largo, he was a man of many faces. But Ethan didn't plan a trip to L Street looking for him.

Throwing black smoke over the line of cars, the engine chugged along the Southern Pacific's tracks, pulling a steep grade crossing through the Tehachapi Mountains. Then southward on the final leg to *El Pueblo de Los Angeles*.

•6•

ETHAN WAS MET by two Wells Fargo agents who took charge of the cargo. One agent, from Joplin, said a wagon train had arrived in Los Angeles bringing a hundred people, the majority of them from Kansas.

"They've camped east of here," the agent said, "past the Los Angeles River. A half mile from San Gabriel Mission, near some pepper trees, we found the wagon train. Friendly folks. One young fella struck me."

"How's that?" Ethan asked.

"The joker, funnier than hell, had a wide gap between his front teeth and whistled when he talked."

Ethan shoved back his tattered Stetson. "Did you catch his name?"

"It's Andrew Love, that's him."

Surprised, Ethan drawled his words. "Andy Love?"

"You know him?"

"Sure do. He's from Topeka."

After saddling Sage, he decided it was time to have a look. He laughed, it had to be Andy; God, in all His kindness, couldn't have made two! "C'mon Sage, let's find Andy."

Andrew Love, who tread on life's brighter side, inevitably charmed ladies into believing he lived up to his name—that was the game he played. Ethan had nicknamed him Boots, because Andy would spend his last dollar buying a new pair. His shiny leather boots often gathered dust beneath a pretty girl's bed.

Andy pleased ladies to a precarious point. Love affairs could have ended his career. The disillusioned plaints of frustrated women often rang in his ears. Rumor had it that Andy left Topeka without saying goodbye. Chuckling to himself, Ethan guessed that Andy left Topeka *dodging a woman.*

•7•

RIDING EAST, ETHAN came upon an orange grove
and a salesman wearing a bright yellow shirt, a red tie,
candy-striped trousers, white shoes, and cocked over his
right eye, a straw hat. Ethan eased Sage next to the
stranger who perched on a crate, shaded beneath a daz-
zling pink and black umbrella.

"Afternoon," Ethan said. "Am I headed for San Gabriel?"

"Straight ahead. Lookit, not so fast. How'd you
like an outstanding buy? This orange grove, a hundred trees, thirty percent off! I'll throw in the umbrella!"

West of the mission, a wooded area ran north to
brush-covered foothills. A stream of clear water flowed
south through pepper trees. Ethan dismounted at the assembled wagons. He asked a man for the whereabouts

of Andrew Love. The man pointed to a path leading toward the stream.

Immediately, Ethan recognized the figure walking ahead of him. His arm around a young girl's waist, Andrew Q. Love worked to convince a tender young thing that he was love personified. "Boots," Ethan shouted, "turn around!"

• 8 •

IN A CLEARING next to Andy's wagon, Ethan and Andy sat by the morning fire waiting for the coffee to perk.

"Andy, I feel awful leaving Kansas." Ethan drew his .45 and checked the load, then he shoved the pistol back in its holster. "If I'd stayed in Kansas, someone would have shot me. Felt like a bull's-eye was painted on my back."

Ethan adjusted the holster low on his hip. "I don't know how often I've done what I'm doing now. How many times I've had to pull that gun. That last time when I saw the coffins lined up, I had to make a change."

"Ethan, once you told me it isn't always the man that draws fast, but the man that takes time to aim that stays alive. But killing four bandits at one time, that is hard to understand."

"Andy, I had the edge. And the experience to use it. In my line of work, sportsmanship never enters my mind."

In Kansas City, Ethan had a master gunsmith, Peter Wick, who kept Ethan's guns in perfect condition. Ethan always had three pistols: one in his holster, a spare in his dresser, and one being checked at Pete's. Pete worked his trigger action smooth as silk, and he'd developed a slug that had less penetration than a factory-made, but on impact burst into a jagged hunk of lead that devastated a man's gut so that one shot usually finished the job.

Ethan said with authority: "I've seen men hit four times with a factory-made that went clean through and the shooter still had strength enough to fire one more shot. And I've seen that last shot kill a man who thought the fight was over."

"Then I guess you use Pete's bullets?"

"Every damned time!" He pulled a shell from his gun belt. "I brought all I could manage, and when I get settled I'll let Pete know where I am. He's the only insurance I've ever bought for myself."

Now Andy understood how one shot painted a robber's brains over the bank's wall. "That woman you killed in the bank, who was she?"

Ethan shoved back his hat and gazed at the sky. "Somewhere, I've seen her but I haven't figured out where."

Boots took a stick and poked the fire; the aroma of strong coffee and fried beans rose with the steam.

"I know you've lived bad times. But, friend, those days are gone. California'll be different. If it ain't, I've carved lots of meat off my ass riding this far for nothing." Andy paused. "I'm sorry about Nora. I thought marriage was a sure thing." He dumped his coffee in the fire. "Women are strange, Ethan. I ought to know!" Andy hooked a cocky thumb to his chest.

"Guess I'll amble over to Kitty's wagon, see how ma honey is feeling. We, uh, got a little picnic planned soon as her folks leave for San Gabriel Mission. Feel safer when her pa's not around."

"Her pa approves you messing with his daughter?" Ethan looked over his shoulder.

"Dunno. He's never said. Fact is, we hardly speak."

Andy pulled the makings from his vest pocket. "I'm gonna roll a smoke, want one?"

"Sure, thanks."

Andy's nimble fingers flew. He passed the first homemade to his friend, the second he clenched between his teeth.

Ethan dipped a stick in the flames and held it for him.

"There's an old newspaper on my bed roll, so relax and enjoy yourself. I'd ask you along, but uh, you know what I mean."

"I know *you*! Keep your eyes open."

"Yeah. Her pa's a farmer but he's built like a blacksmith."

•9•

AWAY FROM THE wagons by the stream at the foot of the San Gabriels, underneath a stand of low-hanging willow trees, Kitty and Andy found a hideaway.

"Say," Andy said, bashfully pointing to a sack behind him. "Care for a little touch to, uh, brighten your day? I got a small bottle of good stuff."

"Whiskey?" she said indignantly.

"Just a sip." He held up a pint of sour mash. "Honey, I wouldn't give you nuthin' bad."

Throwing back her long hair, she smiled. "I don't need whiskey! Andy, *I've got you.*"

She reached over and unbuttoned his collar: her fingers toyed with the curly hair covering his chest.

"We've had a time finding the right place." She placed her fingers on his lips. "So with Pa and Ma gone, well, I wanna do everything you been telling me.

We've only done it once. I'm young, Andy, but I'm not afraid." She smiled sweetly.

"I'm surprised at you." Andy corked the bottle. "And, uh, I'm not sure I understand."

Kitty removed her blouse, allowing the sun to shine on youthful loveliness that made Andy's wide eyes blink. She drew his hand to her breast. Breathing erratically, Andy pulled back his hand.

"What's wrong, don't you like me?"

"I just wanna yank off my boots."

After his boots, he hurriedly undid his cumbersome buckle. Kitty's eyes followed his trousers as they crumpled around his feet.

On top of her, Andy listened to her sighs and tasted her moist lips, while Kitty tugged at her skirt.

"Kitty Bean, where are ya?" a voice boomed. "This here's your pa!"

Locum Bean's husky voice was still echoing through the canyon while Andy stumbled into his pants.

"Kitty, ma God, hurry."

"Don't be afraid, we ain't done nuthin *here*!" Dressed, Kitty shoved a chicken wing in his hand. "C'mon, let's be eatin' if'n Pa comes."

Andrew Love sat staring at the bony wing, then looked at her. "What do you mean, we ain't done nuthin' *here*?"

"The warm nights in the wagon, what we did."

"Kitty, we've only necked around. Nothing serious."

"Serious? I thought it was. I told Ma."

"You *what*?" Andrew felt hot.

"Silly, you know what I mean. Only woman talk. I, uh, told her—"

"Kitty! Look up there, near the boulder. It's your pa. Jesus, here he comes!"

•10•

WHILE PREPARING A fresh pot of coffee, suddenly he heard shouting behind him, and Ethan swung around half expecting to see Billy Largo. Then he recognized Andy's voice. Ethan dropped his cup and rushed toward the commotion.

Near Bean's tailgate, Ethan stopped. His back against a wheel, his arms ramrod straight, Andy stared at Kitty's pa. A yard away, the man leveled a sawed-off American Arms .12 gauge directly at Andy's chest. Locum's fingers played over the triggers.

Ethan's eyes shifted to Bean, then Andy. *It was like old times, bad old times!*

Ethan faced Bean straight on. "Mister, this isn't my affair. But it appears you're about to murder my friend over a young lady's imagination. Because how you're handling the triggers, Mr. Bean, the shotgun's apt to go off. There won't be enough left of Andy for a short hymn."

Bean held firm.

Ethan hardened his words. "Look, Bean, I get paid for using a pistol, and free work doesn't interest me. I suggest you be reasonable. If not, *I'll kill you.*" Ethan took one step back. "I'm not a braggart; it's not my style. Before you move, I can sink two bullets in your chest. It's simple: live or die. *You call it.*"

The cold in Ethan's voice chilled the farmer. Locum was angry enough to kill Andy, but dying himself and abandoning his family didn't appeal. Locum lowered the barrel.

"Damn you, Love, you've fiddled with Kitty's virginity!"

"I only kept her company and allocated her part of my affections."

From the wagon seat, Kitty Bean grabbed a shotgun, raised it, and pulled both triggers, blasting a hole in the sky. With a handkerchief, she wiped her eyes.

"Pa, I lied to Ma." Kitty dropped the shotgun. "I'm not with child!"

Andy felt he'd returned from the edge of death as Kitty hurried to her father's side. "Pa, if you hurt him, I'll tell Ma what I seen. You and the painted hussy in Sante Fe." Pa Bean broke wind, and crashed through bushes to relieve himself behind a tree.

•11•

"ANDREW LOVE, LOOK at me," Ethan said on the way back to camp. "I'll talk, *and you listen*. Boots, I'm not gonna draw my pistol and scare another man half to death. If you get in a mess, especially over a woman, you're on your own." Ethan rested his hand on the .45's butt. "Years back, when I rode with Lefty, even though he was half crazy, he had enough common sense not to get into that kind of trouble. When he planned a bank job that looked too safe, he'd say: 'Boys, even the smartest fox can end up in the wrong chicken coop!'" Ethan leaned back and smiled.

"The next time a father, husband, or irate beau tries to kill you, Andy, I'm walking. If he kills you, I'll bury you. Maybe buy a headstone, very small."

Andy squinted at him. "You mean that?"

"Sure as that muscle 'tween your legs needs a knot, I've trouble enough without your uncontrolled pecker getting me killed."

"Then, uh, ya mind if I ride along?"

"C'mon, let's get out of here."

•12•

AT DAWN, ANDY was snoring in short bursts. Ethan crawled from the wagon, gathered some kindling, and started for coffee. In the east, a layer of deep orange clouds covered the morning's blue, and suddenly a gust of warm wind touched his face.

"Mornin', Ethan. How ya feel?"

"Like a million, half spent."

"I'm glad we're leaving." Andy reached for a cup. "The man that bought my wagon is coming early."

"Didn't you say you'd bought a mule?"

"Mr. Deeter threw one in," Andy said proudly.

"That's good. I've got some belongings at Wells Fargo's in Los Angeles. So a mule'll work fine. Notice the wind?"

"Warm for this early, ain't it? Mr. Deeter says it comes off the Mojave Desert. There's a name for it, Santa Annie, some such word. Hand me the sugar."

"Andy, you think Nora dumped me because of my past, or the other man?"

Andy spilled coffee over his shirt. "I hardly knew Nora. She acted like an intelligent woman. Maybe your days after the war scared her?"

Andy scratched his head. "Lemme put it another way. Had ya married Nora and then if she'd pulled-up fickle, it could have been worse. But as I've said, life in California is gonna be different, you'll see."

Ethan frowned. "You're an experienced sort. Say a man buys a whore, yanks off her clothes, and tells her what to do. He pays for what he gets. Now, take a so-called decent woman. You romance her, buy her pretty things, try to make her happy, and what happens? Likely, she tells you what *she* wants, then makes you feel you're not good enough to give it to her. Andy, I'm not like you. I just can't bounce around."

"Yeah, that happens," Andy said dejectedly.

"Bouncing around?"

"What ya said about the whores. Let's eat!"

They were filled on a breakfast of fried grits and bacon and eggs, when a short man driving a team arrived to collect his purchase. Behind Mr. Deeter's horses, his son had tied the largest black mule either Kansan had seen. He backed his team into the wagon and untied the mule.

"Gents, I call him Peter Balls. Before I gelded him, the animal had the largest pair that ever hung. Smart mule stronger than two his size." He handed the lead rope to Andy and got up on the wagon seat with his son. "Luck to you men. Maybe we'll meet again. I'm going to Bakersfield."

They waved.

"Andy, climb on your pinto, lead the mule, and follow me."

A half-mile from San Gabriel, Ethan gently reined his buckskin, threw his right leg over the saddle and slid down. Sage lowered his head and nibbled at dry grass.

. Gazing over the land, Ethan felt that coming to California was a wise move. Other than Andy, he didn't know a soul. But somewhere he'd find a different way to cut a dollar and meet a woman who'd enjoy him for what he was.

Andy eased back, placed his right hand against the cantle, raised his left arm to the sky, and sang.

Though he couldn't understand the words, Ethan let him ramble on. Andy Love was special.

Born during a Kansas cyclone, with carrot-red hair, robin-blue eyes, gapped teeth, and a cleft on his chin, he wasn't the man people thought. Behind Andy's good-time-Charlie facade lay ambition. Ethan knew Andrew hadn't come to California only to chase women. Possibly in California, Ethan would discover what went on inside the special man's head.

Reaching for the canteen, Ethan took a long pull. He pulled off his Stetson and ran his fingers through thick hair. He dusted the hat, and put it on and relaxed, enjoying the stillness. He looked back at Andy who was rolling a cigarette. "Tell me, Andy, what do you think?"

"About what?"

"About leaving Kansas and traveling to California."

Andy's face flushed. "Oh, Gawd, there's been so damned many things I've thought. I dunno which one punches my mind most. Tell ya this much, hotshot"—Andy scratched his head—"if I know'd it was gonna be a long, ass-bustin' ride, I'd had reservations 'bout traveling so damn far. God knows, with my behind so long on a hardboard seat, I've tacked on a lotta years. Next time I'll ride a train!"

They lingered a few moments looking toward the east where sunlight had brightened the land and the mountains to the north. Easily touching spurs against Sage's flanks, he pulled alongside Andy's mare.

"Still got Kitty on your mind?"

"Ah, not really," Andy said, in an easy Kansas drawl. "Well, that's a lie. She's hard to forget. I'll stick her in the back of my mind." Andy chuckled. "She'll tuck in right nice, too!"

They rode along sharing the silence. Ethan felt a twinge and looked over his shoulder. Only the empty trail lay behind but Billy Largo's face twisted a nerve in the back of his neck.

•13•

FROM A BLUFF, the Kansans gazed down over Los Angeles. On the outskirts were small box houses on dirt streets. The main buildings resembled well-designed structures in Kansas City.

North of Los Angeles, mountains ran east to west, forming a rocky boundary protecting the pueblo. South, soft rolling hills ended at the ocean's edge. Angelenos boasted that in 1880, eleven thousand people had gathered in Los Angeles. At this rate, San Francisco faced a challenge.

"Here it's just another balmy day." Andy lifted his arms up toward the cloudless sky. "Lord, Ethan, there's frost in Kansas. No wonder people are coming. Town don't look like much, does it?"

"I've seen tent meetings with more hustle." Across the street, a two-story, weathered building had a red sign hanging above rickety steps. Hotel Nuevo didn't impress either Kansan.

They led Sage, Gussie, and the mule to a livery stable and went back to the shabby hotel. Upstairs, Andy unlocked the door and strolled inside. Broken lath boards protruded from the cracked walls.

Shiny-black cockroaches scampered along the faded curtain down the wall to a ragged green rug spread underneath a dumpy bed.

"I smell burnt wood." Andy sniffed and looked around. "Musta been a recent fire."

"Maybe sleep on the trail?" Ethan suggested.

Instead they threw saddlebags on the bed and went out, locked the door, and walked down the squeaking stairway to the desk. A sign, "Hot Baths," pointed to the back door. It had been days since they'd seen a tub. They spent most of the day submerged in hot water and making up for lost sleep.

The next day while wandering around the pueblo, they arrived at what the Mexicans called *la plaza*, where Angelenos rested under palm trees, their faces hidden under wide sombreros. At the plaza's west end stood a Spanish church, and down a dirt street, the city jail.

Ethan thought that in a decent town churches outnumbered saloons. So far, here it was even.

A short distance from the plaza was a narrow, cobblestoned street lined with rows of open stands where people busied themselves selling foods, clay pots, homemade candles, and sweet-smelling candies. Farther down, they spotted a faded red two-story adobe, La Cantina Roja.

Suddenly, people began shouting while pointing east to a dust cloud behind galloping horses. Something familiar about the yelling cowboys. Especially the man riding in front who waved his hat. Ethan and Andy stepped back and watched as they rode by.

"Sweet angels in Heaven, smile on us," said Andy. "It's Luke!"

•14•

LAST THEY'D HEARD, Luke Tucker, an old friend, had worked for a cattle baron herding longhorns from El Paso east, half across Texas, then north to Dodge City. Today, he rode point for a bunch of noisy drovers waving arms and hooting as dust settled over willow trees alongside the road.

The thirsty, wide-eyed cowboys dismounted, tethered their horses a few yards east of the cantina, and waited for Luke's word. Laughing and brushing themselves, banging hats together to shake trail dirt from sweaty clothes, they stood ready to stampede the door.

"Damn, I cain't believe my eyes, that Luke's in California." His mouth wide open, Andy stared. "Where'n hell you s'pose they started this drive?"

"Strange," Ethan said. "Luke doesn't bring riders into large towns. Los Angeles must be safe or he wouldn't have let 'em come."

Luke was a no-nonsense, trail-savvy ramrod, who knew more about herding cattle than any man Ethan and Andy had ever known. He didn't worry about hired men as long as they could ride, didn't beat the cook for making salty beans, or think Billy the Kid was sane.

From a taco he held in his hand, thick red juice dribbled off Andy's chin. "Shouldn't we amble down and say howdy?" He looked longingly at the cantina.

Ethan hesitated. "We'll take our time. Even in California, a saloon's *still* a saloon."

There was always a chance of encountering a wild-eyed, ego-stuck cowhand who imagined himself the fastest draw ever, especially in front of a mirror.

"Hell, Ethan, maybe there'll be some old boys we know. It's been a while since we've seen anybody from home, and you've always thought kindly of Luke."

Keeping Andy outside would be like holding a thirsty steer to a pile of sand. So he threw caution to California's ovenlike breeze. "We'll have a look. But remember, Andy, watch your mouth."

•15•

AS SOON AS they were inside the cantina, Luke saw them. Shoving aside a cowhand who wanted an advance, he let out a wild Texas yell, rushed up and grabbed both men. "I'll be, Topeka Sands ... Andy Love. Lord, trade me for a pint of spit!"

Ethan gently elbowed him. "Go easy, Luke, and uh, name's Ethan."

Luke stood back. "You boys ain't on the run, are ya?" He laughed, knowing Ethan Sands wasn't a man to run. "I'll be! If'n you boys ain't a fancier sight than four aces over a payday's pot. God, it's good to lay eyes on ya both. Ethan, you're handsome as ever. Andy, *you* haven't changed."

"We rode in yesterday." Ethan explained how he and Andy had met in San Gabriel. The three Kansans took a table next to the wall and ordered whiskey. For a minute they stared at each other, until Ethan broke the spell. "Sorry about cutting you off. The Topeka Sands you knew took a long ride. I'm simply Ethan."

"I wasn't using my head. Sorry." Luke tipped his hat and sprayed dust over the rough-cut table. For a while they swapped stories. At intervals, the yelling was so loud that Andy cupped his hands so Luke could hear. Luke's eyes watered and wrinkles cut across his face deeper than usual; the trail boss had aged.

"If'n I'm not gouging your privacy, what's your plans?"

Ethan sighed. "Staying alive comes first, but after that, San Francisco. That city has a future. I'm thinking of settling there and looking around until I find something where I can make a living. And I don't mean protecting a bank."

"You have any connections in San Francisco?"

"My ex-boss, Briggs, knows businessmen I can meet, and that's about it. So, I'll take it as she comes."

"Andy, I'll take a guess at yours." Luke winked at him. "Say, upstairs there's Mexican firecrackers, pepper hot. Good lookers, too."

Luke leaned over and punched Andy. "C'mon, old friend, give it a whirl. Gawdy, partner, for such a high-quality lady's man, you still got that boyish peekaboo grin on ya."

Luke poured another drink and glanced down at Ethan's gun. "You know, the law has grown tough; days of packin' a gun are nearin' the short end. And frankly," he said, smiling, "I think it's good. Trouble is, there's been wild tales glorifying the old days. The times when pistol shooters grew reputations. The way I've got it sized, these young drovers today got their heads stoked up on book-stories making it dangerous for a man to carry a gun. They'll read them ten-cent books: most of 'em are walking around living a life that's a pack of lies. My balls tingle from what I read, and worse, from what I see. So if they take away our guns, maybe the old days will fade away. Hell, who knows?"

Luke paused. "Ethan, you recall that young writer fella working for *The Topeka Capital*?" Luke scratched his head. "For the life of me, I cain't recollect his name."

"Andrew Buderman?" Ethan swung a glance at Andy.

"That's him. You've heard what he's done, haven't ya?"

"Quit pounding sand. What'n blazes did he do?"

"He's made you famous, Ethan, that's what he's done."

Luke may as well have punched Ethan.

"Famous?"

"It's rumored Buderman had written one of them pulp westerns. He's called it *The Topeka Kid*! The main character, a shoot-'em-up gunfighter, may not be you, but sure as clocks tick, if'n it ain't, he's closer than bread to butter."

Ethan stared at Luke. "You hassling me?"

"I'll say it on a Bible if'n ya want. One of my hands read me a part and this crazy wrangler's got the book." Luke glanced at the bar but the cowboy was busy upstairs, bleeding the lizard.

"Good Gawd," Andy blurted out. "Ethan, that's all you need. Sweet Jesus be with us. I s'pose that writer fella drew a picture of ya?"

Ethan pushed back his Stetson. His stomach burned, reminding him of four open coffins that he would just as soon have forgotten.

Andy shook his head.

"Luke, you're right as rain, the days of wearing guns

is coming to an end. But as long as there's men and guns, men'll kill."

Luke and Andy eyed each other and didn't speak. Luke said, "I think the gunfighters these young drovers read about, Buderman has made the bastards heros."

Luke took a long drag, pinched his cigarette, and tossed it, missing the spittoon. The old ramrod felt at ease.

"Smart gunmen are careful what they say and do, keeping one thing in mind—that's staying alive." Luke chuckled. "Like you, Ethan."

"For a living, a man can go just so far, pulling a trigger. Though I'd rather face a professional any day than a wild cowpoke waving a pistol at me."

Luke nodded, his eyes slowly scanning the room. "Well, gents, speaking of wild, I'd better mosey about, circulate. Gotta keep an eye peeled because these are as prickly a bunch as I've seen. I don't wanna pay my own hard cash for patchin' this saloon."

Luke stood, aimed, and took a long spit, grazing a Mexican's leg.

"A year ago, most of these yahoos were back East, clerking stores. Now look at 'em! They'll shoot at anything that moves, even shadows and worse. They'll waste a box of lead on any target dead or alive."

The three friends glanced toward the bar and smiled.

"I've got another bunch coming, young hands from Omaha, first haul west for most. Worries me, though. I've got hotheads among them."

Luke had ridden behind cattle longer than he cared to tell. Typically, he had little to show. Thin, hard, sun-baked body, and a bunch of rotten memories to fill a book. Luke's eyes showed his hard life, page by page.

Ethan twisted his finger, "Come dawn, Andy, we're riding north along El Camino Real. So drink up."

The cantina's door flung open. The smoke in the cantina and the stench of unwashed bodies overpowered the whore's cheap perfume and mixed with stale tobacco and beer, the cantina stunk. Through the bluish haze, whores displayed their figures against the stairway leading to the cantina's second floor. The drovers were already half drunk and, when they spotted whores, they burst into yells. Andy and Ethan stood back as the drovers pushed ahead. The last two drovers yelled at their pals.

The shorter man caught Ethan's attention. He had slitted eyes with shiny black pupils; teeth stained yellow dulled his smile. With a pearl-handled Peacemaker .45 hung in a quick-fire rig on his hip, he had the swagger of a man not afraid to draw.

Ethan figured the man had spent every dollar he'd earned buying a weapon to make him look dangerous. The hardware didn't concern Ethan, but the man's eyes bothered him. He had seen that caged look before. The man's sidekick, a husky cowboy with a shaggy beard, bumped Andy's shoulder. Andy shoved back.

"Hey, farmer, watch that shoving!"

Ethan moved between them and, easy like, urged Andy toward the door. Andy wasn't armed.

"C'mon, Buck, don't waste your time," said the short cowboy next to him. "We got whores." Slowly he gave Ethan the once-over.

"Say, mister tall man, you gotta look to ya. Sumpin' tells me you think yer better'n me."

Ethan let the remark slide. "Let's move."

Andy nodded and they walked toward the door. The black-eyed drover blocked Ethan's way.

"Hold it, tall man, I cain't say that lookin' at a man's back suits me." He put out his right hand. "I'm West St. John."

Ethan ignored his hand.

"Good enough, friend. Me and Buck will step outside with you gents."

Ethan and Andy casually walked down the steps toward the street.

"Hey, you ever been in Kansas?" West hollered.

"Ah, God!" Andy whispered.

West's friends followed them outside. Two other drovers stood back, hands resting on their gun belts, and nodded at West. West faced Ethan. "Okay, mister handsome, you call it."

•16•

COWBOYS, WALKING OUT the cantina's door, stopped when they saw West, his arms folded across his chest, facing the tall stranger. They gathered in a half-circle standing behind him. Ethan moved toward West and pointed his finger close to his face. "Kansas mean something special to you?"

Ethan eyed the other men.

"Oh, not much," West said.

"Look! Whether I'm from Kansas or not, that's my business. Cowboy, use your head and don't push yourself." Ethan lowered his voice. "Take my advice, you and your friends go inside and join the others. You'll find plenty of ladies waiting to kick up their heels. So go on, give 'em a try."

Ethan tipped his hat and turned and walked toward Andy.

West lunged forward. "C'mon now, you and your

partner ain't so old ya gotta leave in the shank of the evening, are ya? Maybe we should talk a little, eh?"

Ethan frowned and motioned Andy to back away.

"Look, West, I don't pass time talking. I've spent my evening, and sleep is what I have in mind. It's that simple."

"Hey, tall man!" West whispered. "You been in Topeka? You got them gray twistin' eyes like I've read about."

Cautiously, Ethan signaled Andy to follow him, and as they turned away, the cowboys yelled catcalls.

"Hey, dummies, cain't ya see them old men is weary? C'mon, let 'em be." Buck waved his arm.

West glared at them. "Shut your mouths, ya mindless hens, I'll handle this."

From the rear, someone yelled, "You tell 'em, Shorty, how gutsy ya are." His friends laughed. One snickered and said, "Lookie, West, look at them pig farmers. Scared ta death, ain't they? Go on, tell 'em *who* you are. Maybe they'll hightail it and run." Snickers and laughter drowned his voice.

Luke walked out the cantina's door. His eyes fixed on West and Buck. "West! Listen to me. You've been a burr under my saddle since we rode out of Texas. Now I'm gonna give ya settlers advice."

West winced; the lines on his face tightened.

"You and your loudmouthed friends find whores and bed 'em down. I'll guarantee you'll be safer pumpin' your peckers than shootin' off your mouths!"

West stepped back, sucked in a deep breath, coughed, and spat directly in Luke's face.

Stunned, Luke yanked off his bandanna and wiped the slime from his cheek. The brim of his hat touched West's. "You damned-fool son of a bitch!"

Luke turned to one side as Buck spun around and

grabbed him around the neck, sticking a gun against his spine.

Luke stiffened.

"Steady, Ethan, they're hotheads, they'll do nuthin'," Andy said.

"Stand easy, I'll handle it." Ethan slid over in front of Luke, keeping Buck and West in sight.

Luke said in a husky voice, "Ethan, these are the drovers I was talkin' about. The husky roper wearing the red shirt owns the book."

"By God, I knew it." West grinned. "You're him Topeka's Shooter. I read about the fast draw, how you buried a dozen men, and, oh yeah, that sun-colored hair. Yes sir, boys, a real killer!" He laughed. "Maybe you'll show us how!"

•17•

EVERY MAN'S EYES focused on Ethan. "Damn! To-peka's Shooter," Buck said, his pistol firm against Luke's back. "Ethan Sands, Gawd a'mighty!"

"West," Ethan said, "forget this. Let Luke go, and do as he says, go inside."

"Sure, I'll let him go. "He's a cantankerous old bas-tard who's takin' up space, and he's lived too damned long. Fool's a wore-out nuthin'."

"West, you don't want to kill Luke. I'm the one that'll make your reputation." Ethan paused. "You do know about reputations? There's two kinds: one comes easy, by talking. The other comes hard, by drawing fast before another shooter plants a headstone that'll hold down worms on your grave."

West stood in front of Luke. "Mister, talk is cheap now. Sands, it's my turn." His hand moved.

Two staccato shots slammed into West. Ethan's gun

was so quick West didn't see it. A hot poker burned in his stomach; his knees buckled. West's eyes searched for Buck's.

"Buck, I'm hurt bad."

Buck didn't hear; his own *cold* glassy eyes stared at the moon. From a dented hole in his forehead, blood trickled over his face, forming a puddle next to his temple.

Luke stood looking at the two bodies. "Both of 'em, Topeka . . . Dead!"

•18•

ETHAN FACED HIS friend, his hand on the Colt .45 hanging low on his right leg. He threw back his head and wailed, "Dammit, Andy, the fool wouldn't listen." Ethan felt drenched in misery; two more graves had raised the score.

Slowly he approached the dead men's friends. "*You dumb bastards!* Go on, look at them! You wanted a gunfight, to see a man die. Remember what you see."

Ethan stood with his legs spread. "The four of you next to Luke, you wanted to kill me, c'mon, kill me. Draw, you can't miss."

One man's hand dropped low, then jerked back; the other three froze at Ethan's cold stare. One young cowboy was so frightened that urine trickled inside his pants.

Ethan stepped back. "I'm turning my back, and walking. Go on, here's another chance."

No one moved.

•19•

DRUNKS AND PAINTED whores rushed from the saloon and stood staring at bodies lying in the street.

Luke stood with Ethan. "You saved ma bacon. Buck and West would have killed me. You've spared an old man's life."

"I owed you one," Ethan said.

Luke swung around to the others. "Y'all gonna stand like wooden Indians, or help me load these stiffs in the wagon?"

Before the ramrod climbed on, he waved at Ethan. "I'll meet you in the mornin'. We'll talk with the sheriff. I'll have a witness with me. Don't worry 'bout nuthin'. It was self-defense. Get some sleep."

Luke drove the dead men into darkness over the pueblo's cobblestone street.

Ethan looked at Andy. "Bad way to begin a new life, killing two men—one for each week I've been in California, one for each day in Los Angeles."

Andy took Ethan's arm. "You did right. In my mind, West killed himself."

Part 2

Northward, on the Doughty Little Friar's Road

• 1 •

THE NEXT MORNING the Mojave Desert played an unseasonable trick on Californians. An updraft of sultry air flowing over the mountains had built thunderclouds that covered the basin. The light showers, though, hardly dampened Angelenos' clothing or wet the Plaza's grass.

Upstairs in their hotel room that overlooked a freight dock, Ethan and Andy saw workmen unloading wagons stacked high with hides.

A heavy fist pounded against the door. Brushing shaving soap on his face, Ethan turned to watch Andy, who sat on the bed pulling on his boots. Annoyed to be interrupted half-finished, Ethan strapped on his gun belt and went to the door.

"Who's there?"

"It's me, Luke."

He unlocked the door. "Morning, Luke. You're out early."

"I wanted a word before we go." The trail boss spotted the whiskey atop a rickety table next to the window. "Can I?" Shaking, he managed to pour half a tumbler and threw it back. "You'd think from experience I'd know not to mix whiskey with tequila. But as ya get older everything looks better *at the time*! But it ain't. So come mornin' I began to pay for my mistake."

He wiped his chin and eased down into a straight-back chair. "Are ya renting this closet or are they lettin' you have it for free? Did ya dirty the bed last night or take turns standing up? With three in this pigeon hole, I hate to break wind."

Boys"—Luke pushed back his hat—"I've got a situation I don't like. Sheriff ain't here. Off hunting. They say he'll be back in a week. There's a boy, a pimple-faced deputy who says he is in charge. A tall stalk named Walter Blunt. We had a few words 'fore I came. Yet, after bullin' with him, I see he ain't so boyish as he puts on. In my opinion he's got his eye on the sheriff's job. I don't think he believes a damned word I said to him. Maybe it was because I'm tired. I've been awake half the night burying them cowboys."

Ethan swung around. "You buried West and Buck? Why?"

"Because these Los Angeles undertakers want too much money for what they do. In my time I've buried plenty of men, so that's what I did."

"Anybody see you?" Andy asked.

"Just my night riders, they helped me. But there's more. Blunt says he's gotta see the bodies."

"You mean dig 'em up? What'n hell for?" Andy asked.

"It's the law. Damned-fool one if ya ask me." Luke looked for the spittoon.

"We've got crazy laws in Kansas, but this takes it all. A dozen people saw 'em die." Andy leaned down and dusted his boots.

Ethan put his hand on Luke's shoulder. "Luke, I'd of done the same. But we'd better go see this man."

•2•

DEPUTY BLUNT, SITTING relaxed behind the sheriff's rolltop desk, removed a small black book. He shoved it toward Ethan. "That's my notes on the law. Seems Los Angeles has got a couple of murders. I—"

"Murders?" Ethan cut him off.

"From what I hear, there were two men shot last night. They're dead, ain't they? If there wasn't a killing, why'n hell am I wasting my time?"

"Sheriff Blunt," Ethan said, flattering the deputy, "it's a case of Luke's life and self-defense; nothing else." He sat in a chair next to Blunt.

"Can you prove it?"

"Sure. Besides Luke and Andy, there's four spectators who saw the shooting."

"Fine. Bring 'em here."

Ethan glanced at Luke.

"They're probably sleeping it off somewhere. But I'll get them, Sheriff."

"Sands, I'm a deputy; not a sheriff."

Ethan smiled.

Blunt fumbled with a pencil. "The law will uphold itself the same as if the sheriff was sitting right here. By law, I must hold you men until the facts are clear. See that you don't take a notion to leave town."

He leaned back in his curved chair. "Three things: I need to see the bodies; I want to talk to the other four men; and, for number three, I want the sheriff in on this."

The visitors looked at one another, puzzled.

"I've got some questions." Blunt's tongue touched his pencil.

"I'll need the time and place of the killings, where Luke buried the men, their names, and where they lived."

Luke answered his questions.

Sounding as official as he could, Deputy Blunt continued. "Now, Sands, where ya born?"

Ethan hesitated. "Kansas, Wamego, northwest of Topeka."

The deputy dropped his pencil and leaned back in his chair and, for the first time, smiled.

"Damn, now ain't that a coincidence? I'm from Kansas, born in Topeka. Hell, I know Wamego, been there plenty. Good pheasant hunting in that part of Kansas. You boys want coffee? It's hot."

He grabbed the coffeepot and began pouring three cups. Andy shoved his chair closer to the desk.

"Well, Mr. Blunt, what do you know? *I'm* from Topeka."

·3·

ETHAN HOPED THAT Andy wouldn't say too much.
The deputy leaned over his desk. "I'll be. Whatcha do
in Topeka?"

Andy sighed and put his coffee on the desk. "Worked
for the Western Prairie stockyards. I was assistant foreman of Topeka's holding pens."

"Sam Hank's yards?"

"That's right. Sam's. My brother, Frank, is Sam's
manager."

"Is Sam still with us?" Blunt asked.

"You bet he is. Sam's meaner and richer than ever.
Leastwise that's the way I left him."

"His daughter Minnie married my half brother,
Tom."

"I'll be," Andy replied, trying to sound sincere. "Ain't
that something? Married Tom!"

Blunt picked up his notes. "Gentlemen, tell ya what. If you'll get out of town quickly before any more comes of this, I'll mark it down as testified self-defense. That fair?"

Ethan thanked him and promised that, come dawn, the pueblo of Los Angeles would be behind them.

•4•

PETER BALLS, LOADED and packed, lagged behind
Sage and Gussie as Ethan and Andy rode north along
Main Street. The sky above Los Angeles was blue, and
the sun warm as usual. Andy kept looking behind, just
in case Deputy Blunt had changed his mind.

At the edge of town, a little girl in a green skirt and
a yellow blouse ran out to greet them. Her smile radi-
ant, she held a bouquet of orange poppies in her hand.
"Señores, these are for you." Rising on her toes, she
handed them to Andy.

He swung down from Gussie and held up the poppies. Andy grinned at Ethan. "See, the pueblo cain't be
so evil, not with sweethearts like her around."

Ethan smiled at his friend. "There's good everywhere
but at times it's difficult to find."

They turned northwest and walked Sage and Gussie toward the mountains. After a while Ethan said, "Boots?"

"What's on your mind?"

"Those four cowboys. The ones I talked down after the shooting at the cantina."

"Why them four?" Andy asked.

"They had mouths they hadn't used up. Suppose those boys ride up ahead, and get mouthy with someone they shouldn't, talk about meeting up with the storybook fella, Topeka. Might rile something up."

"Ethan, we're in California now. No one ran you out of Kansas, no one's running us out of California."

Ethan smiled wryly.

"As my old grandma used to say to us children," Andy went on, "get the good out of each day, for when the sun goes down, there's no more good to be had." Andy smiled. "Certainly them boys'll mention your name. But people have talked about you for years, and by God, you're still here. If trouble comes, we'll deal with it. We've a helluva long ride, so let's put the jinglebobs to these animals, and go."

A few minutes later, Andy said, "You're serious about going to San Francisco, aren't you?"

"That's right. San Francisco is a different world. I've got a gut feeling about the place. That's all I can tell you."

"Hmmm." Andy pulled back on Gussie. "You'll think this damned peculiar, but I've got a gut feeling, too. *I'm turning back.*"

Ethan swung around. "Back to Kansas?"

"Naw, Los Angeles. Mr. Bean should pull into Los Angeles today, and Bean's a good farmer, but he's not worldly if ya know what I mean. I thought I'd tag along, make sure the Beans get to where they've planned to go."

Ethan shook his head. "Someday I'll discover what

goes on inside that head of yours. But it's your business. Where's Bean headed?"

"I think to Monterey County. He's gonna buy a farm, is what he said."

Ethan knew it wasn't the love of Kitty's father that concerned Andy. Maybe Kitty hadn't lied? "Look, I'd like to keep the mule. He's packing what I need."

"That's fine with me. I'll yank off my personals. And when we meet again we'll take it from there."

"I've got an extra pistol, a Navy Colt. It's old but it's in fine condition. You'd better take it."

"Thanks, but no, Ethan. I'd probably blow off my foot. Anyway, Pa Bean's got weapons. Besides, I won't be far behind you. Chances are we'll meet up sooner than you think."

Andy untied the mule's pack, taking what he needed. Back up on Gussie, he held out his hand.

"Feel awkward about leaving ya, Ethan. But if any man can take care of himself, it's sure as hell gotta be you."

Ethan watched Boots ride away. He pushed back his hat. He'd never told him about Billy Largo following him. Ethan shook his head and gently lifted his reins. Sage snorted.

"C'mon, old boy, it's you and me.

•5•

WHEN ETHAN HAD arrived in Los Angeles, Wells Fargo's chief inspector, Ray Taylor, had given him a map showing roads, landmarks, and towns along the Camino Real. According to the map, Mission San Fernando was the first mission north of Mission San Gabriel where he'd found Andy.

A mile west of San Fernando, along the banks of a dry creek lined with fool's gold, Ethan pitched camp. He hobbled Sage and Peter Balls, and gathered wood for the fire. After a hasty supper, he spread his bed roll and removed his boots.

For the first time since he'd run into Andy, Ethan fell into a despondent mood. Without Andy's chatter, he'd have time to reminisce, mulling over how things in California were going to be different. "It's different all right," he said aloud. "I'm alone with Billy Largo unleashed."

Sage whinnied. "Sorry, I forgot—not completely alone."

Early the next morning after coffee, stale cornbread, and bacon, Ethan mounted Sage. He rode northwest at an easy lope through the coastal hills. White-flowered yuccas grew above tall brush along the road that had begun at Mission San Diego. Father Serra had forged the trail along the coast in 1769. From San Diego to the north of San Francisco, missions located about a day's ride apart dotted Ray's map along *El Camino Real.*

The Mission Santa Barbara lay less than a hundred miles north from where he'd camped. After another long day atop Sage, Ethan figured it shouldn't be far until the turn to Santa Barbara. He moved ahead at a fast walk, while Peter Balls, the cantankerous mule, lagged.

At noon of the second day, Ethan stopped in a wooded area a half day's ride from the mission's road. Mission San Buenaventura lay farther west along the coast. The weather held so he decided to forget San Buenaventura and continue north.

By October in Kansas, leaves would have turned red and yellow and the really cold weather would be around the corner. By now, he thought, snow would have covered the prairie grass and cattle would dig for feed.

Ethan halted Sage to admire the golden hills dotted with green cactus. To the east, mountains were silhouetted against the pale blue sky. High oak trees offered shade from the sun. He was surprised that the moist air had a salty taste.

Occasionally, Ethan passed travelers riding to the *Pueblo de Los Angeles* and traded greetings.

Ethan looked up over Sage's head. "We'll ride up that hill yonder."

He hauled on the mule's lead rope, pulling the animal closer behind Sage. Peter Balls turned and cow-kicked at the gelding, but Sage nimbly sidestepped his powerful hoof.

•6•

AT THE TOP of the hill was a sight that strained his imagination. The Pacific Ocean resembled acres of Texas bluebonnets stretched farther than a man's mind could reach or a painter could gather on canvas. The blue-green water rolled over the soft sand.

Peter Balls balked, slamming Ethan against the cantle, but Ethan ignored it. Down below on the shore spindly-legged birds raced over the wet sand, skirting the breaking waves, while overhead, a formation of brown gulls hovered, swooped, and dove. Speechless, Ethan sat staring at the scene.

Caught in the Pacific's spell, Ethan camped by the shore. Resting by the fire, he enjoyed the steady sound of surf breaking over the water. The sun settled to the horizon, and Ethan nearly heard the sun sizzle when it grazed the purple water. Damn, he thought, Nora would have loved this. No use looking back; he was here.

•7•

HE AWAKENED TO the cawing of birds above him, while below the waves rolled and hissed.

After a hot meal and a shave, Ethan restored the area. He removed rocks that housed the fire, picked up trash, and buried manure. Then he mounted Sage and headed toward the road. He was refreshed from a peaceful sleep that had carried no dead men's faces. He laughed. There had been one dream: Andy nude, standing in church!

The afternoon sun reflected from Mission Santa Barbara's white walls. Entering the narrow mission road, Ethan saw a dozen Indian children playing near a building whose decaying adobe shed itself over the earth. They hurried toward him, shouting words Ethan didn't understand. Their excitement caught the attention of a short, round-faced priest whose brown robe brushed against his leather sandals as he shuffled over the dusty road.

He stopped in front of Ethan, puffing, a cheerful smile spread over his flushed face. "Welcome, my son, I'm Father Remos. Please step down." The father made the sign of the cross, blessing the stranger. He turned and said something in Spanish; the older boys held Sage's reins.

"My children will corral the animals and bring your saddlebags. You have the look of a man hours in the saddle. We'll sit in the arbor and enjoy the shade."

•8•

"MY SON, YOUR name is?"

"Ethan Sands, Father Remos."

Not knowing whether to shake hands, Ethan just smiled. Father Remos took him by the arm and walked with him toward the mission, entering a patio.

"Ah, there's a bucket of fresh water by the post. I'll find something to dry your face. Then we shall sit and enjoy a glass of wine."

Ethan put his hands into the swollen oak bucket filled with clear, cool water and splashed his face feeling refreshed by washing away the trail dust.

Father Remos handed him a towel. "Please, sit here, next to me." Ethan relaxed in a heavy wooden chair made of sycamore logs tightly bound by thin leather thongs. Above Ethan's head, grapevines with large faded leaves hung below the arbor, touching the rich black soil.

"Ah, the wine is here." Father Remos took the tray from the Indian boy who stood by. "Mr. Sands, try a glass of red wine from the mission's winery. Tell me of yourself."

As they sipped the hearty wine, Ethan spoke of Kansas, his journey, and how he was bound for San Francisco. He described Andy and how they'd met; what he thought of Los Angeles. The priest listened attentively. When Ethan finished, Father Remos thanked him.

"Here at the mission we depend on visitors to keep us abreast of the times."

After refilling their glasses, Father Remos sighed and settled back into his chair. "Your Kansas has quite a history. Our library, somewhat limited, does have a section on American history and I've read most of what we own. Tell me, are you familiar with California's missions?"

"I know very little. I do know El Camino Real began in San Diego and connects missions along the Pacific Coast. That's about it."

"My son, that's the place to begin! Since Father Serra founded the church in San Diego, much has happened. We were the tenth mission built. Even since May 1844 when I first arrived, so much has taken place. I assume you've never heard of secularization?"

"No, Father."

"Rome decided California missions should function on their own and not be completely dependent upon the Church for survival. In 1837 how we managed our affairs, including the Indians, had changed. We had to seek other sources in order to survive. Foolishly, we sold our lands into private hands. While secularization succeeded in other Spanish countries, its application in

California proved disastrous. Ah, but enough of the negative."

Father Remos pointed to the Moorish gray-rock fountain splashing water into a circular basin. "That, my son, is a picture of happier times. The fountain was built in 1808."

"Father, what happened to the Indians, the ones you've converted and educated, are they still here?"

"That is the saddest part. No, most of them have gone. We allowed the converts to do as they pleased, and this proved to be poor advice. In short, their lives became poorer than they had known with us, a tragedy."

Curious, Ethan raised his eyebrows.

"You see, the Church had become their shelter, their very being, so to speak. Free, they've become subservient to the wishes of the white man. And, he hasn't always been fair. Ah, your glass—more wine?"

Ethan learned how the missions had suffered. Fright lingered in the priest's eyes when he mentioned the earthquakes of 1818 and 1825.

"Have you witnessed an earthquake?" Father Remos asked as he refilled Ethan's glass.

"No, and, uh, I'm in no hurry."

The rotund padre smiled. "I'll pray that you never shall. See the buildings over there? Ah, such poor condition. We have neither the money nor people to repair what you see. My friend, as you ride, you'll find these conditions exist in the other missions along the Camino Real." He laughed. "I've nicknamed El Camino the doughty little friar's road!" His eyebrows rose as he reverently glanced above. With a quick bend of the arm, the good father threw back his wine.

"Tonight is fandango. You must attend. It may shatter the boredom of such a long ride. And, of course you'll stay."

Ethan couldn't refuse such an invitation.

"On one condition, Father." Ethan smiled. "Just call me Ethan."

"Very well, I shall. Oh, speaking of Kansas, the day before yesterday four young men visited the mission. They, too, were from Kansas."

"Did they say where they were headed?" Ethan asked.

"Paso Robles. Something about locating a herd, I believe."

"Do you know these men?"

"No, Father, I don't know them, though as you say, everyone coming from Kansas is peculiar."

Father Remos pushed back his chair and motioned Ethan to follow him. Collecting his saddlebags, Ethan walked behind the priest. "Ethan, there was something unusual about one young man. He seemed troubled; he asked me to hear his confession."

"Father, did he mention a gunfight?"

The priest stopped and placed his hand on Ethan's shoulder. "My son, I'm sorry. That's all I can tell you. Confessions are confidential."

They went through a dim passage covered with blood-colored pavers that wove through an arch leading to a thick wooden door whose hinges were held by iron plates bolted to the wood. When he pulled on the iron latch, rust flakes scattered over the tiles below.

"You'll find our rooms plain, but the basics are here. Water, soap, a towel; other amenities are down the passageway to your right. I'll call for you when it's time for fiesta."

Ethan placed his hands against the rough, textured wall and felt the coolness. He sat on a bed made of heavy timbers laced together by husky leather straps. He stretched out as the leather complained under his weight.

•9•

AT FIVE O'CLOCK, Father Remos guided Ethan outside to another patio where people had assembled for fiesta. It began with guitars and dancing. Pretty señoritas dressed in brilliant reds, yellows, and the Mexican greens flashed before him. Father Remos, sitting before him, placed an inch-long, deep green jalapeño on Ethan's plate.

"We have a saying, my son: jalapeños are the devil's angels. Supposedly they cleanse evil from within your soul."

Ethan believed him. A few bites of the fiery peppers sent sweat pouring over his face and flowed down his neck inside his shirt.

The next morning, after a humble breakfast of cornmeal cakes, tea, and dark beans, Ethan was ready to leave. Indian boys held Sage's reins. Father Remos smiled, holding new directions he'd added to Ethan's map.

"On this, my son, you'll find the missions clearly marked. You're welcome even at sanctuaries not under our dominion."

Ethan waved a salute and rode west on the mission's corrugated road. Reaching El Camino, he heard the mission bells ringing over the hills calling those who would pray. Soon the bells faded and the only sounds were of Sage's hoofs, and the saddle's squeaking leather.

Soon a gray mist drifted over him, destroying his contented mood. It reminded him of the dismal day Dirk Largo's gang and his son, Mace, were buried. Among the few attending the humble service, Dirk's brother, Billy, had stood quietly as they shoveled dirt over the coffins. The next day, the sheriff had seen Billy Largo leaving Topeka's Wells Fargo office that Ethan's friend, Matt, managed.

When Ethan had disappeared from view, Father Remos, in a pensive mood, shuffled over the dirt road. Climbing the mission steps, he entered the faintly lighted corridor and found his room. For a moment he sat thinking. There was so much he could have told Ethan, but not wishing to bore the visitor, he had refrained from recounting a litany of events.

Smiling, he reached over his desk and ran his fingers along three old registers. He lingered over one: *The Dedication of Mission Santa Barbara.* Dusting off the cover, he began to read.

The tenth mission, founded December 4, 1786, was rededicated December 16, 1786, by Father Fermín Lasuen. The earthquake of 1812 destroyed the mission and it wasn't until 1815 that repairs began. Finished in 1820 with only one tower, until the second was added in 1833. Disturbing as earthquakes in 1834 the mission was secularized, then sold in 1846, and during the Civil War was returned.

Father Serra, the founder of California's missions, dreamed about building Santa Barbara. But the honor fell upon Father Lasuen. Father Serra had dreamed of three channel missions, protected by a presidio, to gap the distance between San Luis Obispo and San Gabriel. At San Buenaventura the first of the channel missions was dedicated in 1782. Father Remos sighed; that was over a hundred years ago.

Unfortunately, Governor Neve was opposed to the expansion of the mission system because he felt that it gave too much economic power to the padres. Father Remos laughed, always a politician with the idea that he knew what was best for the people. The governor worked hard to block the expansion of the missions.

"And oh, how he did," Father Remos said aloud.

Father Serra was unaware of the governor's opposition, and he did not know that the governor had already persuaded the viceroy to withhold funds for a separate mission in Santa Barbara. He favored Monterey. But Father Serra kept busy preparing three leather-bound registers for the anticipated mission. After three weeks of waiting he was informed by the governor that the mission would not be approved until the presidio was completed. Father Serra was saddened. Before he died, he had visited the presidio twice before a new governor granted permission for the mission to be built.

Someone knocked. Father Remos opened the door.

"Yes, my son, what is it?"

"Father, come. Another visitor is riding up the road."

"A gringo?"

"*Sí*, padre, a strange-looking one."

Father Remos put down the register.

•10•

IN A DINGY Topeka hotel off Main Street, the sun sifting through slits in the green window shade awoke Billy. He fumbled for the gun belt hanging from the headboard's post. He stood in front of a mirror gargling and spitting whiskey into a porcelain bowl next to a rose-trimmed pitcher.

Wiping shaving soap from his chin, he stared in the mirror. Today, Billy thought, is the beginning of the killing of Ethan Sands.

The rusty cowbell over Wells Fargo's door clanged as Billy ambled to the counter. A broad smile covered his narrow face as he spoke to the man sitting behind a desk piled with papers.

"Good morning, sir," Billy said, leaning over the counter. "I'm Burlo Wills. Uh, Mr. Briggs of the First National suggested that possibly you can help me."

Matt eyed the handsome stranger, rugged in a heavy

sheepskin coat with the collar turned up about his neck. The black Spanish sombrero seemed odd to Matt, as did the long blond hair that touched the newcomer's shoulders. Silver conchos dotting the leather hatband caught Matt's eye—though they were less eye-catching than the pistols protruding from his long gray coat; the narrow black eyes—sharp enough to cut glass—frightened Matt.

"What's on your mind?"

"I'm looking for a friend. His name is Andy Love."

"Andy? Let's see. Uh, three months ago he took a train to New Mexico and, from what I've gathered, he joined a wagon train going west—to Los Angeles."

"You're sure?"

"Positive. Because another good friend of mine left Topeka two months after Andy."

"Could you give me any idea where I can find Andy, or maybe the friend?"

"I have a notion he's in Los Angeles—but I dunno."

"Well, uh, about this friend. Maybe he'd have something that would give me a lead. His name?"

"Ethan Sands. You've probably heard of him."

"No, can't say I have. I'm not from Topeka. You got any idea where I'd find Mr. Sands?"

Matt took a long stride to the desk, found the notebook and opened it.

"He left Topeka for San Francisco, then Wells Fargo sent him south, to Los Angeles. There, Ethan quit. Mister, that's the most I can tell ya." Matt waited as the stranger shifted his weight.

"Mr. Turner, when's the next train to Los Angeles?"

Apprehensively, Matt reached for the timetable.

•11•

NORTH OF MISSION Santa Barbara, Ethan noticed the mountains had grown nearer the sea, and a pleasant onshore breeze carried spray from the breaking surf into the hills. The fine mist salted his cheeks. After drinking half a pot of coffee, Ethan mounted Sage and continued along El Camino Real.

On the road for an hour, Ethan noticed Sage's ears lying back flat on his head. Sage broke into a choppy, nervous trot, then stopped, scraped his rear hooves while backing up.

"What's wrong with you, boy?" Ethan spurred him.

Now the mule, sensing trouble, reared back. Sage jerked his head and shied from a thicket of trees to the right of the road.

"C'mon, walk over there. Take a look. There's nothing to spook you."

Sage snorted, his bulging eyes large as dollars. Ethan fell back, nearly emptying the saddle.

"You crazy son of a bitch!"

He slammed his palm against Sage's head. Pain shot through his arm into his chest, pinching a nerve. Nostrils flared, the huge quarter horse—which stood a hand higher than his normal seventeen—stared at the thicket of trees. Taut as steel, the reins yanked on Ethan's arm.

He dismounted, calmed the mule, and loosely tethered Sage and Peter Balls to a tree. Walking into the brush, he heard a crunching sound, branches snapping under a heavy weight. In a clearing stood a horse with its front leg tangled in the reins; above him a body twisted at the end of a squeaking rope hung from an oak tree's limb.

Ethan's eyes followed the revolving body until he had a full view of the man's face. The face was now grotesque, yet he recognized the young cowboy who had closed West's eyes.

A shaft of sunlight shone through the leaves, casting eerie shadows over the dead man's face. And from Father Remos's description, the victim was one of the four Ethan had seen at the Los Angeles cantina. His first thought was that the young man had hung himself. He stood staring at the pitiful sight until men's voices commanded his attention.

•12•

ETHAN HURRIED BACK through the thicket to the road. A wagon rolled toward him. The driver waved for Ethan to come alongside.

"I'm Lester Fern," he said, pushing back his tattered derby, "and this sleepy-lookin' creature next to me is my swamper, Arapaho Jones. Me and him saw the horse and mule and we figured its rider had got thrown."

Before Ethan spoke, he added: "Mister, from the gawk on your face, you've seen a ghost. You all right?"

Ethan introduced himself and asked both men to step down from the wagon.

"I've come onto a dead man, Mr. Fern, and I'd like you to witness the body as I found it."

The men followed Ethan toward Sage. "The tracks you see are mine, and there's no horse tracks leading in or out of the heavy brush."

When Lester and his friend saw the body, they stood quietly gaping.

"Sure as hell, he's dead," Lester said, handling the dead man's boot. "Is that his horse?"

Ethan nodded.

"It looks to me"—Lester paused, picking mud from his hands—"that he rode the horse underneath the limb, tied the rope, spurred him, and finished the job." Lester turned to his friend. "Arapaho, you hightail down the road and track the dead man's horse, see where he entered the brush. Me and Mr. Sands'll cut him down." Lester pulled a skinning knife from his belt.

After Arapaho disappeared, Lester said, "Jones is mostly Paiute, but a helluva tracker. His Indian name is Quiet Stick. Stick'll find out what happened if anyone can."

"I thought you said he's Arapaho."

"No he isn't. He's a Paiute but he thinks Paiutes are stupid. It's complicated. Kindly said, the Paiutes rate poorly on the Indians' social ladder, especially out here in California. Jones, after smoking too much crazy-weed gets his brains crossed and favors the Arapahos. Personally, I find the Paiutes a friendly tribe and easy to know." His eyes lingered on the dead man's boots. "Stand back, I'll cut him down." He stood on a log and worked the blade through the rope.

Ethan helped Lester load the body over the horse and they walked out through the brush. On the road, he untied a blanket from the dead man's horse and covered the corpse.

"Wanna smoke?" Lester had the makings in his hand. "I can see why you wanted us to see the dead fella. That's why I sent Jones to have a look. Though your tracks were underneath the body, it doesn't mean you did it. Strange why a person carrying a gun would hang himself. Grisly way to die if ya ask me." He handed a cigarette to Ethan. "You need this more than I do—go on, light up, I'll roll 'nuther."

"Thanks. Ethan took a long drag, exhaled and glanced up the road. "Here comes your friend. Looks Arapaho, don't he?"

•13•

"WHAT'D YA FIND?" Lester asked.

"A horse went in and came out exactly where you had trailed him from the road. The dead man was alone."

Changing the subject, Lester glanced at the wagon.

"Before me and Arapaho turned legitimate, we were forty-niners during the big one. We've seen lots of killin's. Diggers thought little of a man hangin' from a tree. Hangtown didn't earn its name *building churches*!"

"Ya wanna bury 'im here?" Arapaho asked.

"Hey, not so fast. Mr. Sands, ya ever run in to this fella?" Lester pressed his boot against the cowboy's body.

"No. Never." Ethan had to lie. Explaining the cantina shoot-out would be a mistake. "You boys going south, through Santa Barbara?"

"That's where we're headed, with a load of fence wire for the hardware store in town. Why?"

"It'd be wise to take him to the mission. He'll get a decent burial, and the priest will make a record of his death."

"Uh, hold on, I dunno about that. They'll ask questions, maybe drag the sheriff in on it, and God knows what else." Lester glanced at Arapaho, who shrugged.

It may have been that the former forty-niners were wanted by the law, but Ethan knew this was not the time to ask.

"Oh, what the hell"—Arapaho sighed—"all we gotta do is tell 'em what we've seen. No lawman that's got his nuts and bolts in the same pouch would think we'd have carried a man so far just to *bury* him!"

"Guess you're right, chief." Lester winked. "Okay, it's done, we'll take him."

Relieved, Ethan helped lift the body into the wagon, then shook both men's hands. "Just get him to a priest, and I'm sure he'll understand."

"Mr. Sands, I'd stay out of the brush if'n I was you. It's hard telling what you'll find, especially in California!"

A mile down the road, Arapaho Jones pulled the wagon to the side of the road, tied the reins, and rested one foot on the iron step.

"What'n hell ya doing?"

"I'm gonna dump the stiff, and we'll forget we ever saw him."

Lester scratched his head. "Suppose you're right. Santa Barbara ain't no Hangtown! Here, grab a shovel." He glanced over his shoulder, then reached down and yanked off the dead man's boots. "C'mon, no one's coming—we'll put him away where he belongs."

Arapaho faced his friend.

"Les, sure you ain't half Piaute?"

•14•

SAGE WAS AS good a friend as a well-trained horse can be. The Kansan had enjoyed conversations with cats, dogs, and horses, and compared to dullards he had known, animals were often finer company. Still, while riding a hundred miles alone, Ethan collected dust and lonesomeness.

A hundred miles north from where he had seen the hung cowboy, Ethan rode into a ranching community, San Luis Obispo. He was dry. On Higuera Street, he tied Sage and Peter Balls to a hitching post in front of Elmer's Saloon, slung a saddlebag over his shoulder, and ambled inside. E. J. Rucker, the proprietor, had gone for the day and had left his bartender, Gus, in charge.

Gus saw the saddlebag and laughed. "Mister, either you're hauling gold, or you're looking to wash your clothes." Ethan slid the saddlebag onto the bar.

"Just a beer."

Sensing that the stranger didn't appreciate his waggery, Gus poured and slid an iced beer in front of Ethan. "That'll be a dime."

"Bartender, that sign outside says five-cent beer. How come a dime?"

"From the dust on your digs, I figured you'd be thirsty. That's a large mug. It cost a dime. But don't fret, if'n you want, I'll take it back."

Ethan put the money on the bar and took a long draw.

"You, uh, passing through?" Gus asked.

"That's about it."

"We've got good hotels. One has inside tubs, and the other, the Andrews, partly finished, only has a few. Across the street. It's reasonable. 'Nuther beer?"

"Sure."

Gus gave the bar a quick wipe and filled Ethan's glass.

"Reasonable sounds good," Ethan said. "I could use a bath. It's been a hot and tiresome day." Ethan couldn't cope with summer weather lasting this late in the year.

"Then, mister, you'd better stay. Because after you leave here, you'll climb the Cuesta Grade, and the next decent hotel is twenty-five miles, in Paso Robles."

"Is that about a half-day ride?"

"Depends."

"On what?"

"On how long it takes you to pull the Cuesta Grade. It's a steep run, especially if it's warm. You see, if you only . . ." Gus glanced toward the door, his eyes narrowed to slits. Outside, a husky, raw-faced woman with a jowly face, draped in a sacky dress, a hat shoved sloppily over her head, swept her hard eyes over the bar. Satisfied, she shuffled on.

Gus sighed. "Thank God!" He hurried from behind the bar, raced for the door, and stuck out his head, looking both ways.

"I hope to God I never see that freak again. That's the most vicious woman that ever crawled from the hills. Mean Willa is what she's called."

"Mean Willa's a tiger, huh?"

"A gorilla's closer. Had you been in town a week ago, you'd understand. Willa was in a rage."

"Why?"

"We've a gent in town who's a full-time drunk. He's got a thirst impossible to quench. The fool's married into a fine California family, has a gorgeous wife, and when half-sober he makes a deal of money. He's in shipping or something close." Gus wiped the bar.

"It was Taris McCleary that Willa damned near killed. Picked him up and threw him outside, and the drunk landed facedown in the mud. And Taris is a fair-sized man. Taris offended Willa while she sat next to him, drinking, and Miss Ugly took wrong something he said."

"Hurt him bad?" Ethan asked.

"Damned near broke him in half. Truth is, Taris isn't out of the hospital yet."

The lingering chloroform dulled his vision. Taris McCleary squinted as he tried to focus his eyes on a hand holding a rag.

"Hold still! I've gotta get the vomit off your face," the nurse said. A cold wash rag slopped against Taris McCleary's blotchy skin. "There, that's better. I must prepare you for Dr. La Rue; the doctor wants to see you."

La Rue's name jangled Taris's head. "Prepare? Oh, that's pleasin'. You mean that stiff-necked, soft-mouthed Protestant bastard wants to talk?" His guts were dry, cracked and splintered. "Oh be-Jesus if'n I had a drink." His swollen right eye barely moved; the left eye stayed closed.

"Fair lady," Taris said, "be going to the wall, me pants. Uh, there's a fiver in the right pocket—it's got your name on it, it has." Taris sucked in. *"Get it!"*

The nurse stepped back and glared at him. "You want *me* to get a bottle—for *you*! Mr. McCleary, you *are* crazy. Why, I'd lose my job. Dr. La Rue would skin me. Oh, no, *I will not*!"

"Lass, there's two fives!"

The nurse tossed the rag on the tray and rushed for the door just when it flew open.

Dr. La Rue strode in, warm in his long black coat.

"Taris, what have you done? Never mind, I've heard!"

Taris looked at the ceiling and braced himself.

"McCleary, you've had a serious injury. Your ribs may have pierced your lung, we're not sure yet. Your collarbone is fractured, and you've got a clump of nasty head wounds." The doctor rubbed his chin.

"If you continue to consume liquor, beatings or not, you'll die."

Taris had expected this. He knew the doctor wasn't a man like himself who enjoyed a good drink. The doctor knew little of the Irish! He'd trade all his trite words for a wee, cheap pint.

"Taris, you've got an exceptional wife. Sabonda is an exquisite and charming woman. If you persist, you'll lose her. A man who indulges usually has a hurt, a failure, a memory that clings inside his brain. Thus, when troubled, he turns to drink, but booze only shoves it deeper inside of him. Taris, if you continue you won't solve what's bothering you. Instead, you'll kill yourself."

Dr. La Rue walked to the window and raised the green shade.

"I know of a man in San Francisco who can treat you. You'll have to stay for several months. But when it's over, you can get on with your life, Taris, sober."

Taris frowned. Next he'll be bringing up the Church. "Good doctor, you've got me wrong. I'm a moderate man."

"Moderate! God in Heaven, you don't know the meaning of the word! I've patched you up too many times!"

Too weak to fight back, Taris stared at him. He wondered if La Rue had squealed to Sabonda's father.

"One more word." He held up his forefinger. "If you sneak drinks, McCleary, to hell with you! You can find another physician."

Taris began to boil. The other doctor in town had just died. He wanted to blast out the truth about everything. Whenever doctors can't find out what's really wrong, it's always the booze! Dr. La Rue hesitated at the door.

"Taris, think about what's troubling you."

•15•

TARIS COULDN'T GET the fuzzy images of his departure from Ireland out of his mind. His father's admonitions: "Your brother needs this money. Get it to him as soon as you arrive in New York. Put off your thoughts of California for now. The gold's all dug and in banks. Son, my shipping business on the East Coast must be solid before risking the West Coast operation. It's still dangerous and wild in California!"

Taris never docked in New York. In Boston he jumped ship with $5,000 of his father's money. He boarded a ship for New Orleans and sailed around the Horn.

A year had passed since Taris left Ireland. He'd cut a fine figure on the warm August day he landed in Monterey. After a year, her father, the *alcalde*, reluctantly consented: Sabonda became Mrs. McCleary. Two years ago, come May.

Taris leaned over and lifted the pan. He gagged, dry. He lay back disgusted. He wanted a drink. Hell! With a pint, he'd rise up and walk out of this dreary sick-room. Once again, he'd be alive. He lay pondering, weary, his eyes closed.

He dreamed of Ireland's green hills at dawn, the cold mist spilling over the hills. In his sleep, he moaned. His mind needed the relief that only whiskey could provide.

"One more beer before you go?" Gus nodded at Ethan.

"No, two's enough. I'm going to stable my animals and try a hotel. Though I enjoyed it—good 'n' cold and worth a dime."

Gus picked up the glass. "Speak of the devil, there he is! M'God, he can walk."

In a pressed checked suit, a gold tie, a derby cocked on his head, Taris McCleary stood in the doorway, beaming. Leaning on a cane, with his enlarged, blood-shot eyes he searched the saloon. Satisfied, gathering his energy, he pushed back the door and strolled to the bar.

He dropped his backside on a stool, pounded a heavy fist on the bar, and laughed. "Ya fathead, ya didn't think I'd make it. Damn you, Gus, I'm here! Bring me a bottle and don't dally, making me tongue turn to sliv-ers." Taris gazed at the stranger standing beside him. "Ah, sir, 'tis a celebration I'm having. Please, Mr. Cow-boy, join me for a drink. Gus, the whiskey."

Taris had made a thirsty stop at the German's saloon to fortify himself before stopping at Elmer's.

"McCleary!" Gus shoved a paper in front of Taris. "Before you drink, you'd better have a look at that. The boss said I should give it to you."

It was an itemized bill for the damage Taris's battle

with Mean Willa had caused; below it, a past-due liquor tab. Taris glanced at it and tossed it aside. "That's ridiculous—there ain't that much furniture in the place."

Gus leaned across to him. "That's right, you've busted half, and the boss wants his money."

Taris fumbled with a wad of cash, ripped off four bills, shoved them at Gus, and laughed.

"I've purposely paid that quack La Rue with a bad check." Laughing hurt his taped ribs. "Oh me God, I'd give a hundred to hear the righteous fool squawk. We'll scoot to a table and have a shooter." Taris yelled, "Gus, a bottle."

Gus slammed his huge hand on the bar. "Not so fast." He looked at Ethan. Mister, if you buy a bottle, fine. But if my boss comes in, you tell him it's yours. He'll fire me if'n you don't."

Ethan noticed the pathetic look on Taris's face.

"Bartender, I'll stand him for one drink."

Taris whispered, "Please, get a drink and, uh, I'll take care of it." He slipped Ethan a dollar. "Might you be Irish?"

Ethan poured the drink.

Taris grabbed Ethan's whiskey and threw it back.

Soon Taris was slurring his words. He stumbled to his feet. His glazed eyes tried to focus on Ethan. His cane slipped from his hand and he fell flat on his face. He tried to pull himself up. He looked up into Ethan's face. "Ah, what the devil, least this time I won't be landing in the sloppin' mud!"

"Mister, give me a hand," Gus said to Ethan. "We'll take him across the street. At the hotel, they'll know what to do."

* * *

Leaving the Los Angeles Wells Fargo office, Billy Largo headed for the sheriff's office. He had heard the details of the cantina shooting.

"My deputy is not here—he handled that case. Lemme see." The lawman opened a file and thumbed through. "Here it is. Self-defense, no charge. Two men killed."

Sheriff, was the shooter a man named Andy Love?"

The officer looked again. "No. A fast draw called Ethan Sands. Both of 'em left town." The sheriff looked at him uneasily.

"Much obliged, Sheriff."

For fifty cents, the Mexican clerk at the Nuevo Hotel said Ethan and Andy had bought a mule. Riding out of town, Billy knew they hadn't taken the train to Bakersfield. No one in their right mind would pay to ship two horses and a mule, loaded down.

The thought of pulling the trigger and putting a bullet between Ethan's eyes warmed Billy's heart.

"Big shot," he'd say, "turn around. I'm going to give you what you gave my brother, Dirk. Mister Fast Draw, you're a legend—a dead one!"

Billy, doing right by avenging his family, reined his horse north—toward El Camino Real.

•16•

AFTER THE HOTEL bellman had locked Taris's door, he took Ethan aside. "Gus said that you're riding north over the Cuesta Grade. I've got a suggestion."

The hotel's owner, busy adding his cash, didn't overhear the bellman cutting a private deal.

"Willow Creek is near Cuesta Grade. Hannah, my sister, and her husband, Josh, own a ranch near the creek. Hannah earns a little extra taking boarders, and for the cost of a hotel room, you'll get home-cooked meals, and a clean bed, plus your horse'll have hay free of fireweed."

Ethan thanked him. It had been a while since he'd had a home-cooked meal. "At your sister's, can I take a hot bath?"

"You bet." The clerk scribbled a note. "Give this to Hannah. And don't worry about Mr. McCleary, he's a regular. We know *exactly* what to do."

* * *

At Hannah's farm, Ethan seated himself at a table with breads, jams, and spices and a hefty supper of fried chicken, mashed potatoes, fresh peas, and buttered corn bread. Rounding off her supper, Hannah brought him coffee and a slice of fresh apple pie with a cut of cheddar cheese on the side.

Outside on the porch, Ethan thought about the peaceful life Hannah and her husband had. A comfortable home, love between them, and money enough to get along. He thought of how little money he'd made risking his life protecting other people's funds.

If he had stayed in Topeka dodging bullets, he'd probably have been buried with a bucket of blossoms and a handful of tears from mourners who hardly knew his name.

California took on a rosy glow.

The next morning, Ethan felt brand-new. He crossed the yard to the house. Hannah met him at the kitchen door. "Mr. Sands, you'll need this 'fore the day is gone."

He sniffed the air as she pointed toward the stove. "I've got ham 'n' eggs, sweet bread, fried potatoes, hot coffee and cream. Ethan, if I may, I've enjoyed having you at my table. You strike me as a man who hasn't found time to enjoy himself."

She handed him a flour sack. "Here's a little leftover chicken. Thought it might hit the spot later." Ethan thanked her and tucked it under his arm. The clerk was right. The traveler had been treated well.

"Keep your eyes peeled; there's places on the grade where highwaymen can jump you, especially riding alone. In years past, the stage got robbed nearly every run."

Her eyes drifted down to Ethan's low-slung pistol. "Mr. Sands, I get the inkling you and that forty-five aren't strangers. I'm not asking about your line of work. If you come back, you're welcome to sit at my table." She smiled coyly. "Anytime."

Hannah stood by and watched him mount up and head the large quarter horse and Peter Balls toward the gate.

Touching his brim, Ethan said, "You take care of yourself, and if I ever come back, I'll be at your table."

Down the road, passing beneath the gate's heavy timbers, Ethan swung around to look back. Hannah was pretty with the sun shining on her white apron over a checked blue dress. If she represented California's hospitality, he'd already struck it rich.

Part 3

Sí Señor, California Is a Two-Faced Bitch!

• 1 •

WHEN THE MORNING mist began to lift, Ethan arrived at the foot of Cuesta Grade. He looked up the serpentine road and leaned over to stroke Sage's neck. "Ya ready?" He turned around and checked the mule.

What Gus had said was true. The steep grade demanded energy from both man and horse. The road cut through ravines and snaked around cabin-sized boulders; thick oak trees stood deep in brush that measured saddle-high. Ethan began to understand the railroad's concern for laying tracks over the grade; chiseling these tons of rock, the workers would bust both picks and backs before a tunnel passed through the Cuesta Grade.

For two hours, Sage, Peter Balls, and Ethan worked up hill, and weary of rubbing against leather, he halted the animals.

Ethan looked up at the mountain's rounded domes and tried to imagine how long it must have taken for a wagon drawn by two horses to haul a heavy load over the twisting grade. At last the summit was just ahead. Sage's grunts indicated that he, too, had had enough. At the summit, Ethan decided to rest the animals. The faithful horse, heavily lathered, had earned his keep. Peter Balls, a stubborn animal, took the grade in stride. The mule lifted his head and sniffed the air; thirsty, he had smelled water.

Ethan dismounted and hobbled Sage and Peter Balls. He looked back down over the steep grade, pushed back his hat, and said aloud, "Cuesta Grade, glad you're behind me and not ahead."

The Kansan carefully sprinkled brown tobacco over thin yellow paper, and ran his tongue along the paper's edge, sealing it. He struck a match, inhaled, and let the smoke run free. For a few moments he stood enjoying the aroma of tangy tobacco as the smoke rose lazily overhead. He drifted over to a hump of granite boulders that concealed a stream. Green-white water rushed from smooth rocks buried in the sandy bottom of a cool mountain spring.

From Cuesta's summit, he had a sweeping view of dry brush that covered the mountains running west, and farther north, the mountains that descended to form a shallow valley where golden grass grew so tall it resembled Kansas corn. From the rich grasslands, the earth rose to higher hills. North and east, the lower lands were studded with trees, and shaded pastures molded a ragged green edge against the horizon.

He pulled out a handkerchief and wiped the trail dust from his eyes. And suddenly he saw, off to the side, a man resting against a thick oak trunk. Nearby, a buckskin grazed.

Leaning against the trunk, the old man with a sugarloaf sombrero sat holding a guitar across his lap. His long hair framed an oval face with furrows scrolled into his skin from years beneath the sun. Strapped to his side was a dusty, hot-iron pistol, a friendly relic from other times. Ethan admired his glistening teeth. He lifted his guitar and strummed a melodious chord.

•2•

"¿*QUÉ TAL*, HOW goes it, *amigo*?" He smiled. "*Por favor*, please, come rest yourself."

The stranger reached behind a tree and grabbed a bottle. ¿*Tequila, hombre?*"

Ethan squatted down, resting his arms across his knees. Playing with a leaf, Ethan smiled. "Thanks, old-timer. Do you live nearby?"

The man's clear, dark eyes sparkled. "*Sí*, once I did. When I worked for the *alcalde*, on Rancho Norte Verde." He pointed south, down the grade. "But now I'm going home, to Monterey. You are a *vaquero*? A cowboy, my friend?"

"I guess there's some that call me that. I've had my share of chasing cows."

"A man should know his cows. *Hombre, por favor*, come take a drink!" The old man's arm wavered as he passed the clear glass bottle. Politely, Ethan took a short drink and handed it back.

"*Muchacho*, your horse is winded, his lungs are working like bellows against his ribs. After the Cuesta, it's wise to let your horse rest, and for that he'll be kind to you. Come, let us talk." He bent his finger at the blanket. "Sit, lean back, enjoy yourself against the trunk. This is why God made the trees."

Ethan sat next to the man with hair that mirrored the sun.

"Gringo, you know of the Salinas?"

"No. I'm afraid I don't."

The old man took a long drink that gurgled down his throat. He pushed back the guitar and raised his arm. "Over there, behind those willows, is the river; the Salinas, *muchacho*. She's mean when it rains. She has quicksand that can kill a horse, the river she floods the land. This is why I warn you, señor."

He paused and belched.

"Years ago, when the Spaniards ruled the land, they searched for a trail to Monterey. Then there was grass high as your saddle horn. They failed. Later, on a march north, a smart *soldado*, a Spanish soldier, carried a sack of mustard seeds he'd brought from Spain. On the way the Spaniard scattered seeds in the fresh earth along the river." He paused, held up the nearly empty bottle, and frowned.

"Returning, they had a surprise; the mustard plants in the fertile riverbanks had grown, and tall yellow flowers guided them back to San Luis Obispo. You see, that is why now you can ride El Camino Real." He cracked a laugh. "Ah, when I was young like you, I was a strong vaquero. I rode for the *alcalde*, Señor Juan Bautista Ricardo. I am Jorge Fermín. *Americanos* call me George, at your service, señor."

Ethan moved closer. "Uh, you said, the *alcalde*?"

"*Sí*, he was the mayor when I first joined him in Monterey. You know him?"

"No. But I've heard his name."

The vaquero laughed. "You should. Señor Ricardo is a respected man who has power and owns much land. He has ranchos from San Luis Obispo to Monterey. Some say the *alcalde* may be the wealthiest man in California. But he's a good man."

"Mr. Fermín, does this fella have a daughter? I think her name's Sabonda?"

Fermín held up his hand. "Oh *sí*, that is the señora. Sabonda, oh she is beautiful, like a rose, *amigo*." Jorge sighed, making a fanning gesture with his hand. "It's a shame."

Ethan cocked his head. "I don't follow you."

"Her beauty is wasted."

"Wasted?"

"On her husband. Señor McCleary, he drinks too much."

"His name is Taris?"

"*Sí.*"

"We've met. Funny man. But you're right, he drinks! More than the normal man." Ethan laughed. "How does he get along with this *alcalde*?"

"Juan Bautista didn't approve of the marriage. But Sabonda was in love, so for her sake he gave in. The *alcalde* opened the way for her husband to make something of himself, and for a year he tried. Later, this man changed. I think—and this is only me—he lives with the *diablo*, the devil, señor. The vaqueros on the Rancho Norte didn't like what they saw. Neither did Sabonda's father, but he stands by her."

The old man yawned. He laid the guitar aside and

stuck the bottle in the sand. "*Hombre*, it is time for si-
esta."

Jorge Fermín leaned back and closed his eyes.

Quietly, Ethan walked back to where the animals
grazed and untied their hobbles. Adjusting his saddle,
he heard Jorge's voice. "*Amigo*. Remember, California,
she's like a two-faced señorita, she can be a bitch."

The weary Mexican vaquero waved and closed his
eyes again. The wind blew leaves over the star-shaped
rowels of his Spanish spurs.

Riding down the other side of the grade, Ethan
thought about what the old man had said—California's
a two-faced bitch.

"C'mon Sage, we'll give this California she-devil our
best shot."

In a heavy fog, Andy was riding alongside Kitty
Bean's wagon, humming a tune as they turned up the
road leading into Mission Santa Barbara. A rider wearing a black Spanish hat, with long blond hair hanging
down his back, approached them. He paused, looked
into the wagon, nodded and disappeared into the thick
ocean fog. Something moved Andy to turn around and
look. But all he saw was the stranger's back.

•3•

AS ETHAN RODE northward along El Camino, the sun poked through willowy clouds and cast long shadows over the ravines. Farther east, the Sierra Madre Mountains formed a valley along the highway continuing south past San Luis Obispo. To the west, the Santa Lucias ran north toward Monterey.

He paused to light a cigarette. As he lifted the match, he spotted a wagon, half mile ahead of him, pull onto the Camino Real. There were two men on the front seat and three on horseback, riding behind. They turned left and headed south toward him.

The driver cupped his hands and hollered, "Howdy, stranger. Afternoon to ya!"

Ethan reined Sage and yanked hard on Peter Balls. Cantankerous as usual, the mule skidded to an awkward stop and stood rigid with his legs spread wide. He began to break wind. The series of short bursts saturated the afternoon air with an awful putridness uniquely his.

The men on the wagon seat sniffed, coughed, and gagged. The driver yelled. "Stranger, I'll have to get personal but there's no other way. You've, uh, been away from soap and water too long. You've got a rotten smell, powerful enough to cut grease."

The smaller man, seated next to the driver, pinched his nose while the driver waved his arms, thrashing the air.

Ethan pointed behind him. "That ain't me. That's Peter Balls—my mule. I'm damned sorry, poor animal's got a bad habit. When he's nervous he farts and I'm afraid he's gotten edgy."

The driver focused on Peter Balls. "Well, it's a helluva way to greet a man but, anyway, howdy.

"You headed for Paso Robles?"

Ethan unfolded the map. He studied the worn paper, then returned it to his vest pocket. "According to this, Paso Robles lies just ahead. If it does, that's where I'm headed."

"You must be new; certainly it's Paso Robles."

Cautiously, the driver turned and called to the riders behind the wagon. The three men lowered their hats and rode up to the wagon. After a short exchange of words, they spurred their animals and galloped down the road.

Ethan barely got a look at the riders' faces as they rode past.

"You know those riders, stranger?" asked the driver.

Ethan gazed after them. "I didn't pay much attention," he lied. They were the cowboys he'd seen standing behind West during the troublesome night in Los Angeles. He wondered why they were around.

The big man holding the reins said, "Ya, lookin' for work?"

Ethan shook his head. "If yer holding to pushing cows, no sir, I'm not. Though thank ya kindly; I'm heading north, making tracks for San Francisco, but not to herd cattle."

The driver climbed down off the wagon, stretched his arms, and stroked Sage's strong neck. He stood back and warily checked the mule, satisfied it was safe.

"I'm Jasper Burns, ramrod for the herd that's grazing two miles farther east. The other fella picking his nose, that's Clayton. Clay runs errands for me."

Ethan laughed and put out his hand and introduced himself.

"Good knowing ya, Sands. My boss is Mr. Roy Sedway. Roy's a popular man in these parts." He turned and looked down the road. "Mr. Sedway has a partner, Woodson Dru." He smiled proudly. "Both fine men to work for, both honest men. Say, thinking on it, I believe Mr. Dru hails from your part of the country. It's either Kansas or Missouri where he was born. Sure you don't want work? 'Cause I've got 'nuther herd coming from Texas. Expect them any day. Calling it straight, I'm hard up, I need hands."

Ethan got off Sage and stretched.

"By chance is the ramrod of that second herd a man named Luke Tucker?"

"You know Luke?"

Ethan chuckled. "Jasper, every cowboy, sheriff, working girl, and gunslinger east of here knows Luke. Yes, Luke's an old friend."

Jasper shoved back his hat and cracked a wide smile. "That's perfect. Then, for sure, you'll enjoy riding with him, huh?"

Ethan shook his head. "We're friends but I'm not riding with him. Sorry."

"If I can't make ya change yer mind, I'll offer advice. If I were you, I'd ride north of Paso Robles, maybe an hour's ride. There's a place called the Adobe Hacienda. It has a new owner from Bakersfield, and he's restored the place."

Jasper elaborated on the clean rooms and the tasty Mexican food. "You'll get friendly hospitality, and they've got hot sulfur baths that'll ease your saddle sores and improve your disposition."

Ethan thanked him, shoved his boot in the stirrup, and climbed on Sage.

"Sands, if'n ya meet up with my boss, don't tell him I sent ya to the hacienda. Mr. Sedway and his friend own a hotel in Paso Robles and, uh, you can see what I mean."

Ethan touched his hat. "Jasper, this place got a friendly girl that'll wash a man's back?"

"A fella could ask." He laughed. "One thing more, stay awake. We've got riffraff on the road, sombitches that'll do anything to make four bits."

Ethan waved good-bye, spurred Sage, and headed him past Jasper's wagon.

Fortunately they had moved far enough away when Peter Balls cut loose again.

•4•

THE LATE AFTERNOON air chilled Ethan. He reached behind the saddle and untied the saddle strings holding his coat. To the west, the sun sagged behind the Santa Lucias, casting shadows along the road. To the east, the branches of oak trees twisted as the wind murmured across the leaves as day faded into night. Taking Jasper's advice, he rode through Paso Robles and continued north.

Clearing his mind, Ethan glanced at the evening sky and swung around to inspect Peter Balls. He took a long drag on his cigarette, and smiled as he saw the yellow lamps on the Adobe Hacienda's portico shimmering through branches of thick oak trees. To the east, over the Diablos, a full moon scraped itself against the purple evening sky. He heard a guitar softly playing

melodic sounds that drifted easily over the gentle
breeze.

He turned off the road and rode down easy slopes
heading for the lanterns. Near the building, he reined
Sage and stood admiring what he saw. He'd never seen
a hotel that resembled this hacienda with a wide front,
thick adobe walls, and square pillars that supported the
red-tiled roof. A balcony enclosed the second floor and
its narrow windows. Heavy wooden shutters hung by
iron hinges bolted into thick walls. Atop the roof, three
chimney stacks emitted smoke that drifted lazily across
the hacienda's tiles.

The aroma of fresh beef cooking above an oak fire
tantalized Ethan's nose. Saddlebags thrown over his
shoulder, Ethan entered the hacienda's lobby through a
two-foot-thick arch with dark, hand-carved doors.

He held the heavy doors open while he admired the
colorful room. Lighted candles burned inside amber-
glass lanterns that cast snakelike shadows on the adobe
walls. Bright bullfight paintings decorated the north
wall, and orange poppies in earthen pots sat on striped
gray and blue serapes that covered round oak tables.
The hacienda's atmosphere was a part of California
Ethan hadn't seen.

From a side door entered a man wearing a ruffled
white shirt tucked into gray trousers, shiny black boots,
and a red string tie. "Good evening, I am Victor Dobbs,
the owner, your host." He bowed slightly and made a
sweeping gesture.

"Mr. Dobbs," Ethan said, shaking his hand, "you've
a mighty handsome hotel, and back down the line I
heard about your food."

Ethan looked past the owner at a dark-eyed girl with
red flowers in her long black hair. The señorita lowered
her eyes.

"Buenas noches, señor." She bowed. "They call me Tarita."

Shyly, Ethan turned away. Tarita went into the main room.

"Now, sir, a room?" Dobbs's voice broke the spell. Ethan nodded.

"Sir, I've got a comfortable room with a large bed. It overlooks the hills to the east. How many nights will it be?"

"One. How much?"

"Three dollars," Dobbs said. "Includes everything."

Ethan lowered his voice. "Ah, everything, sir, uh, is exactly what?"

"My rate includes meals, rooms, and hot baths. Everything except drinks."

Two men swaggered through the front door and stood behind them. They wore dark blue seamen's coats over black and white striped shirts. One had a long scar on his right cheek that disfigured his eye.

Mr. Dobbs pardoned himself and stared at the burly strangers. "Rooms, gentlemen?"

"Naw, no rooms," said the lanky man with a mean smile on his pockmarked face. "My name's Diker. This here's Slouter."

Slouter had a dour face so unyielding a grin would have cracked it. His dark sunken eyes seared into those who lingered upon his.

"We want whiskey. You got a bar, ain't ya? Your whiskey is probably bilge compared to San Francisco's booze."

Ethan eyed the gruff pair.

"Are ya landlocked, mate? Show us whiskey."

Dobbs hurriedly led them away. When he returned, he apologized. "Sorry. The road doesn't always bring us pleasant guests."

Upstairs in the clean room with a view of the hills, Ethan was ready to shave and try a hot bath when someone knocked.

"Señor, I'm Paco." The short Mexican boy smiled. "*Por favor*, I'll show you to the hot baths." He carried a towel over an arm, and a bottle of whiskey in his hand. "*Mi jefe* says this is a gift from him, señor."

Ethan pulled the cork and inhaled. "You got a deal, partner. Lead the way. By the way, Paco, thank your boss."

The bathhouse didn't please Ethan. The room stank of old sweat, but the hot water felt good and he soon forgot the smell. He soaked his body and sipped whiskey until he felt his tired muscles loosen, and life pleasantly took on a happier tone.

After a time, he got hungry. He toweled off his body, returned to the room, dressed, and went downstairs to the restaurant.

The black-haired girl, Tarita, seated him. "Señor, a drink perhaps?"

"Make it the same whiskey Paco served me upstairs."

Tarita, giving him a distracting smile, leaned over the table. "Tonight, I suggest the *carne asada*, it's tasty and mild."

But soon he had reason to become annoyed. At the bar, Diker and Slouter drank heavily; their coarse language disturbed the room.

Tarita served her patrons while Paco played soft music in rhythm with her swaying hips.

Ethan smiled as Tarita served his meal. He barely had to press his knife against the tender steak covered with a red sauce that was spiced mildly enough to please him.

He was about to reach for warm tortillas when three men walked in and brushed his table as they headed for the rear of the room. Ethan didn't move. The bearded faces on two of them and the fashionable long, dark coats triggered his nerves. The third man, dressed in a dapper suit and wearing a well-trimmed mustache, seemed jovial. Something about the men in long coats reminded him of Kansas. Trouble was, where and when?

•5•

TARITA BROUGHT HIM coffee, and she smiled as she handed him a clean napkin. He glanced toward the rear; the strangers who had entered earlier spoke quietly as they shared a conversation while passing the bottle between them. Ethan was certain that he'd never seen the man in the checkered suit. It would have been difficult to forget a handsome gentleman who wore a shoulder holster underneath his left arm and two pistols beneath his coat.

The two bearded men reminded him of a picture he had seen, but he wasn't sure. His mind raced back to 1876, to an occurrence along the northern Kansas line.

At that encounter with a group of wounded men, Ethan thought he'd seen his last sunrise. An outlaw gang had just made a costly mistake. Together with the Younger brothers, they'd planned a bank robbery in Northfield, Minnesota. Somehow, the town got tipped off. Entering Northfield, the gang rode into an ambush. From rooftops, windows, behind barrels and wagons, the townsfolk opened fire with lead so dense it darkened the air. The ambush was so well planned that several of the bandits were killed, while the others barely escaped with their lives.

Ethan had just captured Charley, alias Deacon Spoon, who had robbed a bank. Charley was the brains of a gang made up of his two sons and a nephew named Billy Largo. Both handsome and contriving, Largo became a good friend of the gang's leader. Charley Spoon attempted to rob a bank in Lawrence, Kansas. His two sons were badly wounded. Billy ran outside to warn Charley, who acted as cover man. Billy ran for his horse. Ethan got off a lucky shot, wounding him in the arm. Mad as hell, Billy and Charley galloped out of town.

Two weeks later, Ethan caught Spoon on a farm outside Wahoo, Nebraska. The thief was a dangerous old man whom others called amusing. If he was comical, cows milked soda pop; a craftsman at robbery, he was crazy. He'd as soon kill a man while telling a joke, that was Charley's unusual way.

Ethan shackled Charley's feet, and handcuffed his wrists, and prepared the malcontent for the ride home. They had ridden three days, and Ethan had almost begun to like the zany bandit. He was smart, well informed, and knew how to make a man laugh. What Ethan didn't know was that he was being set up. Old Charley was clever.

"Señor, are you all right?" Ethan, staring blankly, had been stirring a spoon in an empty cup.

Tarita looked on, concerned. "Perhaps more coffee, señor?"

"Oh, yes. Daydreaming, I guess." Ethan was with his thoughts. Dying was not what he feared, it was how he lived that worried him. He was not a man to run away, but he was always searching. Suddenly, there came a cold foreboding thought that the past would always haunt him unless he could bury it. The direction of his life would not be solved by killing the Kansan, nor by a change in scenery. If he were to make a change, it had to come from within. He reached for his makings and rolled a cigarette. As he exhaled, smoke stung his eyes, but that didn't bother him nearly as much as the unanswered question in his mind: what was he searching for?

•6•

ETHAN, WITH HIS prisoner, Charley, had camped south of the Platte River that morning years ago when a gang of somber-faced riders rode in. Three of the gang, tied across their horses, had serious bullet wounds, and the riders alongside the dead glared at Ethan who was holding a comrade in arms. Recognizing Charley in chains didn't improve the leader's disposition. He knew Ethan wasn't a lawman, but when he stared at him, Ethan wasn't sure what the outlaw thought. Still, he knew that if there was one bad move, one wrong word, he was dead. The Younger brothers moved in behind him and stood guard while the leader and his brother climbed down from their horses.

For Topeka Sands it wasn't the best of times.

Surprisingly, things were clam. They talked and drank coffee, and exchanged a few meaningless words. Rather than the gang leader, it was Charley that worried

Ethan. The prisoner kept making eyes at the Youngers and cracking sly remarks.

If he could have shut Charley's big mouth, it might have been easier. The outlaw chief and his brother stood in front of Ethan while the others stood behind. He knew that if he'd been lucky and shot both men, the Youngers would have punctured his back with lead and left his naked body hanging from a tree.

"Someday, Topeka Sands, we'll meet again. Take care of my friend Charley, ya hear?"

Then they turned and rode out of camp. Charley laughed at Ethan who stood shaking in his boots.

Later, after one joke too many, he shot Charley; the sly old fox tossed hot coffee in Ethan's face. Ethan fired, then tied his corpse over the horse's rump.

• 7 •

ETHAN GLANCED AT the men in the dining room; suddenly it came to him. If the two bearded men were the ones he had met with Charley, they'd pick the time and place to let it be known. Patience was the key; he decided to sit tight.

In spite of the feeling he had, California living brought out the relax in Ethan, and the hacienda's atmosphere worked pleasantly on his mind. Wiping his mouth, he glanced at Tarita. Damn, how she reminded him of Nora. He had the silly thought of inviting her for a walk along the Salinas River—maybe clear his mind about things that shouldn't have concerned him.

Caught with his thoughts, Ethan was embarrassed when Mr. Dobbs pulled up a chair. "Is everything satisfactory, Mr. Sands?"

"First-rate, Mr. Dobbs, first-rate," Ethan said quickly. "I'm sitting here preparing myself for a long night of ups and downs if you know what I mean." He pointed to the coffee and pushed back the cup. "Your cooks have the know-how when it comes to fine foods."

"Good. Care for a cigar?" The owner held several in his hand. "I have these shipped from San Francisco by stage."

Ethan put a cigar between his teeth. "Do you know those men sitting behind me next to the wall?"

"In a way. Two of them have been eating here for nearly a month. Quiet men. I don't know where they live, but the tall one said they're here on business. They know a deal about railroads; they've asked interesting questions."

"What do you mean by 'in a way'?"

"The man in the checked suit, I know him, or of him."

Dobbs explained that before coming to San Luis Obispo County, he had lived in a town fifty miles north of Bakersfield, a town called Potterville. It was as wild and immoral as Bakersfield. He moved west to get away from the violence to be found in both towns.

"Bakersfield, Mr. Sands, is to California what Dodge City was to Kansas, maybe worse. It's an outpost for outlaws, killers, pimps, whores, and no-goods of every sort. The Chinese have opened josh houses where opium is smoked and the Chinese use their own girls for sport. Mildly put, it's the hellhole of sin."

Dobbs struck a match, held it a moment, then blew it out.

"When I tell you the man's name"—Dobbs lowered his voice and shot a glance over Ethan's shoulder—"I want you to keep it to yourself. And if you should meet him, don't mention we've talked. Frankly, I'm surprised to see him with the others. Chances are he's using a different name, hiding his true identity. Even though he's sober, I recognize him."

"Well, what's his name?" Ethan asked.

"Jim McKinney. From Bakersfield. A dangerous man, probably the worst. Some call Jim the shotgun killer. Sober, he's quiet and often amusing. Drunk, that's something else. He's killed men for simply disagreeing with him over nothing. Women? He loves 'em. There's a rumor that handsome Jim, in a moment of urge, convinced a naive preacher's wife that she had been sleeping with the wrong man. But drunk, and feeling mean, he'll pull both triggers to kill a foe. Unfortunately, the kind of women Jim courted, most men wouldn't have been seen with. He's a breed unto himself." Feeling he'd said enough, Dobbs excused himself. "Pardon me, duties need my attention. Enjoy yourself." As he walked by the bar, he gave Diker and Slouter a closer look. Rolo, the bartender, looked frightened.

Slouter barked, "Hey, Diker!" The stocky man grunted. "Get that Mex to pour us rum!"

"Slouter, the fool says he don't keep rum, only whiskey and tequila," Diker replied. Rolo poured them each another glass of whiskey. As Tarita approached the bar carrying a tray of dishes, Diker poked Slouter. "Watch this!"

•8•

DIKER FLIPPED OUT his leg, tripping her. Dishes scattered everywhere as Tarita's head struck the hard tile.

Rolo started around the bar.

"Hold on, peon." Slouter sneered. "Diker here'll help the wench."

Diker leered at Tarita as he sunk down on his knees. He placed his hands on Tarita's bare leg and pushed up her skirt. His fingers squeezed her soft thigh.

Tarita was terrified, and tried to push him away.

Diker tugged at her blouse.

Suddenly, a boot slammed down, pinning Diker's right hand against the tile floor. Diker yelped and looked up into Ethan's cold face.

"You bastard, you're busting my hand!"

Ethan didn't budge. Slouter started for him. Ethan's

.45 flashed out. Slouter threw himself back against the wall.

"Let him go, ya son of a bitch," he growled, "or I'll kill ya."

Ethan's boot remained jammed on Diker's hand, whose face flowed with tears of pain. "You've crushed my hand."

Tarita pulled herself over against the wall. "Mister." Ethan spoke slowly to Diker. "If you ever want to use that hand, get up. Pick up that towel on the bar and wipe up the mess."

Diker appealed to Slouter. "Jesus, I can't do it! Get the towel and help me. My hand is surely broke!"

"You smart-mouthed sissy," Slouter snarled. "Do it yourself!" He spat on the floor.

Cautiously, Ethan backed up. Behind him, the room was still. Paco's guitar went silent. Two of the men from the rear ambled forward and stood there, their long black coats pushed back to clear holstered pistols; the third, not far behind them, unbuttoned his tight coat.

"Slouter, down on your knees," Ethan said calmly.

"Up yer hole, cowboy. I ain't moppin' up no woman's mess."

"Fat man"—Ethan's controlled voice echoed through the dining room—"clean the floor, or go for that gun sticking out of your gut. I don't care which, but you'll do one or the other."

Slouter's fingers twitched; he wanted to draw.

"You're spitting wind, Slouter. I'm counting, one, two—"

At the same instant that Slouter's hand moved, Ethan's pistol crashed on his head with a dull thud like a hammer whacking a sun-baked pumpkin.

Slouter sank against the wall and slowly crumpled near Tarita's feet. Blood trickled down from his temples, spotting the tile. Diker's shocked eyes fixed on Slouter lying next to the girl. He wondered why the gunman hadn't shot Slouter. Cautiously, Ethan slid his foot off Diker's hand.

Diker lifted his damaged hand. He moaned like a whipped dog. Ethan lowered his gun to his holster. He tapped his boot toe against Slouter's ribs. He was unconscious.

Diker painfully began removing broken crockery from the tile pavers, his fingers slipping in the juicy sauce.

Dobbs watched the three men standing nearby. By their eyes he knew that death was not a stranger to the men dressed in black.

One of them knelt down next to Slouter and poked him in the gut. Ethan looked up; Dobbs was standing there, his face pale. "Mister," the man in black asked Dobbs, "where'n hell do ya want this trash?"

"Out back, gentlemen, I'll lead the way."

Ethan started to help, but the tallest of the three stopped him. "You've done enough. We'll handle this," he said in a Missouri drawl. He directed the bartender, Rolo, pointing to their table. "Son, we'll need a bottle."

Ethan felt strangely uncomfortable. He thought, I should have killed him. I should have finished it.

"When my friends come back, we'll join them in a couple of whiskeys," said Jim McKinney. The two other men returned. "I'll introduce you to my friends."

Ethan swung around. "If you please, after you."

"That's Avery Dru. The man next to him is his brother, George. I'm Fred Stall, from the San Joaquin Valley, visiting. And you, sir, are?"

"Ethan Sands."

The four men pulled back their chairs and silently faced one another. Finally, Jim spoke. "We gonna sit, piddlin' around like prairie chickens waitin' for a train, or have some drinks?"

Tarita arrived. She placed a bottle surrounded by four shiny glasses in the center of the table, smiled at Ethan and withdrew.

Jim, seated to Ethan's left, said, "Let's don't be bashful!" He began to pour.

Like old friends the four sat peacefully and conversed while Paco played and the candlelight cast mysterious shadows over their faces.

Jim McKinney, the one calling himself Fred, said Avery and George had an uncle who lived in Paso Robles. He'd been showing Avery around looking at various business opportunities that might interest him. "Isn't that right, Avery?"

Avery nodded. "I'd like to find a business, and besides"—he held his glass to the light—"I like this part of California." Then he put his hand on George's shoulder. "But my brother's homesick."

His brother raised his glass. "To Missouri."

"How about you, Ethan? Got a job?" Jim asked.

"Sure do—*staying alive!*"

Avery and George just smiled. Four glasses clinked over the table.

In his room, Ethan enjoyed a last smoke. As he climbed into bed and lay looking through the window at the moon, he wondered why George and Avery had come to California.

Victor Dobbs stood on the hacienda's portico saying good evening as his customers departed. The three men who earlier had been talking with the Kansan stood in the shadows speaking quietly among themselves.

One man shook hands with the others, buttoned his

checkered coat, and walked over to Dobbs. Dobbs froze as Jim McKinney pulled out a small cigar.

"In a few minutes," he said in a deep voice, "I'm walking your waitress, Tarita, safely home. And Mr. Dobbs, put your mind at ease. That's all I have in mind."

When he had gone, his two companions swept into their saddles, adjusted their weight, and casually tipped their hats. Then they goaded their mounts away from the hacienda.

It had been an exciting day for Victor Dobbs, a peaceful man who would feel content, and safer, when Jim McKinney had boarded the Bakersfield stage.

• 9 •

THE MOONLIGHT SHOWED the way for the two men who rode south for Paso Robles. They had ridden a mile without saying a word. A distant coyote's howl accompanied them. The last bright star in the sky shone.

"Say, you got any makin's?"

The rider on his right reached in his shirt pocket. "Here."

"When was the last time we saw Topeka Sands?"

His partner rubbed his chin. "It was coming back from Minnesota. Sands had captured a friend of mine, remember?"

"I do. I'll never forget Northfield. Bad!"

The other man blew smoke thinking on it, bad was not *bad* enough.

"Sands is a steady hand. He didn't kill here, but that doesn't mean he won't! In a showdown, he's got guts.

That shooter's a man to have around. Maybe he'll join us."

"He won't! He's been on the straight road too long," he said with a smirk.

"I wonder. He's like an old hound dog I had. Best hunting dog I ever owned. Until the day he died, poor hound never changed. Sands won't change—count on it!"

They stood in front of a ranch gate. Up on the hill, their uncle's home overlooked the valley filled with almond trees. The moon slid behind a cloud, flooding light over the riders.

"I've got a question. Say we're back home, busy at our business, and you meet with Topeka Sands. You're both toe to toe—would you shoot him?"

"I'd kill him!"

Silently, they headed toward the ranch house.

In front of the tie rail, they dismounted. Each untied his saddlebag and threw it over his shoulder. The shorter man smiled, looking at his brother's face.

"Good night, partner. At least for tonight, nobody's bothering us."

"That's right. But say, in the morning, for the hell of it, I'm going back and have a talk with Ethan. You've given me an idea. Sleep well."

Miles away across the Great Divide, in Missouri, men talked about the James brothers. One in particular, a likable young man, felt warm sweat between his hands when he heard the outlaw's name. Bob Ford, among other noted Missourians, knew another outlaw, dangerous as the legend itself—*Billy Largo*.

Part 4

The Blood of San Miguel

• 1 •

IN THE 1850s, an obliging place for a breather between Santa Barbara and San Luis Obispo was a town located on a site the Chumash Indians called Ne-po-mah, which meant at the foot of a hill or mountain. During California's early history, travelers found Nipomo warm and friendly, a refuge from rigorous days spent traveling along El Camino Real. And when Andy and the Bean family arrived in Nipomo, the custom held.

Andy thought that the Beans, especially Kitty, had appreciated his companionship and had made the strenuous journey from Los Angeles easier. The journey wasn't as friendly or exciting as traveling from Santa Fe; since Andy's controversy with Kitty's father, their relationship varied from unsociable to hardly speaking. While Kitty's mother had taken a liking to Andy and treated him fairly, Locum seldom allowed the Kansan out of sight.

When the wagon arrived near Nipomo, Andy found

an excuse for leaving. He saddled Gussie and rode into town, rented a room at the Chumash Hotel, and treated himself to a hot bath.

He enjoyed eating supper with his feet under a table. Being away from Pa Bean's watchful eyes eased his tension.

The next day, the sun rose over the Sierra Madre Mountains and spread its warmth over the level land surrounding Nipomo. Upstairs in his hotel room, Andy awoke in a homelike bed. He lay back, noting the wormholes in the ash beams above him. It was the inspirational time of morning when a fella should be nestled close to an obliging woman. Or a soubrette whose feminine logic allowed her to relish the hoop-la of the fluttering sheets.

When he rolled out, his bare feet tingled on the cold floor. Andy's sensual thoughts vanished as a chill ran up his bare legs, tickling his vitals. He wondered about Ethan and how he had fared.

Leaving the hotel, Andy thought back on the many pitiful mornings he'd left a woman's tenderness. Bedding a lovable woman definitely was no jack-rabbit affair, not for Andy Love. Traveling with the Beans, his romantic meetings with Kitty had become ticklishly limited, and fatherly Pa Bean didn't miss a trick. Kitty was demanding more of his attention, so much so that he now thought of leaving her.

Approaching the wagon, Andy reined back on Gussie and took a deep breath. Today he would talk to Kitty. It was time to get on with his life. Also, Ethan was still not too far ahead, and riding alone he'd find him. Feeling comfortable with himself, Andy urged Gussie toward Bean's wagon.

•2•

"MORNIN', MR. DOBBS, you're up early." Ethan smiled and asked for the bill.

With a flourish Dobbs tore up the bill. "It's the least we can do. Everyone had appreciated your courage."

"You're generous. Thank you."

"There's coffee and fresh sweet bread in the kitchen." At the kitchen table Dobbs poured two cups and placed hot breads and honey between them. Ethan asked what he might expect to encounter riding north.

"Well," Dobbs said, dunking sweet bread in his saucer, "El Camino, from Soledad south to Santa Barbara, has been a dangerous road. During the wild days of the fifties, bandits became more than dangerous. Now, thanks to the law, it has improved." He paused. "In fifty-one, folks in San Luis Obispo County formed a committee, and loaded pressure on the sheriff to reduce robberies. Then, the Civil War settled bandits down.

During the mid-seventies, despite the depression, the damned bandits returned. California roads swarmed with what the newspapers called 'stand and deliver men.' Highway miscreants who stole your goods, roughed you up, and had little fear of getting caught."

Ethan buttered another slice of sweet bread and washed it down with coffee.

"On the Cuesta Grade there were more holdups than you could imagine. They'd come riding out of the Santa Lucias' canyons, robbing stagecoaches easy as they pleased, then they'd vanish, hiding out in Las Pilitas, a devilish place to corner bandits. Many of our lawmen got killed flushing them out, using the Camino Viejo, an escape road that has been used for years."

Dobbs's guest listened carefully. "After Spain and Mexico had occupied California, the new American government demanded that patrons prove title on lands they held, land grants that had been owned for generations. Hundreds of Americans poured in from Eastern States, most with the idea of getting hands on good land at cheap prices." He pushed back his chair and laughed.

"Cheap, hell! Some wanted the land free! Squatters arrived to find that others had an abundance of land, so they defied the owners and moved onto other folks' properties. Then, we had trouble."

•3•

ETHAN SHOVED HIS cup against the breadboard and looked out the kitchen window. The sun cast westerly rays through the trees, telling him it was time to quit talking and hit the road.

Oblivious, Dobbs continued. "Squatters continued to arrive, and the owners didn't take to this. Bloodshed was plentiful. The federal government moved in. When Uncle Sam found an old Spanish or Mexican land grant had a clouded title, things turned sour. If the owners couldn't remove the squatters, they stood a chance of losing their property. If a rancher couldn't prove owner-ship or pay back taxes, his property was confiscated and put up for sale."

Itchy, Ethan checked the time. Dobbs didn't run down.

"Smelling bargains, aggressive businessmen charged in, paid the unpaid tax bill, and claimed the land. In my view it was legalized stealing." Dobbs poured himself another coffee. "Californians have gone through unhealthy times. Human trash from the world over accumulated in California seeking gold from the Sierra. But eventually these dregs learned that digging for gold was hard and chancy work. And besides, living in gold country was nothing like many of 'em figured: cold, expensive, and deadly is what they found." Dobbs wiped honey from his mouth.

"Finally, thank God, the gold ran out. Forty-niners, weary and broke, drifted away. Some traveled east into Nevada after silver."

Ethan's host reached for the freshly cut bread and passed it over. "It's a twist of human nature: when gold takes over a man's soul, whatever goodness he had before disappears. In its place, greed is born and hell breaks loose. Tell you, though, many of these men arrived with no good in them and left the Sierra the same way, mostly broke and with sour dispositions."

Ethan laughed.

"Oh, there was good folks who sought the diggings. Luckily, some stayed. God knows, we're going to need the smart 'n' able to mold California into the state that'll make us proud. Mr. Sands, men such as you!"

•4•

"YOU WOULDN'T GO wrong, settling here, near Paso Robles." The owner placed his hand on Ethan's shoulder.

The Kansan smiled, pleased for the education, but anxious to move on.

"Now, about the road. The first landmark you'll come on will be Mission San Miguel, another mission falling apart from lack of care. It's a shame. Two businessmen own the shambles."

Ethan recalled Father Remos mentioning the Englishman and his partner who owned San Miguel. The owners had built stores and living quarters, and there was a rumor that soon a saloon would occupy the mission.

Dobbs sighed. "The mission's owner is a friendly man. Sometimes too much so. He and his family offer shelter to El Camino's travelers. I think he's asking for trouble; he's braver than I am."

Before Dobbs continued, Ethan stood and put out his hand. "I appreciate everything that you've told me, and I'll keep your advice in mind. Mr. Dobbs, I've got to move on. But if I return we'll talk some more. So until then, take care of yourself."

Dobbs grabbed his hand and shook it firmly. "Good luck to you, Ethan. I'll walk you to the door."

•6•

DRESSED IN AN open shirt and work trousers, Avery today had the look of a hired hand.

"It's time I rode out," Ethan said. "I'm halfway, but I've still got more than two hundred miles ahead of me, according to Mr. Dobbs."

Avery rolled a cigarette and watched Ethan brush Sage's legs.

"Fine horseflesh. Had him long?"

"Since he was a foal. Trained him myself. Yes, he's a good horse. Good friend too."

"Back in Clay County, I own a horse like that, miss that horse. I trust him more than certain men I know."

"Hell, I talk to Sage."

Avery had picked the place and time, for talking with Ethan alone.

"I'd like a few words."

"You bet. Shall we go inside?"

"I'd rather not; this is fine."

Ethan laid the hairbrush aside and faced him.

"What's on your mind, Avery?"

"Making money. You interested?"

"I'll listen."

"Good! I'll go on. California is opportunity. And besides, it's a damned good distance from Missouri." Avery said. "Since I've been here, I've spent a good deal of time with my uncle, and Ethan William Dru is a knowledgeable man."

"I've heard his name. Good businessman is what I hear."

"He is. He's opened my eyes to several things."

"Money?"

"Money. Plenty of it. For openers, he introduced me to a wine maker named Pesenti. He's Italian or Swiss, something like that, but he knows his business. Mr. Pesenti owns land west of Paso Robles on the road that crosses the Santa Lucias to the sea. He plans to build a winery, probably next year."

"What's it got to do with me?"

"He says that this land here will produce wine grapes good as any in California. I'd like to stay in California—right here to be exact—get into the wine business. Bring my family here, get away from Missouri."

Ethan leaned against the wall and rolled a cigarette. Avery rolled one for himself, and lit it. "I'll need men who can handle themselves, and who I can trust." He smiled. "You can't believe that Avery Dru is changing his way of life and coming to California trying to do something worthwhile."

"It's curious. If Californians ever discovered you weren't Avery Dru, what would happen?"

Avery took a final drag on his cigarette and blew smoke away from Ethan's face. "Why, I'm surprised at you, Mr. Sands. That'll never happen. Why should it? If it ever leaks out, well, I would have a dispute."

Ethan took a long drag. "Avery, I'm not looking for disputes. With you or anyone else. I don't like threats. You want to talk about men, I'm listening."

Avery smiled. "Good! Then we understand each other. Here's what's on my mind."

•7•

FOR FIVE MINUTES Ethan listened. In his deep Missouri drawl, Avery spelled out what he wanted to do. He didn't waste words. When he quit talking, Ethan was amazed. Avery had a plan that would allow him to live and to be an old man . . . a rich old man!

They mounted and left the barn together. Avery would ride along so they could talk more without being overheard.

With Peter Balls behind Sage, Ethan pointed ahead. "Let's hit the road, Avery. I've set a goal of forty miles."

"*Haven't we all!* C'mon, work 'em," Avery said, smiling.

A low fog had come in from Cambria making it difficult to see ahead. The fog hindered their visibility and they missed the turn-off to San Miguel. Turning right they ran into the mission's south wall. Behind the wall they barely made out buildings farther back. The dense fog concealed what the years had engraved on the weather-worn adobes.

"Damn! It's got a bedevilment to it, weird." Avery peered into the eerie fog.

·8·

"ABOUT NOW, I could use warm Missouri sunshine," Ethan mumbled.

"The place has a haunted look. It's dismal." Avery pulled up his collar.

Through the fog they saw twisted pear trees, and a wall facing the mission's front.

It was too calm. Birds fluttered nervously among the trees, while a cottontail scurried for safety in the grassy fields nearby.

"Not a cheery sight this time of morning," said Avery.

Both men stared at what time and nature had done. The once proud walls had crumbled, and the San Miguel was badly in need of repair. San Miguel had suffered. The buildings had been built by Catholic converts: Indians who had toiled to complete what the priests had planned.

Swinging down from his saddle, Ethan remembered what Dobbs had told him about the mission. Once, more than three thousand of San Miguel's wards lived on the surrounding lands. Thousands of cattle, horses, and other livestock grazed, and the land prospered under the guidance of the mission's fathers. In time Indians and livestock disappeared. The stillness of lost years lay heavy on the land.

"I don't figure this." Avery frowned. "There's no sign of life."

"Dobbs told me a family lives here," said Ethan.

"Let's take a swing around back, have a look-see." Avery shoved back his hat and scratched his head.

"We'd better. It's peculiar."

They walked their horses to the back, dismounted and tied the animals to a tree.

"There's supposed to be servants, too," Ethan said.

"If there's anyone here, by God they're making themselves scarce," Avery said.

"Hold on, Avery, there's a door open." They heard a dog whimper. "Listen, it's coming from inside," Ethan said.

They approached the doorway.

"It's a kitchen." Avery stuck his head inside.

Across the floor came a dog, whining, his round eyes glued on the strangers.

"That pooch is trying to tell us something. Look at them eyes." Avery patted the dog's head.

The pooch quit whining, rose up and barked at the door. Following the dog, they entered the kitchen. Ethan had tripped over a woman's body, lying face-down. He had stepped on her outstretched arm.

"Ma God!" He knelt down. "Gimmee a hand, we'll turn her over."

Locked by death, the woman's glassy eyes stared at the ceiling. Down from her right ear, under her chin, to her left ear, a deep cut split her flesh. The savage wound had dumped a pool of dark blood on the tile floor. Ethan found an apron and covered her face.

•9•

DEATH'S ODOR SATURATED the mission walls, causing the dog to sniff as he walked along the hallway. Following closely behind him, Ethan and Avery entered a large room and Ethan struck a match to a candle resting on a table.

The flame cast grotesque silhouettes over the coarse adobe walls. On the floor sprawled a man's body, its arm stiff against the wall as if he had reached for something. On the tile next to his left hand lay a leather bag the kind miners had used to carry gold.

Stab wounds covered him, blood sopping his open shirt. Avery lifted the candle. A woman's body lay face up, spread over the bed, both hands tightly bound to the wooden posts—so tightly her wrists had bled, and were purple and swollen to double their size.

Rivulets of blood trickled over her white outstretched arms. Death had surely been a blessed relief from the vicious knife wounds plunged in rows across her breast. One deep gash exposed the heart.

Avery shuddered.

"Damn. Cover her, Ethan."

Ethan pulled the thin rug from the floor and placed it over her.

"Get that pooch away." The dog had found his master on the floor and was licking the dead man's face.

The men lunged back into the hallway and sagged against the wall. In another room, dead bodies as railroad ties stacked in a pile. There was one cruel exception to the pile. Lying in front of the blood-spattered fireplace, where his small head had been bashed against the stone hearth, lay the body of a young boy.

Nine or ten years of age, it was difficult to determine. Ethan counted the malicious carnage: two women, one quite young, three men, one much older, stacked on two younger men with arms dangling toward the floor. Eyes fixed, mouths twisted, frozen by fear's final words.

The wretched fetor of blood from carved flesh permeated the dark room. Ethan sucked for air, but this room lacked windows.

"C'mon; let's get outside." Avery's stomach churned. They ran down the dark hall, past the dead man's reaching arm, into the kitchen. Carefully stepping over the dead woman, Ethan threw his full weight against the half-open kitchen door. Outside they gasped to get air inside their lungs.

Ethan heard a voice in his head.

"*Amigos*, California . . . *sí*, she can kill."

•10•

OUTSIDE MISSION SAN Miguel, Ethan tried to accommodate the nauseating obscenity he had witnessed.

The butchery was as gruesome as either man had ever seen. It was a picture that would contaminate Ethan's mind for years. As for the murderers, they considered Indians, but that didn't make sense; Indians—Chumash, Salina, or the Yokuts—were peaceful. Besides, butchery hadn't been their style.

Lost in thought, neither man had noticed how the sun had dissolved the morning fog.

"Avery," Ethan said, "that torn cloth clutched in the boy's hand."

Avery frowned. "Well, what about it?"

"Last night? Diker and Slouter wore black and white striped shirts. That cloth in the boy's hand looked the same."

Avery stuck a cigarette between his teeth and struck

a match. "Men would have to be loco to torture people that way. That woman was raped. Maybe they forced her husband to watch. Ethan, that's grisly." He took a deep breath and spat.

A minute passed before Ethan spoke. "We've stumbled onto a massacre, and if we don't find someone to witness what we've seen, they might think we had a hand in it. Avery, that's a poor deal."

"*Suspects?* Us?" For a moment he thought about riding back and finding the sheriff. "Where's them converts or other folks who live here?" Avery shook his head.

"We've got no damned reason being suspects. As the day warms up, it's gonna smell worse than putrid inside." Ethan rubbed his neck. "We can't just leave the dead and ride off.

Suddenly, Avery pointed. "Look by the wall . . . riders! Coming this way. That big fella, that's Jasper, the ramrod I know. Next to him is my uncle's partner, Roy Sedway." He faced Ethan. "Friend, in front of Sedway, not a word about Jim McKinney."

"Whatever you say, Avery Dru."

•11•

"I'M ROY SEDWAY." He waved toward the six others. "These are my men. Avery, surprised to see you."

Jasper leaned over the saddle. "Mr. Sedway, this is Sands, the man I met south of Paso Robles. He hails from Kansas and is headed for San Francisco. Says he's a friend of Luke's."

Sedway studied Ethan's face, then looked around at the mission's yard. "Something's wrong. You men seen my friend Walter Brian?"

Uneasy, Ethan nodded. "Perhaps I can have a few words." He pointed toward a bench beneath a pepper tree. They walked over and sat.

"These words I'm about to say come hard, but there's no other way. Inside the mission—everyone's dead."

The boss jumped to his feet. "Everyone?" His voice cracked.

"Women, children, men, all murdered." Disbelief grew in Sedway's hazel eyes. "Are you telling me that Walter's entire family is dead?"

"That's what we saw. Avery and I rode in an hour ago."

He gave the details. Sedway's eyes remained focused on the kitchen door. "Any tracks?"

"We haven't looked." Ethan kicked at the dirt. "Let me make this clear. Neither of us has anything to do with this."

Sedway shook his head. "I understand. I make no such insinuations. You two are as shaken as I am."

The rancher gave orders for two men to ride and find Bolo Joe and Dr. Flanders. Bolo Joe, an Oklahoma Chickasaw, was an expert tracker. He told his men to find the sheriff and form a posse. He turned to Jasper. "It's time we go in . . . have a look."

Jasper flinched. He looked at the other men and back at his boss. "Anytime you're ready," he said.

"You men coming?"

"Naw, Mr. Sedway," Ethan said. "We've seen enough."

•12•

SEDWAY AND HIS men came out of the mission ashen, and gagged. One cowhand, hand over his mouth, lurched through the door and leaned against the wall. Coughing, he splattered vomit over his boots.

"God help us!" Sedway mumbled. "Living in a world where men are that evil is beyond comprehension. I don't understand!" He mopped his forehead and mouth with a white handkerchief and threw it in the dirt, and stood staring. He lowered his head and spoke softly. "That poor little fella, Matthew, and oh—God—his mother, Ella!"

"Was that everyone in Mr. Brian's family?" Ethan asked.

"Yes. Three were servants."

For several minutes no one spoke. Finally, Sedway shook his head. "They've been dead for several hours, so I figure this happened last night or early this morning. Whoever did it took the entire family by surprise."

The small dog was sitting on the step looking at the men.

"Wished that pooch could talk." Roy whistled to him. "You're right, it wasn't Indians. I've got to think this out."

Ethan swung around. "Mr. Sedway, I believe those misbegottens I saw in the hacienda last night were sailors." He explained what had happened. "They had the look and talked like seamen and their shirts were striped."

The men gathered around him. "Jasper, get riders over the hills to Cayucos in case the killers try to escape by boat. Check anyone strange, especially seamen." Sedway frowned. "Seamen have been jumping ships, landing in Monterey, and traveling up and down the Camino Real."

He pointed at Jasper. "Get another rider north. There's a telegraph crew working on a spur just north of here. Have the operator pound out news to San Francisco, and make sure the word hits every station along the line. We'll find them. I'm posting a six-hundred-dollar reward for any of these killers, walking or dragged in dead. Understand?"

Jasper nodded to his riders.

"Sands, which way are you headed?"

"North, but I'll ride in any direction that will help."

"You can ride north and find the spur. Good."

"I'll lend a hand," Avery said. "I've had experience tracking. I'll ride back with you."

A group of converts had drifted in out of curiosity and approached two of Sedway's vaqueros. They talked excitedly. The vaquero thanked them and reported to Sedway.

"One Indian said that yesterday he saw two gringos ride into the mission."

"Did he get a good look at any of 'em?"

"Yes, sir. He says one was short, stocky. Near sundown he and a tall man came out of the mission and rode north. The face of the man had the sickness marks on both cheeks."

"We're in luck," Ethan explained. "The skinny one is Diker and the stocky man is Slouter. Both were at the Adobe Hacienda."

"Maybe they're the gang of cutthroats we've seen hanging around," Jasper said, touching his gun.

Ethan kicked the dirt. "I should have killed them both. Damn!"

Roy instructed the converts to form a digging party and bury the family. "Mrs. Brian had a relative living in Monterey but there isn't time to reach her. If that cemetery's full, kick down the wall and make room."

Roy's men spurred their horses and rode south.

Ethan suggested they move back into the shade.

"Jasper says you're heading to San Francisco," Sedway said. "I'm planning a big cattle operation near Paso Robles. If you're interested, we'll talk. Sorry we didn't meet under different circumstances." Roy lifted his head toward the sky. "We need rain. Maybe it'll clear the stench."

"What'll become of the Mission San Miguel?" Ethan asked.

Roy gazed at the sky. "Probably up to his partner. *I'd burn the son of a bitch!*"

"If I'm going to make the telegraph spur before dark, I'd better ride. Sorry to leave you stuck with this miserable job."

"Sands, keep the wind to your back and your pistol cocked. I'd enjoy handing you the reward."

Avery walked with Ethan toward Sage.

Roy called to them. "Say, you ever been in Topeka?"

Ethan glanced at Avery. "I've been there."

Roy smiled. "Next time you're here I'll introduce you to a friend of mine."

As they walked toward Sage, Avery lowered his voice.

"Ethan Sands, you're a straight man, and I'm glad that you've met up with Avery Dru. Uh, Avery's a conventional gent compared to the outlaw you've mistaken him for."

Both men laughed loudly.

As Ethan rode away, someone was ringing the mission's bells. The sound spread sadness over the land. For Topeka Sands, the sadness dug deep. He pulled on Sage's reins and stood for a moment watching Avery ride south following Roy's party. Avery stopped and waved.

Interesting, Ethan thought, what makes men ride the direction they do.

•13•

THERE WAS LITTLE to do but ride, leaving the crumbled walls and memories of what used to be, and the dead, behind. Ethan rolled a cigarette as he rode along. He said aloud, "Guess no matter where a man goes, things don't change. Some people are bad. Others I've seen are worse. God made everything, but I think he misfigured people."

Ethan brushed the top of Sage's head. He reined left and turned around, looking back toward San Miguel. Then he glanced up at the blue sky and sighed. "California has lost something today." He leaned forward, resting his hand on the saddle bow. Ethan thought of Avery Dru, a thin shadow of who he really was.

On April 3, 1882, Bob Ford did to Jesse what he had done to others: he shot the outlaw in the back.

When the Missourians gathered to pay their last respects to the famous outlaw, many held mixed opinions of Jesse and his brother, Frank. When the Civil War came, Frank joined William Quantrill's guerrillas. Quantrill became known as a notorious plunderer and murderer.

In 1864, Jesse took his brother's lead and joined the guerrillas under "Bloody Bill" Anderson. During this time both men did ruthless acts that were far from heroic: the shooting of seventy-five unarmed Union soldiers. In 1865, attempting to surrender, using a white flag, Jesse was seriously wounded.

After Jesse was well, in 1866, with Frank, they began their careers of crime. They robbed a bank in Liberty, Missouri, killing a bystander. Their life of crime went on until 1876, when riding with the Younger brothers, Jesse made a terrible mistake. One that damned near got him killed.

By this time the fame of the James boys had spread. It grew when they began to rob trains. There was public sympathy for the brothers as they gave portions of their loot to the poor. Throughout the land, Jesse became the Robin Hood of Missouri, much to the displeasure of the law. Lawmen called him a thief and a killer. A folk hero blown out of portion by those who worshiped him. And the outlaw put fear in the hearts of others who feared the legend, Jesse James.

In 1881, the state of Missouri placed rewards of $5,000 each for Jesse and Frank. Two members of Jesse's gang made a deal with Governor Thomas Crittenden to assassinate Jesse.

As they lowered the box holding Jesse into the earth, some people cried. While others walked away shaking their heads, praising the Lord.

•14•

AT RANCHO VERDE, Sabonda's father joined her for the evening. She enjoyed her father's visits, particularly when he stayed for supper. During the meal this evening, he carefully avoided conversation regarding Taris. The *àlcalde* was disturbed by what he had learned from Dr. La Rue, and he didn't wish to upset her. Respectful of Sabonda's feelings, thus far he had let his opinion remain unspoken.

Since her mother had died, he had always taken time to talk and be attentive to her. Juan Ricardo hadn't asked directly, but tonight he sensed Sabonda's unhappiness.

"Sabonda, my dear, yesterday I had a conversation with Dr. La Rue. He said you had made a call."

"Yes father, I did."

Juan folded his napkin. "My love, may I speak openly? Taris's drinking worries me more than ever, and Dr. La Rue disclosed that if he doesn't quit, well, it's alarming. I dislike having you unhappy, and I don't wish to interfere, but I don't like what I see."

Sabonda wasn't surprised by her father's directness, and she knew it would be difficult to make him listen. "But my love, Taris must be stopped." Juan said.

"Father, he doesn't know, the word 'stop.' "

After her father had gone, she readied for bed. Her maid served peach brandy, placing it on the table beside her, and put an extra blanket over the bed, as fall had come early and the evenings had grown cold. She added two large oak logs to the bedroom fire.

Melancholy, Sabonda relaxed as the flames swirled between the embers. As the peach brandy softened her spirits, she recalled how as a little girl she had worked with her grandfather planting fruit trees in the orchard. Now, she enjoyed the brandy derived from the trees she had played beneath as a child.

The flames cast shadows over the sitting room, while Sabonda's dark eyes there was sadness. Her father knew that she was discontented, pretending about her marriage. Helplessly, she had watched Taris become consumed in booze, quavering in a cavern of self-pity.

Since they had married in the Church, divorce was impossible. She would not disgrace her father's name. The family had prospered by the management of thousands of acres that had produced substantial wealth. She and her father valued their birthrights as early Californians. Land brought privilege that someday her children could appreciate, but with Taris, the thought of having children was impossible.

* * *

Sabonda strolled to the balcony and opened the veranda door. The moon cast yellow shafts over the Santa Lucias and stars pinpointed the sky. She gazed at the purple heavens, dreaming. She wanted to reach out and grasp a palm full of stars; instead she whispered a soft prayer for Taris and for herself.

She heard a guitar's subtle tones lifting above the evening's breeze. Her eyes misted, blurring the distant hills. The music continued as she slipped into bed, spreading her long black hair over the pillow. Her thoughts followed the pale moonlight that outlined shadows on her walls, while deep inside she ached from the pain of unspent desire.

Sabonda cried on the nights she had waited for Taris to come to her, yet when he was beside her, anger replaced anticipation. His clumsy actions and flagrant excuses were always the same, and the odor of whiskey repulsive. Taris's drinking chilled his emotion as surely as his cold hands fumbling over her breasts iced her. At first he had been gentle and considerate. She longed for the love they'd once shared; she wondered why he preferred the passion of whiskey to being with her.

She pounded her fist against a pillow, and started to cry. Harsh, choking sobs. Eventually, the soft evening breezes caressed her face as sleep released the misery that had bound her.

•15•

ON WEDNESDAY MORNING, the nineteenth of October, 1881, Americans were still recovering from shock. President Garfield had died on September 19th from an assassin's bullet taken eleven weeks earlier. In California, it rained.

In Monterey County it rained hard enough to send water gushing down the Santa Lucia mountainsides, flooding streams that emptied into the widening Salinas River.

In late afternoon, Ethan located the telegraph gang where the line boss assured him he'd wire every station along the line to San Francisco.

"Sands," he said, standing in the mud, "we've been so damned busy fixing the line, we haven't paid attention to strangers traveling the road." He paused, glancing at the highway. "Though we did see a covered wagon with a rider behind it, driving north, and it was unusual only because we don't see many prairie rigs up this far."

The rain splattered off his hat brim as Ethan saluted the linemen. He urged Sage forward. Sloshing through the thick mud, Sage made his way back to the road. According to the padre's map, King Ranch was fifty miles from the telegraph camp; Soledad was half again as far.

Ethan cursed, trying to roll tobacco that mushed against damp paper. He fumbled with a match, and after breaking two, held a light.

He wondered if the tales about the Salinas were true. The Camino Real curved toward the river, and he realized the predictions about the Salinas were not fantasies. The Salinas flowed swiftly northward carrying trees and shrubs, scattering debris along the shore. He didn't have to be a native to determine the river was dangerous, so he took his time trying to find a safer place to cross.

He adjusted the collar on his slicker. He couldn't believe it was the same river he had seen farther south. The water had chiseled away earth pushing to the edge of El Camino Real. Ethan was grateful that poisonous water snakes didn't breed west of the Great Divide. Upstream, the Salinas wasn't as wide. When he urged Sage near the river, at first the horse balked and pulled back. He had to yank Peter Balls hard to make him move. He disliked gouging Sage but it was the only way. Halfway across he heard a sickening cry.

•16•

A CALF'S BAWLING made Ethan swing around. Fifty yards upstream, the young steer had bogged down in the suction of quicksand. A wall of water rushed over its head. The calf's nostrils sucked air above the swirling water; then quick as a heartbeat the calf disappeared and was lost.

Ethan fought to stay in the saddle as the mule behind them on the line tried to rear. But, weighted down, his hooves dug into the sandy bottom. Defiantly the mule braced himself against the current. If Ethan had had a heavy board he wouldn't have hesitated busting it over the mule's head.

Sage lunged ahead; Peter Balls followed his smarter friend that was up to his belly in rushing water. Finally reaching the far bank, Ethan spotted a deserted barn, and headed for it. He saw washed-out tracks, indicating that a rider had passed. The rider had ridden south and hadn't crossed the river. He followed the tracks until they ended near the barn's closed door. His first thought was of Diker and Slouter.

Ethan dismounted, pushed back his slicker, and drew his .45. The rusty hinge squeaked as he pushed against the door. He smelled burning wood. His eyes went to a glowing log that cast a little light in the dark interior. He heard a horse nibbling hay. Close to the fire, a man lay asleep against a saddle, a blanket over his head.

Softly, Ethan moved over the stale hay that had matted the earthen floor until he stood two feet from the man by the smoldering fire. He held the barrel of his Colt slightly above the sleeper's head. "Mister," he said in a low voice, "easy like, open your eyes. If you make a foolish move you'll sleep forever." A gust blew in across the ground and fanned the fire, shooting a flame up the log. Shadows danced over Ethan's hands as he lowered the blanket.

"Andy Love—*what 'n the hell!*" Ethan's .45 dropped to his side.

•17•

"OH, MY GOD, am I glad to see you!" Andy stumbled quickly to his feet. "Good buddy, let me touch your hand."

Ethan shook his head. "Are you okay? From what I can see, you look hard put. Let's shake up that fire—I'm wet through 'n' cold."

He pushed sticks underneath the log. His hands shaking, Andy reached for his makings and rolled a smoke. Using the flaming stick, he inhaled and blew smoke above his head. "Me and Kitty had a run-in. And uh, I thought it best to put distance between me and her temper. On the way this storm got worse and, by luck, I found this barn."

Andy took five minutes to explain how traveling with the Beans had begun to wear thin. The long journey, cold food, rain, and close quarters had taken its toll on everyone. "Before I fell asleep, I looked around the barn, and someone has been here before me. Look, I'll show you."

Andy showed Ethan an empty bucket with a red-stained rag flung over its side.

Carefully Andy lifted the filthy rag and held it to the light. "It's bloody." He threw it down. "Somebody dressed a wound."

The rain played a drum beat against the barn. Ethan gave him a rundown on what had happened at Mr. Dobbs' hacienda and about San Miguel. "Think Slouter and Diker were here?" Andy asked.

"Could be. Tell you this, if it is them, they're not far ahead." Ethan kicked at the fire.

Andy cocked his head. "Are you sure they killed the family?"

"No. All we've got is a torn shirt and plenty of suspicion." He pointed at the bucket. "The bloody rag could be anybody's." He walked to the door. "No use wasting time standing here, wondering. Oh, where's Kitty and her folks?"

"I left them up the road, oh, maybe six miles. They're headed for King's Ranch but the rain has slowed 'em down. I'm worried. These killers, they could be up ahead, close to the Beans."

"Yes, that's possible." Ethan rubbed his chin. "Riding south you might have passed them."

"In this rain, it hasn't been easy to see. Hell, they could have ducked behind trees I'da ridden by. I should have stayed with the Beans."

Ethan tapped Andy's arm. "I appreciate how you feel, but you didn't know about these men so don't condemn yourself. I've got fresh grub on the mule, so we'll stoke this fire and fix some eats. Then we'll get a little rest. Then at daylight, we'll ride north."

"Uh, maybe we should just eat and go." Andy had a nervous twitch in his voice.

"Partner, it's so dark you can't see your hand on the horse's head. I'll get Sage and the mule, you poke the fire. You got a gun?"

Andy still didn't wear a gun. It wouldn't do him any good. He couldn't hit a bass drum with a handful of marbles.

"Well, Andy, California's not all sunshine. This state has growing pains, and like it or not, that's the way it's going to be."

After enjoying the hot meal and a short sleep, Ethan opened his eyes. Outside, the rain had slowed to a drizzle. Through the warped siding he could see orange streaks of dawn over the dull, charcoal-white clouds. Andy awoke and quickly the men saddled up, packed, then smothered the fire.

After two hours heading northwest the road curved over hills and passed an occasional ranch gate with the owner's name painted on wooden crossbeams. Among the thick oak trees, cattle grazed along the hillsides.

Ethan needed relief. Sage halted near a stand of trees.

"Feel better?"

"Always do. Even better if you'd roll us a couple."

Andy rolled two cigarettes.

In an hour, the road passed a clearing surrounded by high brush and oak trees. Quail darted from the brush and ran in front of them, made a flapping sound as their wings spread for flight. In a split second, nature's beauty had turned ugly.

•18•

BANG! SHI-U-OOP! A rifle sent a lead slug whistling down over their heads. *THUD!* The second shot splattered mud a yard in front of them. Both riders yanked their horses through the bushes toward a large oak nearby, dropped off and hugged the ground.

The Kansans couldn't see who was shooting at them.

"From how fast that shooter fired that has to be a Winchester forty-four," Ethan said, "and if it's loaded he's got fifteen rounds left. That rifle is out of my forty-five's range." He carefully raised himself.

"What are ya doing?" Andy whispered.

"Without losing my head, I'm going to try for my Sharps. I've got it scoped at eight hundred yards and I shouldn't have any trouble laying one in." Ethan reached up and pulled the rifle from the right scabbard; a Winchester nestled in the left. He flopped back down and narrowed his eyes to sight.

"That second shot Ethan, uh, was a little too close. That shooter's got an eye. Without getting my ears greased, I'll sneak a look." Boots snapped his head back and barked. "Ethan, *put that cannon down!*" That's Locum Bean's wagon. With the hundred-weight charge you're loadin', you'll blow 'em apart."

Ethan slammed the trigger guard forward, ejected the shell, and ran his finger along the breech.

"Andy, how'n the hell do you know about a Sharps?"

"I've seen 'em shoot."

"If that's her father shooting at us, I wouldn't be sticking out my head." He shook his head and wanted to laugh. "You know, lover, problems we've left behind are often found just ahead." He rolled over and leaned back against the tree.

"Okay, now what?"

Andy grunted. "I'm gonna holler at 'em."

"It's your head." Ethan wiped a leaf from the rifle barrel.

"Mister Bean!" Andy yelled. "It's Andy Love 'n' Ethan Sands . . . ya remember?"

Andy stuck his head out a little farther; Ethan yanked him back.

"Locum almost blew out your brains once. C'mon, use common sense." He pushed back his hat, took a deep breath, and waited for Andy's next move.

"I'll be smart and tie a bandanna to a stick. Wave it at him."

Ethan handed him a long, thin branch.

"Uh, now hold on," Andy said. "Why don't *you* wave this stick first? Then I'll step out and show ma-self. Then again what if he don't see good? Common sense could get me killed!"

Ethan chuckled. "Hell's bells, you were about to step out before I yanked you back! And if you'll recall,

Boots, I was the one that promised Mr. Bean he'd never see you again."

Reluctantly, Andy tied the bandanna to the stick, eased around the tree, and vigorously waved. "Ethan, why'n hell don't you say somethin'? Tell 'em who we are."

Ethan pulled up his Sharps and hooked his Stetson over the end of the barrel. He stuck it out from behind the tree.

Andy snorted. "Wow, ain't we brave?"

A woman's voice pierced the air.

"If'n that's you, Love, what's ma daughter's name?"

"Go on, answer her." Ethan pulled back the Sharps.

"It's Kitty . . . Kitty Bean!"

"Ethan, "*that's Kitty's ma!*"

Kitty's mother had her fingers wrapped around a Winchester .44 rifle.

"Andy, here's what we'll do." Ethan peeked around the tree. "We'll walk slowly. I'll lead the horses while you stay in front and keep up a steady chatter, say anything that comes to mind, but keep talking, because Mrs. Bean can shoot straight!

"You want *me* out front?"

"They *know* you!"

His heart kicking against his ribs, Andy walked toward the wagon waving his bandanna, and began a soft, slow chatter.

Ethan held their horses' reins. Both men breathed easier when they saw Emma Bean lay the Winchester down.

When they were twenty feet from the wagon, Emma yelled. "Oh God, boys, I am glad to see ya both. I thought it was them bad 'uns coming back." Fear grabbed Emma. Her red eyes searched aimlessly for something she couldn't see. Kitty pulled back the wagon flap. Her once beautiful face had bruise marks turning it to blue and yellow. Cuts crossed her skin and one eye had been punched a sickening eggplant purple.

•19•

BLOOD MATTED KITTY'S long blond hair, and her cracked lips quivered.

"My God, Mrs. Bean, what's happened?" Ethan asked.

Kitty's mother slumped on the wagon seat and began to sob. The bun at the back of her head was undone and her stringy gray hair fell around her shoulders. The Kansans stood calmly, waiting for her sobbing to wane.

Kitty spoke unsteadily. "Help me and Ma, please Andy." My pa's real bad." She pointed inside the wagon.

Climbing up on the seat, Ethan looked closely at Emma Bean. Pitifully, she looked back at him. "It's Locum. Please go to him. He ain't gonna shoot ya."

He entered the wagon, stepping past Kitty, whose hands covered her face as she huddled against the canvas side. On the wagon's floor, covered with a worn quilt, was Locum, unconscious. The big man was pale and had been beaten about the head. Blood soaked through a rough bandage loosely tied in back.

Ethan stepped back outside and leaned down to Andy. "Bad in there. Both Kitty and her father need help." He turned to Kitty's mother. "How'd this happen, Mrs. Bean?"

Kitty's mother told how two men had set upon them. "It was mealtime, I was cooking. At first they only wanted food. We offered to share, but that wasn't all they wanted. They wanted everything. While one was arguing with Pa, the shorter one went behind him and struck Pa hard with an axe handle he'd pulled from the wagon. When Pa went down, they began to beat him." Emma wiped her eyes and continued. "Kitty, God bless, went for Pa's shotgun. That's when the pock-faced one attacked her."

Ethan glanced at Andy. "Emma," he said slowly, "was the other man short and heavyset?"

"Yes. My God, how do you know them?"

Ethan explained how they'd met south of San Miguel. Not wanting to frighten her further, he mentioned nothing of what had happened at San Miguel.

Andy climbed over the seat and checked if he could do anything for Kitty. Emma, forlorn and confused, was close to shock. She sat staring down the road, holding the rifle across her lap, running her fingers nervously over the trigger.

Andy came out shaking his head. "That poor girl has had more than a beating, Ethan. She's bad off." He whispered, "Locum's near dead."

Andy climbed down, gazing at the road, a team pulling a freight wagon headed toward them closer, the man holding the reins eased alongside Emma's wagon.

Ethan told the driver about the attack. The man kindly offered to transport the family into King Ranch, figuring he could make good time. "Sometimes there's a doctor at King's," he said. "If the family needs rest, my spread's not far from town. After they've seen the doctor, they'd be welcome to stay."

"We'll load the family in his wagon," Ethan said. "I'll ride guard with the Beans. Andy, you follow us with Bean's wagon."

Diker and Slouter were closer than they had thought.

When the necessary belongings were loaded into the stranger's wagon, Emma said, "Thank ya, boys, I'm owing ya both."

The Kansans carefully lifted Kitty into the wagon and made Locum as comfortable as they could. Emma sat on the stranger's seat, nervously looking over her shoulder. The heavy wagon squeaked forward as the tall, iron-rimmed wheels splashed mud and began to roll for King Ranch.

Before they separated, Ethan whispered, "Andy, keep Locum's shotgun across your lap and have the pistol I gave you at your side, and if anyone gives you trouble, pull both triggers; then empty the forty-five on what's left. Don't stop for anything."

Andy nodded. "See ya at King Ranch."

As the freight wagon pulled away, a breeze blew around him, and Andy felt lonely. He began to whistle, attempting to lift his spirits and clear his head. Kitty's beaten face kept coming before him.

He hoped someday, somewhere, he and Ethan would face Slouter and Diker. When that day came, they wouldn't worry about the law. He slapped the reins over the backs of the horses then glanced up at the sky; rain could pour anytime.

Beneath the low rain clouds, immense black hawks flew above Locum's wagon—sinister omens of death circling around and around. Andy didn't like what he saw, nor what he thought: no matter where man touches the earth, evil prevails including California.

Part 5

Kiowa's Prairie Justice

• 1 •

ON THE KANSAS plains, the Kiowa have a legend: *"Death and danger ride the south wind."* The Kansans, friends of the Kiowa, understood. The south winds gathered dark clouds over King's Ranch. The doctor wasn't in town, and even if he had been, it wouldn't have mattered. Locum passed away shortly after the freight wagon arrived in town.

Emma Bean was a widow; Kitty was fatherless. Legends contain truths. California had taken him, the tempting señorita had smiled on Bean, and unfortunately, Kitty's pa had returned her smile.

Luckily, despite cracks, the roof of King's Hotel held back most of the rain. Leaks laid yellow streaks over flimsy wallpaper. Ethan threw back the comforter and yawned, reached over and shook Andy. "Talker, how's your fat head?" Andy tucked the cover under his chin and grimaced; he wasn't well. The men had hoped that come morning, the rain would have stopped.

Once a useful hay barn, King Hotel had been rebuilt. During the remodeling, carpenters had been supplied with inferior lumber. When the first downpour blew against the hotel's walls, the cheap lumber leaked.

From a window, they counted ten buildings facing east, and on El Camino's west side there was mostly empty land with one exception, a gathering of lean-to shacks.

"Any whiskey left?" Andy scratched his behind.

Ethan held up the bottle, shook it, then tossed it to him. " 'Nough maybe to wash the stink out of your mouth, though it won't make you feel any better."

Andy drained the whiskey, belched, and dropped the bottle on the floor. "Dammit, Ethan, that's a horrible way for a man to start the day, but . . ."

"But what?"

"I feel injured. All over. It's like mice are nibblin' at the roots of ma hair. I'll tell ya, it's a terrible feelin'. Ya ever get the feelin'?" Andy, disgusted, used his foot to roll away the empty bottle through a puddle of water. It crashed against the wall.

"No. I never let myself get that bent." Ethan laughed. "Count your blessings, Old Boot, it could be worse, I guess. Don't step in the broken glass."

"How worse?"

"A dissatisfied, ugly-mouthed woman could be laying beside you asking you to do something you'd already done." He laughed louder than before.

Andy threw his naked legs from underneath the covers and shivered. "Hand me ma pants, please!" He rubbed his hands together trying to get warm.

Fast Draw threw the trousers, hitting him across the chest. "C'mon, get your butt inside these."

Sitting on the bed's edge, Andy held his head and began pulling his hand through hair so matted that halfway through, his fingers stuck.

"Damn, I need a haircut. Ever cut hair, Ethan?"

"No, I haven't. But I'm not starting with yours, either."

The delays so far had been costly; sleeping in rooms and eating in cafes had created a vacancy in Ethan's bankroll. He thought that had he shipped Sage and taken a seat on the train, he would have been sleeping in a comfortable San Francisco hotel by now: clean sheets, towels, a roof instead of an edifice that should have remained a barn.

"Boot." Ethan sat next to him. "I know you're miserable, but we need to talk."

"Now?" Andy replied.

"Now."

"About what?"

"Money."

Andy fumbled with his shirt, searching for tobacco. He smiled. "Hey, look here. I found two dollars. Here, put it in the pot." He handed over the cash.

Ethan fondled the coins. "Least it'll pay for the room. Maybe breakfast, too. Boot, from here north, we're camping out. Rain, snakes, or snow, whatever they've got, understand?"

"That figures." Andy fumbled with his fly. He leaned over and painfully pulled on his boots. "But right now I need coffee, bad!"

"What you need is my boot across your skinny backside, a swift kick to each cheek would start your day. Last night you sucked everything out of the bottle 'cept the label. I got sick of hearing ya ... Kitty this ... Kitty that!"

Events hung on their minds. Both had whiskey'd

heavily, using rotgut as a crutch against events. California wasn't much of an improvement. The San Miguel murders, Kitty's rape, her father's death, and the killing of two drovers warped their dispositions. Last night, the cheap whiskey and yards of talk reduced their misery to what it was—mostly their imagination.

"Sure ya won't cut ma hair?" Andy flaunted his gapped teeth with an ivory smile that wiggled his dimples.

"Stuff your saddlebags, we'll hit the road. Move."

Outside the hotel they felt better. The cool air refreshed them. While passing wagons splashed mud and the heavy wheels sank, people moved about the town as if the day were special.

Andy held out his hand. "Hey! I've found a half-dollar."

"You want another whiskey?"

"No, I don't want *whiskey*! This'll git coffee. C'mon, Ethan, act like ya had breedin'."

Two doors down from the hotel, they found a cafe that had been split in half. One side was given to dry goods, while in the other half the owner served food. Sitting at the counter, they ordered coffee. Bacon frying in a large pan aroused the Kansans. Andy smiled. "Shall we shoot it all?"

"If'n I'm going broke, let it be on a full stomach."

Andy tossed it on the counter. "Mister cook, give us all that'll buy." The cook fingered the coin. "That'll get you bacon 'n' eggs, fried spuds, and a stack of hot bread, plus all the coffee you can swallow." He stuffed the coin in his pocket.

Once full, Ethan held a cigarette between his lips. "What's going to happen to Kitty and her mother?"

"I hope, as the good book says, 'the crooked places shall be made straight.' "

Ethan snorted. "Where'n hell does it say that? C'mon, be honest, you made that up—didn't you?"

"Of course not! It's in there." Andy looked away. "Kitty told me that they had kin living near San Jose, on her father's side."

"Bean got any money?"

"Said they did. Locum intended to buy a farm near San Jose, somewhere."

Andy pushed back his empty plate and dumped cigarette ashes on the dirty floor.

Ethan stood and walked to the window. The cigarette in his mouth fell to the floor. Three long strides and he was back beside Andy, pulling on his arm. *"Andy, hold on—look outside!* That's them! Slouter and Diker— across the street!"

•2•

BIGGER THAN SIN, the wanted men leaned against the rooming-house wall enjoying the sun. Casually they pushed away from the wall and ambled down the street. They stopped in front of a store window to admire a Hawken plains rifle.

"Andy, listen. Beat it out back, fetch the horses, and make your way to the far end of the street, and keep out of sight until you see my signal. I'll tip my hat."

Andy raced for the back door and vanished, while the killers watched King City's citizens milling by.

Calmly, Ethan moved outside the cafe to the store next door. The killers crossed the street where they had horses tied to a hitching rail.

Sooner than expected, Andy appeared holding Gussie and Sage's reins. He waited. Boots turned up his collar and quickly moved the horses across from the sailors.

He studied the two men and noticed Diker had used

his bandaged hand to untie the horse. Facing the sun, hats pulled down, the sailors backed their horses into the street. They walked slowly toward Ethan.

He waited. Timing was important. He signaled Andy by tipping his hat. Andy spurred Gussie and charged forward. Andy's lasso whipped the wind, swinging big circles over his head.

•3•

WHEN ANDY'S LASSO fell around Slouter's torso, Gussie pulled up short. Digging in, she yanked the rope taut, separating the rider from his horse. He landed facedown in the muddy street.

Straightaway, Diker did what Ethan had expected. He spurred his horse into a run. Ethan leaped from his hiding place and stood in line with Diker's charging horse. He grabbed Diker's arm and jerked him from his saddle. Air gushed from his mouth as he hit the street, belly first. Ethan stood over him as Diker painfully rolled over and looked straight into the ominous eye of Ethan's .45.

"Go for it, Diker. One twitch and I'll bury you in the mud!" Ethan reached down and twisted Diker's collar, choking him. "Diker, you pervert—squirm. Because there's words I want to hear. About San Miguel! About the man's wife tied to the bed, how you raped her like you raped young Kitty." Ethan tightened his grip. "You did a good job beating her father. He's dead! You and Slouter killed him!"

Diker's face was beet-red. Desperately he tried to loosen Ethan's hold. Ethan spat in his face. "The little fella with his brains dripping from his skull, which one of you sick morons did that?" He glared into Diker's scarred face. Before I'm finished, you'll beg to tell me everything I want to know. Otherwise none of your bones will ever fit, and when you bend over your nuts'll pinch. Think about it!"

Sweat flowed down Ethan's face. He slipped a rope around Diker and jerked it tight. "Feel pain, Diker? I'm going to drag you until your guts scrape your skin, you'll wanna die."

Diker wiped mud from his face. Racked with fear, he looked back and yelled, "Slouter?"

Andy had Slouter under rope and was dragging him backward behind Gussie. Slouter's cursing screeches filled the air and caught people's attention. They stood and gawked at cowboy's law alive and well in the center of town.

Rope in hand, Ethan mounted Sage. "C'mon, Andy, let's give 'em a taste of prairie justice."

•4•

"RIDE! GIVE 'EM hell." When Ethan's arm came down Sage and Gussie felt spurs jabbing their flanks. They thundered forward and the ropes snapped taut. Diker and Slouter yowled as their bodies plowed through the muddy street while bystanders cheered the riders on.

Ethan yelled at a spectator. "Where's your jail?"

"To your right, cowboy; next corner, ya cain't miss it."

Slouter, the stronger of the two, tried to pull the lasso back. Andy spurred and with a burst of power Gussie's eleven hundred pounds thrust ahead, jerking Slouter in a spine-chattering haul.

Diker hollered to Ethan, sputtering, "I'll tell ya . . . for God's sake, stop! I'll tell ya whatcha want!"

"Shut up, ya damned fool!" Slouter yelled.

Ethan eased off on the reins and turned. "Haven't heard it yet, Diker. My horse is an all-day horse, he'll run till I tell him to quit. Diker, he's only started." He spurred Sage; the rope burned, cutting into Diker's flesh.

Diker's body, racked by pain, throbbed at every bump. Mud filled his mouth; he urinated down his leg. His bones pulled at the joints. He screamed. "We did it . . . We killed them . . . Christ's sake, stop!"

They reined Sage and Gussie in a wide circle, dragging their captives near the jail's door. "Folks," Ethan called to the crowd, "what you see are the San Miguel killers; and these bastards killed the old man and attacked the women in the wagon."

A cheer filled the street. People hollered at others to come and see. Boys began throwing rocks at the thugs behind the horses and men fired guns into the sky. The noise brought the sheriff and his deputies from the jail. Slouter was still cursing when Ethan and Andy dragged the muddy culprits in front of the jail. Diker had passed out.

Ethan leaned back in the saddle and pointed to the Wanted poster nailed to a post. "Sheriff"—Ethan grinned—"these stinking bastards are San Miguel's killers."

Leaning over the saddle horn, Ethan said: "These men killed Locum Bean and raped his daughter. Both the girl and her mother will identify them."

Nearly everyone in the small community had gathered around the jail. Citizens offered to stand guard outside the jail. "I'll guarantee that the prisoners will stay locked inside my jail. My men can handle the job." The local residents had faith in the sheriff, but after talking with him, Ethan felt differently. A week ago during a high wind, half the jail building collapsed.

He turned to Ethan. "I'll send a rider out where Mrs. Bean is resting. Incidentally, I'm Sheriff Clay," he said, proudly sticking out his hand.

•5•

ETHAN FOLLOWED THE sheriff's men carrying the prisoners inside. Andy remained outside telling onlookers how his partner single-handedly had fought these men in a barroom brawl outside of Paso Robles. Ethan overheard him, rushed back, grabbed Andy's arm and yanked him inside the jail. "Skip that bull. They'll wonder why I didn't have sense enough to kill them!"

Inside, the battered door, the paper-thin walls that covered the cells, were in need of repair. In front of the sheriff's desk, two barrels had been fashioned into uncomfortable chairs. Overhead, thick cobwebs held dead moths and flies. Ethan had known stronger-looking jails. Two deputies shoved the two prisoners toward a cell.

Ethan and Andy waited at the sheriff's desk. The sheriff asked Ethan and Andy to sit. "Boys, I believe you're in for fresh money for what you've done." Sheriff Clay looked over at the Wanted poster hiding the faded calendar that advertised ladies' garments—which a devoted man wouldn't see. Ethan looked twice: it was dated 1879.

"I'll get a wire off to Paso Robles. Let 'em know." The sheriff rescued a half-burned cigar from a rusty can, stuck it in the corner of his mouth, and scraped a match across the top of his termite-eaten desk. " 'Course, these men will haveta stand trial. That'll take place in the county seat where the first crime took place in San Luis Obispo, or maybe Monterey. Tell me, all-ya witness any of these killings?"

Ethan explained about San Miguel and how he'd met Roy Sedway.

"Why, I know Mr. Sedway. He thinks a lot of me." Clay struck another match. "These prisoners, they do any talking?" He raised his eyebrows.

Ethan got up and stood by the window. "Confess? Sheriff, you should have heard Diker sing while I was dragging him."

"Good! Under California law, if there's no witness, nor a confession, they've got a chance of getting off. But that's the court's job, not mine." He turned and spat into a spittoon. "Sheriff, I know Mrs. Bean and her daughter will testify," Ethan said. "Now as for San Miguel, Diker told me they were in on it."

The sheriff wiped a tobacco bit from his chin and pulled a cracked mirror from his desk, then curled his sloppy mustache. "Yeah, I heard about the old lady Bean. Tough."

"Sheriff, give me a pad and pencil and I'll get a confession in black and white. Diker will talk. So will his pal."

The sheriff thought a minute. "I gotta say it's irregular, but if I'm a witness to it, why not?"

In less than an hour the lawman and Ethan were back at his desk with a full confession signed by Diker; Slouter wouldn't sign. "Sheriff, if you'll give me ten minutes more with him, I'll get Slouter's too."

"Son, bet a hundred you would. I think we've got enough. Diker spilled the beans good, it's on the paper." He held up the pad. "So let's settle back. He'll testify against Slouter."

There was another poster lying across his desk. Ethan casually picked it up. "When did you get this?"

"Oh, that came in maybe a week ago. An out-of-stater, Billy Largo was seen in Los Angeles, then in Santa Barbara. Guess he's headed north."

Ethan nodded and shoved back the poster. *Yes*, he said to himself, *you'd better bet your filthy shirt, Sheriff, that you never meet him.*

"I've met Billy."

Clay put on his specs.

"Oh?"

Outside the unsecure jailhouse, folks waited to see the men who had dragged in the killers. When Ethan and Andy stepped outside, everyone cheered and a photographer snapped a picture. The Kansans mounted their horses and were about to leave.

"Hold on." Sheriff Clay held up his hand. "You boys'll get subpoenaed, least you should. In any event, I want you both to stay put until I hear from San Luis Obispo. Look, you've still got to pocket your reward."

He smiled. "Truth is, that's more cash than I see in a year. So, men, like it or not, you've just become heroes! Pretty damned rich heroes, at that."

As they rode away from the crowd, Andy looked back.

"What'n hell is Sheriff Clay up to?"

Ethan turned around and shaded his eyes against the late afternoon sun.

"He's passing out something to folks on the street. Now look, he's shaking hands."

What Ethan hadn't seen was the poster hanging outside his office door: a picture of the lawman, a white Stetson hiding his shiny head as he held a .45 across his chest. Sheriff Clay, the unassertive and humble small-town lawman, was up for reelection.

•6•

LESS THAN ONE-HUNDRED miles south of King Ranch, on the Rancho El Norte, Juan Ricardo asked his guests to join him in the library. Among them were Eddie Ho, Enrique "Henry" Hernandez, chairman of the landowners' committee, Judge Paul Gordain, and distinguished county officials. Juan made his apologies to those who had remained, and summoned Sabonda to assume his position as host and see that everyone was graciously entertained.

Sabonda invited the ladies into the sitting room while the gentlemen enjoyed private conversations, or played billiards in the next room.

In the library, Señor Ricardo passed cigars from a silver box while a servant moved about serving his favorite Napoleon brandy.

Juan formally introduced Enrique and Judge Gordain to Eddie Ho. Edward Ho was an impressive young man: his wealthy Chinese father, a member of the British queen's court, his English mother a cousin of the royal family.

Before sailing to San Francisco in 1877, Eddie Ho, with honors, was graduated from Oxford.

In San Francisco, Ho was alarmed by the bigotry against Chinese which reached from San Francisco to the Sierra peaks. Hard-working Gum San coolies had been targets for San Francisco's unions, hard men who discouraged and attacked them at every opportunity.

Eddie Ho was fortunate. He was handsome, intelligent, and ambitious. He had personal entree to the British consulate that provided opportunities an Oriental of lesser stature would have never enjoyed.

Enrique Cañada Fernandez owned a great deal of land in and around San Luis Obispo, including many original properties granted by the king of Spain. Judge Paul Gordain was a superior court judge in Sacramento. The *alcalde* tapped his glass, seeking their attention.

"*Señores, por favor*, there are problems I wish to address. As Californians, we know history is alive and being written daily." Juan winked. "Though some of us shouldn't have been written about." His audience agreed. "The rush for gold has long since subsided, and another took its place. This rush, of course, is for the accumulation of land, and ways to capitalize on it, other than from digging gold."

The *alcalde* tasted his brandy and continued. "The United States government has occupied itself by inspecting land titles and qualifying Spanish land grants. Some titles are clouded, forcing thousands of acres to change hands."

"Forgive me, Juan," the judge said, "but we've all known unscrupulous attorneys who have gained advantage over Californians by charging abysmal fees for legal services. These services often have concluded by the attorneys owning the land." Juan nodded and sipped his brandy.

"I'm stressing this point, gentlemen, because today we still face uncontrolled danger: the Southern Pacific railroad and the men who have manipulated it as they pleased. My friends, we have been witnesses to a monumental land grab, one of the worst California has ever known. It's disheartening when a railroad tycoon can dictate California's policy. These men who have built the railroad over the Sierra are strangling California."

Indeed, every man listening knew the odious *dramatis personae*: Mark Hopkins, Leland Stanford, Charles Crocker, and the frugal man who held them all in the palm of his hand, Collis P. Huntington. These men had replaced the earlier leaders of California men of importance: Sutter, Vallejo, Larkin, and the famous guardian, Fremont.

It was Huntington's incredible act of legerdemain that had cheated the Congress by charging mountain rates for tracks laid at lower, level land, divesting taxpayers of $100 million.

Leland Stanford had wangled political privileges and licenses with the dexterity of a ferocious tiger. Mark Hopkins and Stanford moved heaven and earth in San Francisco to get supplies for Crocker as he busted his back as a hands-on foreman driving his crews laying tracks in conditions that would have killed lesser men.

Scrooge Huntington, not a patriotic visionary, never dirtied his hands while building the greatest monopoly California had ever suffered.

•7•

JUAN PLACED HIS cigar in an ashtray. "Gentlemen, if we are to share in California's future, we Californians must unite! We know we have land, we have cattle, and we have energy. Totally, we have strength. But we don't have a *railroad*!"

The guests nodded and grumbled agreement. The railroad aimed toward San Luis Obispo had been terminated in San Jose. According to Huntington, the lucrative Southern Pacific tracks running from San Francisco to Los Angeles through the San Joaquin Valley were enough.

The railroad tycoons had maneuvered to stall construction along the coast. The cost was prohibitive, wrote the newspapers.

The judge raised his hand. "Juan, are you implying that united Californians can build a railroad? Lord, that's like God parting the sea, Juan. You can't be serious."

"*Mis amigos*, of course I don't mean build a railroad," Juan responded, "but our future still depends on the railroad. Without it, San Luis Obispo County lacks the means to exist."

Guests turned to one another, commenting. All were aware that without a connecting railway, California's future was bleak.

"Gentlemen, there is a way. Our lands have unexplored wealth. Food and water, gentlemen, is power! Our lands north to Monterey have rich, fertile soil; to the south, we have equally productive lands, and to the east the power machine—the San Joaquin Valley. Food will grant us an unexpected potency to compete against the railroad, and, gentlemen, the San Joaquin can grow that food."

Eddie Ho placed his brandy aside and studied Señor Ricardo. He realized that the Southern Pacific had the means to reach California's distant produce markets, if the markets became lucrative enough.

Henry Hernandez threw up his hand. "My good friend, are you saying that if we unite, there would be enough capital to buy the entire San Joaquin?"

"Yes, Henry," Juan said. "There's money available to buy a major part of the valley, enough to gain control. And the land is not all we must have. Someday, we must harness water from the Sierra's runoff; irrigation will provide a system that will enable the valley to become a food center for the state—perhaps the nation. My friends, a hundred years from now, the man, the company, the corporation or city that owns water in the San Joaquin will control California. Judge Gordain leaned forward. "Not only must we own the lands and raise foods, Juan, we must have markets in cities to sell produce and we must control them."

"Judge, you're correct. This is the reason we must form a coalition to protect our interests now."

Juan Ricardo looked at Eddie Ho. "With Mr. Ho's expertise and cooperation, we shall have markets in San Francisco. Mr. Ho has the labor sources, and gentlemen, this is only the beginning."

Juan walked to the window and stood silent for a moment.

"Now, gentlemen, my second reason for this meeting. To further this plan, I am announcing my candidacy for state senator representing San Luis Obispo County." The men stood and cheered.

Señor Fernandez requested their attention: "Gentlemen, I propose a toast to our next senator, our *compañero* . . . Juan Bautista Ricardo. Viva!"

In the next room the ladies who waited for their husbands overheard men's voices and smiled. They had gathered bits of what Señor Ricardo had said. In the living room, women prepared to reunite with their husbands. While in a sinking mood, Sabonda knew how much her father desired to bring this coalition into reality; she was so very proud of him.

Exhausted, she experienced an emptiness. While her friends politely commented on Taris's absence, an anger grew within her. Frowning, her lips met in a harsh line tightening the skin between her eyes. She was tired, drained from loneliness and the humiliation provided by a man who obviously didn't care.

·8·

AFTER THE EXCITEMENT over the capture of San Miguel's murderers, the townsfolk of King City planned a beef barbecue as a celebration, and every woman was asked to bring her favorite dish.

It was a gala occasion, warm and friendly, and it gave the town a feeling that law and order had prevailed. Leastwise that was the theme of the sheriff's lengthy speech. Standing on a barrel, he gave a windy talk that bored most of the folks who knew he had little to with the killer's capture other than to lock them up in his lean-to jail.

Following the festivities, Ethan and Andy ducked out and spent time resting.

When the sheriff asked the heroes to join the posse hauling the prison wagon to San Luis Obispo, the Kansans had mixed feelings. Returning south to San Luis Obispo wasn't what Ethan had in mind. Still, considering that the prisoners had a chance of being freed for lack of eyewitnesses it seemed important that they should cooperate.

Then, too, Sedway's cash reward would come in handy. San Francisco would have to wait. Ethan chuckled when he imagined how Avery Dru might have felt if he were to accept part of the reward. And if ever they should meet, Ethan would make the offer. He had never fully explained to Andy about the time he had spent with Avery. Like himself, Avery was seeking a different way of life.

•9•

IN KANSAS, BOTH Andy and Ethan had witnessed trials where a man should have hung and didn't. Criminals broke out of jail; often culprits simply disappeared without benefit of a trial.

Before Andy left King Ranch, he learned from Mrs. Bean that when Kitty was stronger, they planned returning to San Luis Obispo where she intended to buy a small ranch that she had seen while passing through. Though healing, Kitty still refused to venture into town.

The deputies rode alongside the jail wagon as it made its way south toward the Cuesta Grade. Eight men, including Sands and Love, made up the posse.

Passing time, a friendly deputy in the posse volunteered tales of disreputable events that occurred on El Camino Real. In the 1850s, he said, Joaquin Murietta harassed the travelers, making life most uncomfortable.

Joaquin possessed an arbitrary sense of justice: he only killed his victim if he deserved to die.

"Yes, Joaquin, he's a legend in these parts," said the deputy. "They say he stayed where we're going, San Luis Obispo. In 1851, the local newspapers warned everyone that Joaquin's gang was headed for town. But the gang rode in without its leader. Some said they didn't do much except send quivers down people's spines."

Ethan asked, "Where was Joaquin?"

"Who knows? He was clever at disguise, and may have been one of them. Slippery is the word."

The deputy unloaded a soggy wad of tobacco and wiped his mouth. "Then we had Tiburico Vasquez. He was a bad 'un, a bandit and a killer, and people hated him. He was captured in 1874 and executed in Los Angeles. Luckily for San Luis Obispo, he only passed through town."

The deputy rolled a cigarette. With a smirk, he raised his hand. "Here's one for you. There's a rumor in Paso Robles that's hard to believe. They say there's been a character hanging around impersonating Jesse James. Hell, it's gotta be a pile. Who in their right mind would be so damned foolish?"

Ethan shrugged his shoulders and agreed.

Three days later, at thirty minutes past noon, the party arrived at the bottom of Cuesta Grade. Near San Luis Obispo Creek, several riders approached the wagon. Men rushed to shake hands with friends and in turn were introduced to Ethan and Andy.

"Boys, the town's ready for a helluva shebang," the leader said. "You're heroes, and folks are gonna show ya a time!"

Ethan looked at Andy. "Oh my God. We're not heroes."

Andy whispered privately, "I don't know 'bout you, Fast Draw, but I ain't ever been no hero, and I'm ready and willing for a little change of pace. Spreadin' joy never hurt anyone." He grinned. "Sensibly put, this trip has been as festive as watching a fire in church."

Andy eyed the gathering crowd. "Yes sir, for a change, if'n I must, I'll playact. Watch me, Ethan—I'll be a hero!"

Highly decorated, San Luis Obispo resembled the Fourth of July and New Year's Eve combined. Red, white, and blue bunting draped the buildings and crisscrossed over the streets. Near the courthouse, the band unpacked their instruments and readied themselves.

On Palm Street, in front of Ah Luis's building, Chinese children shot off firecrackers. When the prison wagon pulled into sight, the band oompahed smartly, and began to march. From ranches and farms, the Carissa Plains and the ocean towns west and south of San Luis Obispo, people had traveled to see the killers of San Miguel and to welcome the men who had captured them.

Andy pulled off his hat and slapped it against his trousers, trying to rid himself of dust. He ran his fingers through his hair, brushing out what dust he could. Ethan sat in the saddle staring at the crowd; never in his life had he ridden in a parade. Sabonda, Taris, and Juan Ricardo enjoyed reserved seats in front of the courthouse.

Cheers welcomed the guests of honor riding on their nervous mounts behind the discordant band. Clashing cymbals frightened birds from the trees, and gulls flew higher than usual over the street. In front of the band, dressed in Union blue, veterans proudly carried the colors. As the parade passed by the courthouse, Sabonda's eyes were drawn to the good-looking stranger wearing a buckskin shirt with his pistol tied low on his leg.

"Be Glory!" Taris jumped to his feet. "It's him! That's my friend. The one, me darlin', I mentioned only a few weeks back." In his exuberance he almost reached inside for his flask, but he didn't dare.

She smiled, looking toward her father.

The *alcalde* placed his hat over his heart as the color guard passed in review.

Andy smiled, showing off his gapped teeth, stood on his stirrups, making himself taller, and waved. He threw kisses to girls and, pointing at himself, called out: "Andy Love—Kansas—*that's me!*"

Ethan laughed. "Andy, you're a damned clown. Quit yelling your name."

Andy swung around. "Ethan, I've been a clown before, but I've never been a hero. Who cares?"

•10•

AT HALF PAST three, the parade returned to where it had begun. In front of the county courthouse, the mayor and Juan Ricardo were on hand to greet Andy and Ethan. Ethan's eyes met Sabonda's. He couldn't remove his eyes from hers.

Taris's voice broke the spell. "Mr. Sands, this is me wife, Sabonda, and her father, Juan Ricardo." Mechanically, Ethan's hand went out to her father.

"Señores, Californians are proud of what you have done. *Muchas gracias, amigos*," Juan Ricardo said. "Now you must bathe and refresh yourselves. He pointed to the hotel across the street. "Please, gentlemen, I've ordered iced champagne for the occasion."

Inside the hotel's lobby, the *alcalde* arranged space enough for the makeshift bar. He signaled the waiter.

Andy pulled on Ethan's arm, "I'm drier than a knot-

holed fence. C'mon, let's hoist a few. I've never in-
dulged myself in champagne."

A waiter sporting a crimson jacket stood in front of
him with a tray. Andy eyed the long-stemmed glasses.
Sabonda raised a glass. "I salute you, gentlemen. To
brave men everywhere."

The bubbles tickled Andy's nose. He emptied the
glass and took another. "Gents, here's to fancy boots,
fast horses, and pretty women. Oh, yes. Here's to Señor
Ricardo." He hoisted his glass, wobbled uneasily, and
looked to Ethan for support.

The small room darkened with smoke while men
talked and, in gracious California fashion, wine flowed.
Politely, Juan Ricardo excused himself and stepped into
the next room.

The Kansans walked to the bar. Ethan noticed the short,
rotund gent in a formal pin-striped suit staring at his pistol. The man's eyes swept over Ethan's tall frame.

"Something wrong, mister?" Ethan felt uneasy being
appraised by a stranger.

"Oh no, Mr. Sands, only curious. Uh, is that the
forty-five that killed them?"

Ethan took a long look at the peculiar man. "Mister,
no one got shot. They're going to hang."

The man gulped and put down his glass, turned and
disappeared.

Ethan signaled the bartender. "Who was that?"

The bartender leaned over. "That's Arch Hanson,
town's richest undertaker. Besides filling graves, he's
got a finger in most everything, including a piece of the
bank."

"Greedy son of a bitch," Andy said. "There's a citi-
zen who gets rich on both sides of the street."

Ethan smiled and filled his glass.

•11•

JUAN RICARDO RETURNED. "*Señores*, Sunday, in your honor, I've arranged for a fiesta at my son-in-law's ranch, the Rancho El Norte. Beef cooked over coals, dancing, wine, and"—he paused—"people who will enjoy meeting you. My vaqueros will escort you to El Norte."

"Good!" Andy lifted his glass to Juan Ricardo who politely bid adios.

Andy finished his fourth champagne. "Ethan, there's no women in here."

"*It's not that kind of a hotel!* Besides, if I was a woman, I wouldn't stand near you." Ethan laughed. "I'm headed for a hot tub. Behave yourself."

The hotel clerk handed Ethan the key and informed him that the room had a private bath. "Like a bottle sent up, Mr. Sands?"

"Yes, suppose you'd better."

Andy, cornered a well-dressed man. "Say, partner, how's the women in town?"

"We have adequate women. Between the town's ladies and the ones arriving from the country, you'll see. I'm George Wickers." He turned to introduce a man. "This gentleman is my good friend Able Strats. We're both deacons. The Community Gospel is our church."

Andy hiccuped and blushed. Mr. Wicker explained that a dance had been arranged that evening to celebrate the day's events. "Mr. Love, you'll enjoy yourself. Speaking for myself and Deacon Strats, we're excited about the festivities.

Andy smiled, his face red. "Nice talkin' to you, deacons." The champagne and the long day's ride had begun to tell on Andy.

•12•

ACROSS THE STREET from Big Ed's saloon, Reb Dunkin, the hotel's owner, watched a tall man clothed in black, a sombrero cocked to one side, swagger in. He strolled to the desk and slammed both hands flat on the counter. "I'll take a room."

Reb blinked. "Mister, there's just no rooms to take. Sorry. Everybody around has come to town for the parade."

The stranger's hand shot over the desk, grabbing Reb's collar. "Bullshit! I don't give a damn over a parade. Kick someone out 'n' quit stallin', and make sure I got a bath. Now, how much?"

Reb, a sensible man, figured there was a friend of his he could move. "That'll be five dollars." He picked up the pen.

"Five dollars!" The man shook his hat, spilling dust

over the desk. "Here's three. If'n it's good, we'll talk about it. Where do I stable my horse?"

The belligerent guest brushed back his long blond hair and shoved back his hat. "Oh, yeah. When I get back, have a bottle on the desk—make sure it ain't cut."

As the front door closed, Reb looked at the stranger's meaningless signature. Somewhere he'd seen the man's face.

Part 6

The First Dance Is Forever

• 1 •

THE NEXT MORNING after a refreshing rest, Ethan and Andy left the hotel and wandered to the creek flowing past Mission San Luis Obispo. Ethan leaned down and took a drink. He smiled. "Water's fresh and clean. It must have come from those hills over there, eastward."

Invigorated by fresh air, the Kansans returned to their room. Andy admired himself in the mirror. He parted his hair, a few strands curling over his forehead.

"I'm gonna wear my new shirt. Lookit, ain't that a pretty yellow color?"

"But, uh, those corduroy trousers," Ethan said, "they look a size too small."

"Perfect fit. What'd you buy?"

Conservative with his reward money, Ethan had bought a white shirt, a gray coat, and a new Stetson, all on sale. After dressing, he checked the load and strapped on his .45.

Outside the hotel, they faced Monterey Street as a dozen smartly dressed vaqueros rode in followed by a carriage. The gray-haired leader, with a youthful face and dancing blue eyes, smiled and climbed off a high-tailed palomino. The handsome vaquero walked toward them.

"Señor Sands, my *jefe*, Juan Ricardo, sends his compliments and his carriage. I'm Jorge Fermín, at your service."

The other vaqueros dismounted and stood in a line showing off their skin-close *pantalones* that flared at the bottoms and wide sombreros stitched with silver that glistened in the morning sun.

Ethan looked at him. "A short time ago I met another Jorge Fermín."

"Did this *hombre* have silver-white hair, and look much older than me?"

"Why, yes. You know this man?"

"He is my grandfather, a wise and wonderful man. Where did you meet him?"

Ethan explained how he had come upon the old man resting atop the Cuesta Grade.

"Did he tell you a great deal about this country, señor?"

"Indeed he did. Very interesting, too. He said that he had worked on the Rancho El Norte."

"For many years, he did. Now he is going back to Monterey, the place of his birth. He is one of the finest horsemen this country has ever known. All of us on the rancho have learned so much from him. Not only about horses, but of life itself. But, señor, I have been sent to get you and your friend. Are you ready?"

* * *

Juan Ricardo's carriage was a classy rig with shiny black sides, tall wheels with red lacquered spokes, and two polished brass lanterns in front. Inside, soft glove leather covered the seats and tasseled shades hung above the windows.

"Gawd," Andy said, putting his cherry-colored boot on the step. "Ain't this the way to go? Style is the word!"

Ethan closed the door and sat back, whispering, "Partner, in those tight pants you fit right in."

Juan's carriage assured Ethan they'd arrive free of road dust. In less than an hour, they turned into Rancho El Norte's gate, a working ranch stocked with cattle that grazed on tall grass, fat beeves that stacked dollars in the owner's account.

"Ethan, those are Kansas cows, look at 'em."

Ethan pushed back the window shade. "Well fed, but I doubt if they ever saw Kansas."

The carriage pulled behind the hacienda. Dark green oaks and pitch pines made a path to the hills, east of the ranch. They walked toward a group of men who stood by the corral.

No matter where they found cowboys, vaqueros, or penniless cow-waddies the job of punching cattle is much the same. Providing there's plenty of animals with men eager and tough enough to sit a horse chasing the beasts. Mean critters that do nothing but throw dust and fear into a cowboy and make him sweat every time his backside slaps against the saddle.

Observing the vaqueros working the corral, the Kansans agreed that the Rancho El Norte's vaqueros were superior horsemen. When swinging into a saddle, the rider landed smoothly as a Cheyenne.

"They've a swanky style," Ethan said as a rider tipped his sombrero.

Ethan and Andy politely followed their noses and walked over to the busy cooks who prepared the beef, done with spicy green chiles dipped in batter fried a crispy golden brown. And served with beans on a plate stacked with warm tortillas. Andy quickly named them "Mexican Come Back Beans." Come Backs were spooned from round clay pots.

Since coming to California, they had learned to heap food into warm tortillas, spread them with cheese and hot sauce, roll it together.

Across the patio, Mexican musicians began to strum guitars. Andy's spirits wakened when people began to dance. Strolling about looking for partners, he asked every woman in shoe leather, from the judge's sedate wife to chubby señoritas taking time out from their kitchen chores. "Sweet *muchacha*, how's a twirl to paradise please ya?" Andy continued until a sultry pair of Mexican eyes flashed a signal he couldn't resist.

Ethan laughed, watching Tricky Toes getting dust on his new boots keeping time to the feisty Mexican music. Ethan danced several slow tunes with members of San Luis Obispo's Ladies' Aid. Each time he danced by Sabonda, he had to resist the strong impulse to leave his partner and pull her tightly to him.

By late afternoon, when the sun settled over the western Santa Lucias, Ethan had finished dancing with the sheriff's wife and had politely escorted her back to her husband. While making small talk with the sheriff, he felt a gentle touch on his sleeve.

"Are you free?" Sabonda smiled. "I would enjoy this dance, Señor Sands."

Ethan was stunned, foolishly delighted, so flustered it was difficult for him to select words. "Why, uh, yes, ma'am, I'm free, and it would be my pleasure. Uh, there's one thing, it has to be a slow dance." He extended his arm.

Her eyes sparkled as she led him toward the musicians. She whispered to the leader, who bowed. She said to Ethan, "You'll enjoy this. It is a favorite of mine. In English, it's called 'Guitars of Love.' Shall we?"

Ethan watched her eyes as she placed his hand behind her back. Drums beat inside him, a chill tickled his spine, his palms tingled, moisture gathered on his neck.

In his arms, Sabonda moved as gracefully as bubbles on a brook. For a moment, only shadows passed before them, people ceased to exist.

During a pause, Sabonda began a Spanish love song in her low and husky voice.

Then the mood blew up.

"Well, glory be to heaven, now what do we have?" His face flushed, Taris stepped next to his wife.

"Smooth as baby clouds ya are, me lad." In a sweeping gesture, he bowed. "You're a fine dancer."

Sabonda's face tightened and the tenderness disappeared. "Taris, you're staring." She stood erect, a tight smile across her lips.

Tension stretched between man and wife and Ethan felt helpless.

•2•

"CARE FOR A drink Mr. Sands?"

Off guard, Ethan swung around. "That sounds fair." Relieved, he looked into the face of Eddie Ho, the friend of Señor Ricardo.

"She's quite beautiful, isn't she?" Eddie paused. "Señora McCleary."

Ethan self-consciously nodded.

Overstepping a sensitive subject, Eddie Ho changed the subject. "Mr. Sands, if I may have a word?"

Eddie led Ethan to a table away from the crowd.

"Our host tells me that you and your friend are traveling to San Francisco. Is this true?"

"Yes, we are."

"Do you know San Francisco?"

"No. I spent two days there, and that's not enough."

"I see." Eddie talked about the city. He spoke of many things, but he always came back to the hatred and bigotry he had found against the Chinese, how life had been in San Francisco during the Sierra's gold rush until now, how Orientals were harassed on the streets, about the tongs and josh houses that supplied Chinatown with vice. He explained *Gum-san.*

"During the late 1840s, Chinese rushed to the Sierra seeking fortunes. The words *Gum San* mean the Land of the Golden Mountain. Thus, *Gum San* was a slang born in people's minds."

Ethan listened attentively.

"The railroads are the problem," Eddie said. He explained how beginning in the 1860s, his Chinese countrymen had worked for the Big Four—Charles Crocker and his industrious friends, ambitious entrepreneurs who had built tracks over the mountains that in 1869 connected the West to the eastern United States via a transcontinental railroad. "The price my countrymen paid became high—not in cash, but in lives."

Suddenly, Eddie changed the subject.

"Señor Ricardo and I have a business situation that may interest you. We've purchased a gold claim in the Sierra, northeast of here, which may be a profitable investment. We know it's dangerous because the claim has been unworkable. The mine is flooded. Finding gold will be more than difficult." Eddie paused. "You see, the claim is on sacred Indian land, and if mining problems aren't enough, the Indians' curse hasn't helped. Superstition is a hazardous thing."

Ethan interrupted him. "But I thought you said the gold had run out."

Eddie nodded. "Mostly it has. Miners have fled to Nevada searching for silver. But with skilled engineering there's a chance we'll be lucky." He studied Ethan's face. "Possibly not a bonanza like that of the forty-niners, but certainly worth the gamble." Eddie put down his glass. "We have the man for the engineering; protection is what we lack."

"Protection? I don't follow you."

"I shall provide the engineer and ample Chinese labor to work the claim. You see, the miners who are working the area resent the Chinese. Many see the Chinese—even those in San Francisco—as no more than coolies. Killing Chinese, during the gold rush, became a sport and not a crime. To succeed now we need strong men who can protect our laborers from being needlessly slaughtered. As I've said, Ethan, it's dangerous. There's gold in the Diablo mine, but, again, the price to find it will be high." He smiled. "Would you and Mr. Love consider this proposition?"

"Mine gold? Andy and I aren't miners."

"We don't need miners. We need men with courage, men like you."

• 3 •

"MY FRIEND LEE Sung, an accomplished engineer, has developed a plan to restore the mine."

Eddie tapped his fingers on the table in time with the music. "But first there's something we must consider—the weather. Winter is not far away, and in the high country during October twenty-foot snows are not uncommon. Both men and animals have been found frozen to death. Roads are impossible. Everything stops. Winter's pain bogs both body and soul."

"When's a good time, Eddie?"

"First of May, at the earliest."

"Uh, that's a problem. Before May Andy and I have to find work."

"Certainly between Juan Ricardo and myself we can find something for you until then. Meanwhile, don't allow the delay to worry you." Eddie raised his glass toward him. "We're willing to pay for protection. Particularly against murder."

"Murder?"

"Chinese get murdered when caught alone in uninhabited areas such as the Sierra. I know thirty years after the railroad was built that must sound strange, but believe me, it still happens."

Ethan relaxed and leaned back in his chair as Eddie continued with his ideas on generously sharing profits. He was beginning to trust Eddie Ho.

"You say that you're interested in San Francisco?" Eddie asked.

"I saw things I liked. It's a city of opportunity that's only begun to grow. In many parts of California there's opportunity."

Eddie informed him of the meeting when the *alcalde* spoke about the future.

Ethan was pleased that Juan Ricardo was a candidate. "Eddie, I think he'll make a fine senator."

"Yes, California needs him. When San Luis Obispo is connected by railroad with San Francisco and Los Angeles, this area will expand beyond everyone's anticipation. I'd investigate buying this land. In time, you'll be well rewarded." Eddie paused. "If you take my offer, your finances should improve. This gold mine is only a part of what we have in mind. A very small part."

"Your proposition is interesting, but I'm not sure that Andy and I are your men. However, the monthly pay and profit sharing is attractive. Señor Ricardo, I'll assure you that earning money with a gun deserves good money." He paused and threw back his whiskey. "It sounds more than fair but I'll have to talk with Andy before we decide."

"My friend, the Chinese are gamblers. Frankly, I plan to invest heavily in California's future—buying land, businesses, anything that I deem profitable. I'll not mislead either of you, because what I've offered has risks. But that's California. She is for those who dare to reach out," Eddie said.

He stopped and thought for a moment. "You said earlier that you came to California seeking change. Don't feel alone; half the people here, including me, came for the same reason. For me, California is the future, it's a land where one success points to another, and it's wild, but wildness combined with ability can make a man rich—especially if he's willing to roll the dice."

•4•

ACROSS FROM ETHAN'S table, Andy was kicking up his heels as if he had invented dancing. Eddie lifted his glass to Ethan's and nodded toward Andy. "Talk to your friend."

Juan Ricardo passed their table. "Gentlemen, it's time to go inside. I've something you'll enjoy, and besides, it's growing cool and inside there's a warm fire."

Ethan rolled a fast cigarette, and walked toward Andy who stood waving his hands in front of several girls. Ethan yanked him aside. "The *alcalde* wants us inside. Eddie Ho's got a helluva proposition. C'mon, this is important."

"*Important?*" Andy said, indignantly. "Cain't you see what I've got? This, Fast Draw, is damned important. I've got the girl's attention. Hell, man, it's surefire! Topeka, look! I been hustlin'. I've got us pleasured for the evenin'."

Ethan stared at him and slowly shook his head.

"Tell ya what," Andy said, "you stroll in, and I'll be right behind."

Eddie Ho stepped in front of Ethan. "Pardon me, Andy, but have you ever considered becoming wealthy?" he asked in a crisp British accent. "It does have advantages, old boy."

Andy had placed his hand on one girl's shoulder when one word stung his ears. "Uh, excuse me, honey." He patted the girl's head and swung around to Eddie.

"Uh, you did say—*rich*?"

•5•

ANDY BEGAN TO laugh. "We're going inside, Ethan. Care to join us? Perhaps we can chat? About money."

After the men disappeared into the hacienda, the señoritas' expressions changed from heated anticipation to frigid disappointment.

One said, *"Amiga, gringos locos."*

"Sí, I know. Gringos talk big. Use cow-pen Spanish, and this *hombre,* he does nothing. *Americanos* drink too much . . . *Borrachos!"*

•6•

JUAN RICARDO POSITIONED himself between Ethan and Andy as they strolled about the hacienda's spacious living room. The host explained to his guests how these honored men had captured the San Miguel killers.

Eventually overcome with praise, the Kansans slipped away from the crowd and ambled toward the stairway. As Ethan glanced at the stairwell Sabonda stood at the top smiling at him. She had changed into a long maroon velvet skirt, gathered at the waist by a silver sash. Gracefully, she began to descend the stairs. Shiny black hair hung loose about her tanned shoulders; a low-cut blouse enhanced her lovely breasts.

Andy caught his breath and spoke in a low tone. "Ethan, that there's a woman that'll haunt you. That's a gorgeous woman."

The *alcalde* took his daughter's arm and escorted her to them. While Sabonda greeted Andy, Ethan's eyes never left her. When Sabonda faced him, he took her hand in his.

"Pleased to see you again, ma'am," he said, wishing he could hide his clumsiness.

Sabonda stood at his side. "Gentlemen, it's an honor for me to entertain brave men in my home." Even her raspy voice pleased him. Andy was amused at Ethan, who was struggling with himself. He'd never seen Topeka Sands so completely unnerved. This look of a helpless child was not the face that Andy had seen facing a bandit's gun.

Sabonda sensed Ethan's awe and it strengthened her attraction. How she had stared at him during the San Luis Obispo parade! For an instant she thought her emotions would bubble out and reveal her thoughts.

Juan Ricardo politely eased Sabonda away to speak with neighbors. "My dear, you're blushing." She looked straight ahead.

Andy tapped Ethan's arm. "Uh, you all right? You look like ya been mule-kicked."

Ethan tried to smile. "*Andy*, shut up!"

"Ethan? Your wine."

Ethan had spilled red wine on his white shirt. He tried not to appear disturbed. With a handkerchief he cleaned what he could.

"I swear, you look feverish."

The musicians entered the hacienda's rear balcony and began to play. Soft guitars pleased Juan's friends as they gathered into smaller groups.

Taris stood on the second floor leaning against the banister and looked over the crowded room. He stumbled as he descended the stairway. A few heads turned toward him. He pushed through guests, nodding at those who smiled at him. He saw Sabonda standing by the fireplace. He moved close and kissed her cheek. He stepped back.

Sabonda stared at her husband, wishing that just for this evening *he wouldn't embarrass her.*

•7•

TARIS WAS SPEAKING with Ethan. Seeing them together, Sabonda thought how much less a man Taris was, and ashamed of her thoughts, she cringed.

"Boys," Taris said, beaming, "good to see you both." He looked them over. "Aye, you're a handsome pair to see. Fancy duds you're sportin'. Fine new fancy boots, Andy. You know, lads, a man could grow belly-sour drinking wine. Awful it is." He cleverly eased them toward the brandy. "Glad you're here, lads. This beautiful ranch was a wedding present from Sabonda's father." His eyes shifted from his wife to her father, and back to the glistening brandy resting on the table. Quickly, he took a glass.

"Boys, do me a favor. Stand together and form a wall, to shield me, if you please."

Andy stood next to Ethan. Taris tried to hide himself from his father-in-law, Sabonda, and Dr. La Rue who were passing.

"Ah, me wife worries too much." Taris smiled. "When I was ill, I took awful medicine that didn't agree with whiskey, but as you can see, lads, I'm sounder than a dollar." He looked at Sabonda. "A loveliness, isn't she? Let's drink to her."

Taris toasted his wife before either Kansan said a word. "God, but that's good!" Eddie Ho approached. "Gentlemen,"—Eddie grinned, raising his glass—"to the queen."

Taris spotted Sabonda walking toward them. Immediately he refilled his glass and fled through the crowd, sloshing brandy.

"Pardon me, gentlemen, have you seen my husband?"

Andy smiled. "He's, uh, excused himself."

"Oh Mr. Sands, perhaps later you and Mr. Love will have a moment?" She touched Ethan's arm. "I'd love to hear of your adventures. Until then?" Her eyes flowed over Ethan, then she walked away.

He rubbed his arm where her hand had touched him.

"Guess we put our boots in it again, Andy," he said grimly.

"Always steppin' in something, ain't we?"

"In spite of his drinking, Taris is a crafty man. He hides his feelings with a sense of humor," Ethan said.

Andy added, "That haywire Irishman moves like a loony with acorns in his boots! Did you see him scoot when he saw her coming?"

Eddie Ho smiled, trying to imitate Andy's Kansas drawl. "B-o-y-s, h-e-r-e's beans in your barn!" He raised his glass.

Andy put his arm around the Eurasian. "Eddie," he whispered, "in the West we say, *that's hay in your barn—not beans*!" All three laughed, forgetting about Taris.

Taris ran for the kitchen, clutching the pilfered brandy bottle close to his chest. He slammed the pantry door against the wall. With shaking hands he lifted the bottle to his lips. Relief followed the soft gurgle as the brandy filled his insides. Gulping desperately, he drank to quench the fear that burned within him.

•8•

BRANDY FLOODED HIS stomach and brandy-blood rushed through his veins. His eyes blurred and memory dimmed but he was marvelously warm, and the painful dryness had faded away. Sobriety, Taris's eternal foe.

He slumped down on the cold floor. In the darkness of his mind, there was a shimmering glow; it was his father's face staring at him.

God! How he had lied. His guts stung from what he'd done. Thoughts jabbed pitchforks from every side. Go back! Go back! The thoughts battered his sanity. He shook the empty bottle and cursed it. Then caressed it against his cheek.

Suddenly a flash of light blinded him. He fell back against the rocky wall; fruit jars fell and broke and rolled across the tile floor The glare from the open door had blinded him.

"Mr. McCleary," Mrs. Kelly said from the open door. "You'd better come out."

Unsteadily, he stood up looking at her. He bent low in a sweeping bow. Taris pulled back his shoulders, adjusted his tie, took a step out of the pantry. Now, again, he could face Sabonda and the others because he had regained the courage he'd craved. He coughed, staggered, and fell. Sweat ran freely over his face.

Motionless, he sat looking at the broken glass. He was cold as a grave in an Irish bog.

Kindly Mrs. Kelly moved away, and closed the door, protecting Taris from a world he couldn't confront.

Outside the hacienda a rogue wind whipped against the barn, slamming the doors and spooking the horses. One vaquero looked at his friend.

"Amigo, that's a mean *viento* from the High Sierra. Hear how she screams. She's cursing someone—maybe a gringo inside the hacienda."

His friend shook his head. "C'mon, forget it, *vamanos*. Let's go, two *muchachas* in the hay, one for me, *y amigo*, one for you."

Juan bid his guests good night. He turned to Eddie Ho.

"Did you speak with Ethan about working for us?"

"Yes. They're considering the offer."

"Good! In the morning ask again. We need them."

•9•

EDDIE HO, SENATOR Ricardo, and the Kansans reviewed plans for reworking the flooded Diablo mine. Eddie's engineer, Lee Sung, had sent an outline of his plan.

Through the winter, waiting for snow to melt from the Sierra trails, the Kansans worked at jobs Senator Ricardo arranged. On the Rancho El Norte they put in saddle time on Sage and Gussie working cattle; they pounded nails into new holding pens. For a few weeks they herded cattle with Luke.

The aging ramrod, weary of tiresome cattle drives, had met an agreeable woman who offered him a deal better than eating cow dust and breeding saddle sores.

For those who knew him, it was hard to believe that Luke was about to cut loose and travel the matrimonial trail. After Luke's wedding, his friends attended what was to be an afternoon reception. His bride, who didn't approve of drinking, served a fruit punch. Cowboys, being what they are, sweetened the punch. Later in the afternoon, most everyone including the preacher had embibed to a point where the reception got out of hand and lasted until dawn. Several months elapsed before even the boldest dared call on the bride and groom *socially*!

•10•

ROY SEDWAY, WHO had admired the Kansans since meeting them at the tragedy of San Miguel, employed them on an irrigation project he had arranged with Juan Ricardo's coalition. Working various jobs, Ethan and Andy were satisfied; fresh money padded the bankroll.

Ethan was fond of the area and had acquired new friends, yet he had reason to leave. Being around Sabonda disturbed him. Sharing casual visits with her became perplexing. Embarrassed, she told Ethan how Taris had treated her. Drunk, the man disgracefully slobbered over her and in front of her friends. And in the privacy of the bedroom, Taris became violent.

On occasion, Ethan had to control himself. Andy saw the pain and knew Ethan was feeding on trouble.

Kitty Bean and her mother had purchased sixty acres south of San Luis Obispo. In his spare time, Andy helped by building fences, clearing ground, and bending his back on odd jobs. He spent a deal of time with Kitty helping to free her mind of all she'd been through.

She seldom spoke of her father's death or of her horrible rape. She was cautious with strangers, especially of older men who admired her figure.

"Kitty, time and patience and love." Andy held her hand. "This'll kill the pain. Sweetheart, you gotta trust in what I say."

Kitty Bean convinced herself not to look back.

Part 7

Women of Any Kind Are Scarce

• 1 •

ON APRIL 2, 1882, one year after James Garfield became the twentieth President of the United States, Ethan Sands and Andy Q. Love heard the whistle of a train bound for Sacramento. The newspaper article Ethan held in his hand said the mountain roads were passable; although, at higher elevations, deep snow lingered on the Sierra Range.

Senator Ricardo thought it wise to leave Sage, Guissie, and Peter Balls at Rancho El Norte. In the foothills east of Sacramento the men could outfit themselves with horses and mules that were adapted to the High Sierra.

From Paso Robles, they took the eastbound stage to Bakersfield, then a train north that carried them to Sacramento. Ethan got the same conductor he had met when he'd left San Francisco headed south for Los Angeles.

"I'll be damned, it's good to see you again," the conductor said. "Didn't you like Los Angeles?"

"Well, yes and no. It's kind of a long story. How's the railroad business?"

"Busy, busy, all the time. More people coming to California every day. Say, did you buy any land?"

"Not yet."

"I did" —the conductor beamed—"near San Luis Obispo."

"Thought you were pitching the San Joaquin Valley."

"I was. But it's too damned hot. Besides, I don't wanna farm."

Andy asked, "How's things in Bakersfield?"

"Bakersfield? Dead!"

"Ah, c'mon, never saw so many people. Busy as hell from what we saw. What do you mean, dead?"

"Figure of speech. There's probably as many underneath the ground as walking the streets. Mister, that's the wildest, most dangerous town in California. They've got gun-happy characters like Jim McKinney, the kind of men you wouldn't want to meet alone. Oh, don't buy in Bakersfield."

A fat lady with two obnoxious children yelled at him. "See you gentlemen later, we've a stop to make."

•2•

THE DAY THEY arrived in Placerville, people on the dirt street gave them the fish-eye like they couldn't believe what they had seen. Lee Sung, the Chinese engineer, sat proudly on a horse between Ethan and Andy. An old digger, resting in front of a saloon, expressed himself. "Damn, ain't it weird to see two whites riding with a coolie? Especially when the chink ain't walkin' or followin' 'em on a mule!"

Another miner pointed. "Jesus Christ, that wagon's filled with pigtails!"

Catcalls rattled Ethan's ears. They regretted leaving Peter Balls behind; the mule they'd bought was not only angry, he was dumb. This lazy animal preferred standing rather than going in any direction at all.

Eddie Ho had recommended an experienced guide, William Henry. Searching for Mr. Henry, they tethered the horses in front of a rustic saloon with only one swinging door; the other hung cockeyed, ready to depart its hinges.

Ethan told Andy and Lee Sung to wait outside. He adjusted his gun belt and, mindful of the hanging door, strolled inside.

A faded sign hung over the bar: "The Bitter Gold Saloon." Farther back was another name: "Hangtown's Last Chance Saloon." The burly, bald bartender pursed his mouth as if he were about to spit.

"You want something, tall man?"

"You the owner?" Ethan asked.

"No. He's dead."

Evidently he was wary of men with questions, as if his words cost money.

"I need information and I'm willing to pay."

The bartender sloshed a soggy rag over the bar. "Stranger, sometimes information is scarce. Sometimes it's dangerous."

Ethan forced a smile. "I'm interested in meeting a man named William Henry. Got any ideas? It's worth a few dollars to me."

"How few?"

"Try two."

"Five's better." Twisting the ends of his waxed mustache, the bartender waited. Ethan begrudgingly scattered silver dollars over the red mahogany bar. "Now, this Henry gent, he's supposed to be a guide and I've heard he's competent."

"Competent!" The bartender threw the wet rag behind him and leaned close to Ethan's face. "Mister, there's diggers in camp, and there's those who claim to be beyond what they are. Especially 'fore they climbed the Sierra looking for gold. Some work; some are worthless as hell. There's good diggers and there's others who would chop your hand for a pinch o' dust. Ya need a guide?"

Ethan's eyes didn't blink. "Yes. But first I want to talk to the man."

The bartender's eyes slid over Ethan's husky frame, stopping at the .45 hung low on his leg. "You law?"

"No, I'm only looking for a guide. That's all."

"Sounds fair, stranger. You see, in gold country we're savvy on watching out for each other—you can understand that, can't ya?"

"You know this Henry?"

"There's no William Henry." The bartender scratched the wiry stuble on his chin. "But there's a Red Rock Henry. When Red's sober, he might be the man you're looking for. But mister, I don't relish trusting flat-landers and you, partner, got flat-lander all over you." He scooped up the silver dollars and stacked them.

"I'll have a whiskey," said Ethan.

"That's what we sell." The bartender reached for a bottle. "That's eighty cents." His forefinger scratched a brown spot on his baggy pants just below his rear cheeks.

Ethan reached in his pocket. "Whiskey brings a cat's-tail price up here, don't it?"

"Stranger, you just learned your first gold-country les-son. Talk's the only thing that's cheap. That's the way it is. Take it or leave it." He poured Ethan a shot. "If you really wanna find Red, go outside, turn right. Go four doors, you'll see it. It's called the Grubstake. He's most likely inside. If'n he's not, then you'll have to start over. If you're lucky and he's there, he's easy to spot. He's got bright red hair, and if he's drunk, his face'll match it. And uh, don't bump the loose door." He chuckled.

Ethan finished his drink and threw down a dollar.

"Bartender, I hope your information is better than your watered whiskey."

The bartender laughed. "Life's tough, mister. You'll find worse to bellyache about—like getting yourself shot."

On his way out, Ethan kicked the door so hard it tore off its last hinge and clattered on the warped sidewalk planks in front of the saloon.

•3•

ANDY SAID, "WHAT did ya do in there? Punch somebody?"

"Could have."

The three men untied the horses and walked to the Grubstake's sign. Inside the dingy saloon, the man called Red Rock wasn't hard to find. Ethan went over to his table and held out his hand.

"Mister Henry, I'm Ethan Sands."

Looking up, the redheaded man belched. "So? Have a chair." He eyed Ethan carefully. "Drink?"

"Small one."

The man lifted the bottle. "There ain't no small. Besides, it's good stuff, ain't been cut. Barman says it's out of San Francisco." Red Rock pushed an empty glass toward him. "Now, Sands, what's on your mind?" Red poured. Sipping his whiskey, Ethan told Red he was interested in a guide. When he asked him what he knew about the Diablo mine, Red's back stiffened.

"Mister Sands, I know plenty. Most if it bad. If that's the place you're asking me to take you, I hav'ta think on it."

Ethan nodded. "I've been schooled about the mine."

"You didn't buy the claim, did ya?"

"No. I have a deal working, that's all."

Red threw back his whiskey and wiped off his mouth with the back of his hairy hand. "Smartest thing you never did. That claim's on Indian land. Them cock-headed braves ain't had good thoughts about the whites digging up their dead kinfolks, especially for gold." Red's bloodshot eyes focused on his empty glass. "It's none of my business, but you don't have the stance of a digger."

"I've got diggers, Chinese."

"*Ya got China-boys?*" Red spit whiskey on the wood floor. "Ma God!"

"Got something against Chinese, Red?"

"Naw. Not me. But there's plenty up here that still do." Red looked around. "Years back, during the wild days, things were ugly for Chinese. Killin' was cheap. Now with miners leaving, looking for silver, China-boys work the railroad tracks. They're still killin' 'em for meanness or anything that fits. How many ya got?"

"About twenty."

Red's eyes sparkled. "Jesus, Mr. Sands, that's a lotta *dead Chinese*! *How much ya payin'?*"

Ethan told him.

"Not enough! Not for the Diablo it ain't."

Ethan pushed back his hat and listened as Red Rock named his price. "And, uh, I want my cash up front."

"Mister Henry, that's a deal of money." Ethan folded his hands.

"Lotta mean chances, friend. Only got one neck." Red smiled. "Another drink?"

Ethan's hand covered his glass. "We have a deal?"

He pushed back his chair and stood leaning forward with both hands pressed on the table's edge.

Red's glass clinked against the empty bottle.

"Sure. It's dumb and powerful ugly, but ya gotta deal." He put out a rawboned hand; they shook. Ethan tipped his hat and walked outside. Red stuffed in his shirt, winked at the bartender, and followed him.

In front of the Grubstake, Ethan introduced Red Rock to Lee Sung and Andy. Red's eyebrows raised with surprise when Lee Sung didn't speak in a singsong Pidgin English. Red stepped up to Ethan's horse. "If ya wanna eat, I've got a good cafe. But leave him outside." Red nodded at Lee Sung. "It's safer."

Lee Sung smiled, made an uninspired bow, and walked away.

Red removed his Montana hat and scratched his head. "Changing the subject, you got mules and supplies?"

"We have horses and one mule."

Red laughed. "Fer twenty chinks? Lemme see your supply list." Red studied the paper. "Let your friend, Andy, buy what you need. Then we'll go mule tradin'. I know a place south of here. Hangtown's too costly."

"Hangtown?"

"Before it was Placerville, it was Hangtown. Folks said the name sounded too active; hangin's came easy." Red smiled. "Back then, by God, they did! Law's a trifle better, but even nowadays you'll see a rope dangle over a husky branch. Besides, I like Hangtown."

They ate at Red's cafe.

Afterward, Red said, "You boys care for a hefty belt

'fore we start downhill?" He pointed at Jake's sign across the street. "Ah hell, I forgot; Jake's is closed."

"How come?" Andy asked.

"Got shot dead. They plugged him last night. Two drifters." Red climbed on his horse. "'Sides, we better git for the mules 'fore dark."

Andy thought a minute before he asked, "Red, what's a man being shot got to do with good whiskey?"

"Everything! Jake made the stuff himself. None of us knowed where he hid the whiskey. That's why the saloon's closed. Every drunk in Placerville is trompin' the brush, searching for his factory."

Andy shook his head and laughed.

"Look, partner, when you're buying supplies, watch what you pay. These bastards know you're green, and they'll skin ya alive. Tell ya what. You pick stuff out and when I return, we'll settle."

Andy rode off toward the store. Ethan, Red, and Lee Sung rode the trail out of town. Red looked over at Lee Sung. "Sorry 'bout that eatin' business, Chinaman. Didn't want to take chances, you being a chink—er, Chinese—uh, sorry!"

Lee smiled coolly at Red. "It is not the first time, Mr. Henry. I *live* in San Francisco."

Red grinned at the Chinese. "You're okay, pal. It's my bad habit saying wrong things. Now, gents, we'll ride for Hollow Meadows." Red laughed.

•4•

"HOW FAR IS Hollow Meadows?" Ethan asked.

"Less than an hour, straight ahead. C'mon, spur 'em."

Red kept laughing to himself off and on. Ethan wondered what was tickling his mind.

Riding through a meadow, they crossed a stream. Scattered clumps of snow clung to the banks, melting into the fast-running stream, and flowers broke through the wet grass, the yellow petals drooping in the snow. The meadow, at the crest of the ridge, was scattered with pin oak, buckeye, and madrone. Ethan asked about snow in the Sierra.

"Here, it melts off. 'Cause the sun warms quicker down where it's lower. Farther east, higher in the Sierra, there's tons of snow. Beautiful and miserable. It's a sight to see, but it's deadly if ya get trapped." Red chuckled. "Tricky. Sometimes I've seen it freeze in August."

When the mule ranch came into view, Ethan's eyes widened. Beside the barn was an Indian woman smothered in fat. She was the largest squaw he'd ever seen. She was taller than Ethan and she outweighed him. Shoveling manure over her shoulder, she didn't look up.

Red Rock reined up. "You men, pull off the road and gather around." He kept one eye on the squaw. "Boys, there she is. *Big'un, ain't she?* Guess I can begin by sayin' it's different up here. *Women, any kind, are scarce.* Winter months are long and cold and worse. It's too damned lonely! Cranks a man into thinkin' 'bout things he shouldn't be thinkin' ." Red reached for his makings and rolled a smoke.

Ethan did the same.

Lee Sung watched quietly, fascinated by the white man's conversation.

"Fess'n up to ya, me and this hunk, ya see, we sorta share ourselves, comfort one another. Like I said, winters freeze yer ass. Passin' time and keepin' warm is what ya try to do." Red blushed and paused. "Cuttin' it to facts, Squaw Woman figures when she sees me it's *always* winter!"

The two others laughed.

Red's eyes rolled sideways. "Men, when we get closer, I'll handle her. Don't pay her no mind. Just keep your eyes on me. Nuthin' to it. Stay calm. Oh yes, she knows her mules—money, too!"

•5•

ETHAN AND LEE Sung followed him in. Red put his weight on the stirrups, cupped his hands around his mouth, and called: "Hey, sweet princess, we've come to buy mules."

The Indian woman jammed the pitchfork in the manure pile and lifted her trunklike arm to shade her dark dollar-sized eyes. Then she began to run, pounding over Mother Earth like a rolling boulder.

She thundered past Ethan's and Lee Sung's horses, her eyes locked on Red's pinto. Suddenly, lines in Red's face tightened and his jaw clenched. His eyes twitched. He prepared himself for the charge about to strike his body, one that already had been struck too many times.

•6•

THE MONSTROUS SQUAW grabbed Red's thick belt and with a gorilla's grip sent the guide out of the saddle. He landed with a resounding thump on his butt. Paralyzed for a moment, and though his pride had been hurt, he tried to smile.

"She's sensitive." Red Rock appeared to have lost all dignity in one swoop. The Indian planted her wide hands on her bulbous hips and stood over him; her eyes burned with fiery pleasure. Red pushed her canoe-sized moccasin aside and came to his knees. He crawled to retrieve his crumbled hat in the dust.

Red Rock, the skilled mountain man, had been taken by surprise.

Within inches of his hat, Squaw Women raised her powerful leg and smashed her moccasin hard, pinning his hand. "You lying white sumbitch! Why you not come sooner? Me wait long time! You say make Squaw

Woman feel plenty good. No short-time Charlie stuff!" She lifted him, patted his face, ran her callused hands through his matted hair.

She spun him around and shoved him toward the barn door. When he hesitated, her heavy fist knocked him against the wall.

Lee Sung looked at Ethan. "If this is *handling*, Mr. Henry's in trouble," said the Chinese.

"Red," Ethan said cautiously, "you need anything?"

"Naw! I'm okay."

Squaw Woman ambled up and pinned him against the wall using her fat body for a solid wedge.

"Uh, Mister Sands, there is one thing," Red gasped. "Start talking about money. If'n that don't do it, *shoot her*!"

Ethan reached inside his pocket, grabbed a handful of bills, and waved them at her; bills floated to the ground.

"Plenty money, Squaw Woman. I need twenty mules, pay you good!"

Squaw Woman turned away from Red. She gazed at the money. Bending down, she gathered it, fondling each bill. She stood next to Ethan's horse.

"Forty dollars each," she grunted.

"Thirty-five."

"Done!" She put her hand on Ethan's leg. "I like long hair. I make tall man tingle. Next time Little Cloud take cold eyes in barn! You feel good—plenty warm."

Ethan felt his horse tug backward.

Counting her money, she eased toward Red Rock. "You get mules, husky man. Get off ranch. We go barn later." Ethan turned to Lee Sung. "I'll bet you fifty that come next winter, Red's on time!"

•7•

ETHAN AND RED began to cut twenty mules from a herd behind the barn. Red kept his eyes away from Squaw Woman's. He nodded to Ethan.

"Let's get out!"

Ethan hunched over in the saddle and casually pushed back his hat. "What we seem to have here amounts to the crushed feelings of a love-starved Indian. A savage who wants your favors, Red, she wants them today!"

Red mounted his horse and they herded the mules out the gate.

The men rode along thinking to themselves. Red Rock's head sagged over his chest.

"Mr. Sands," Lee Sung said, "I am trying to think of a Chinese proverb that would describe this situation, but I've never heard of one!"

Ethan smiled at Red Rock. "Red, why didn't you defend yourself? Push her off. For a time, I was worried."

Red Rock Henry turned downwind and spat. "Well, I tell ya. Sure as hell, winter's coming." He looked back at Squaw Woman. "Cold and lonely, with a cargo of whiskey in ma belly, Little Cloud don't look too bad! C'mon, we got a long ways to go."

When Billy Largo heard the parade was for Ethan Sands, he cussed aloud and headed for the saloon. He met a cowboy from Rancho El Norte, and bought him a beer. He learned more.

"Hell, mister," the cowhand said, "several months after the big shebang, him and his sidekick pulled up and left the ranch. The *jefe* says they went north. Got no idea where they're headed."

"Does anyone know where they went?"

"S'pose."

"Are they hiring out there? I could use a job."

The cow-waddy looked Billy up and down. This gent dressed in black, with yellow hair hanging down his back, didn't have the look of a man who punched cows. "Oh, they might."

"Who do I ask for?"

"Jorge, he's foreman. Mexes call him *el jefe*. Boss."

"Nuther beer?" Billy asked.

"Nope, ain't got time. You from these parts?"

Billy put one foot on the brass rail. "No. I'm here on sort of a hunting trip."

Outside, Billy Largo turned up his collar against the wind that blew from the hills east of town. He didn't care how far Ethan had gone; time cost nothing, and killing Ethan Sands would be worth every minute he'd spend riding through California.

•8•

RED CORRALLED THE mules not far from town. He liked Ethan. What worried him was how to hide the Chinese until it was time to leave Placerville.

Ethan was concerned that the dynamite Lee Sung ordered hadn't arrived from Sacramento.

Lee Sung stood waiting by the wagon.

"Mr. Sands, I don't understand. I personally arranged for the shipment." The sanctity of his word was important to Lee Sung.

"No sense moving until we get everything we need, and you can drop the mister. Ethan'll do."

Placerville had dynamite but to Lee the stable dynamite available in Sacramento was superior.

"You seen Red?" Ethan asked Andy.

"He's out checking the mules." Andy turned up his collar.

"There's nothing we can do, so let's you and me go to the hotel and have some hot coffee."

They found the lobby a comfortable room in which to kill time.

"Wanna sweeten that?" Wilbur, the day clerk, wiggled a pint of sour mash over their cups.

"Thanks, no," Ethan said.

Andy covered his cup. "Why'd they change the name here?"

Wilbur poured one for himself, shoved the bottle in its hiding place, and stepped from behind the desk. "Now, about the town. Placer means 'ground with minerals in it.' Gold is a mineral so they changed from Hangtown. Funny though, before Hangtown, they called it Dry Diggings!" He waited for a comment, but the Kansans casually sipped their coffee.

"But the forty-niners were a crazy lot. Happy-go-lucky bastards, wild yahoos who worked like hell digging gold. Then they either gambled or screwed it away on women. Some of the men drank themselves stiff till there was nuthin' else to do but go out and dig again."

Lee Sung threw open the front door and headed directly for Ethan, whispering, "It's here. There was a mistake."

"Let's go outside where we can talk." He took Lee Sung's arm and gently turned him around.

"It came yesterday, packed like soap, and looked like ordinary supplies, and the driver dropped it off at my friend's laundry."

"That's good news. Andy, go find Red and tell him to get the mules up here. It's time to start earning our pay."

Inside the hotel the Kansans paid Wilbur what they owed. Wilbur cleared his throat. "Mr. Sands, one word. Up here we don't ask about a man's business, where he's going or what he does. But looking out for one another, we break the rule."

"What's that? Ethan asked.

"We ask for a guess when the digger plans to return. We mark down the date and if he doesn't show we put out the word, ask men coming in if they've seen him; and anyone going out to keep an eye open."

Ethan and Lee Sung met Red with the mules behind the laundry. The Chinese workers stood by ready to go. Red said they'd take the wagon as far as possible, then each Chinese would be on foot leading a mule. Ethan and Andy mounted and looked over the line of mules and glanced at Red.

"Anytime you're ready, Red," Ethan said.

Red Rock Henry spat and sighed. "Where we're going, there ain't no perfect time. So, tighten your guts and suck in. It might as well be now! C'mon, diggers! Let's go find pay dirt!"

·9·

TARIS HAD DISAPPEARED! Sabonda's face was ashen when she spoke with the sheriff. At first, he had suspected foul play. After he'd visited the saloon and had spoken with Elmer, the lawman thought differently.

The owner was the last to see Taris, who'd been in the saloon the night before in the company of two strangers, supposedly businessmen from San Francisco; they stayed late and drank heavily.

"Elmer told me," the sheriff said, "that when they finally left, they were going to eat, but Sabonda, nothing in town is open that late."

The sheriff had telegraphed up the line and put out Taris's description. "Sabonda, you want me to wire your father in Sacramento?"

"No. I'll do it. But thank you, Sheriff."

After the sheriff left, she went upstairs to her room and sat by the window. Two nights ago, she and Taris had argued. He became violent and nearly struck her. He insisted his drinking wasn't a problem. "It's your imagination," Taris had said, lifting a pint from inside his coat.

Sabonda had told him: "You'll never again come to my bed drunk, Taris McCleary!" When she awakened the next morning, Taris was gone.

•10•

THE FOOTPATH TO Diablo was buried in the minds of Indians, dead miners, and God. Still, what lay before the Kansans was real. With Red Rock leading, they moved cautiously for three hours higher into the Sierra. The twenty Chinese, hunkered low in the wagon, peeked over the side at the men on horseback who trudged forward on the dangerous road.

Red Rock Henry relaxed in the saddle. The wind stirred the pines, shaking cones over the rocky trail. Red sang along with the wind.

The days were getting longer, thoughts were turning to spring. It was cold, and in this part of the Sierra, patches of snow remained. Higher and farther east, Donner Pass was closed.

Red imagined that down at Little Cloud's ranch, in fresh, green pastures, colts kicked their heels and jack-knifed, running wild. Spring's winds blew warm air over the lower hills. Early gully-washers widened streams, following a course into the valley below. Above, vapor-thin clouds dusted the Sierra's peaks.

For Red, the mountains sheltered him from the outside world. When the jig was up, this was where he'd chosen to die. But today, that didn't matter; there was a job at hand and dying could wait.

The late afternoon sun cast long, dark fingers over the dusty road. Red pointed to a clearing. "Hold up. We'll make camp."

Red hadn't said much, but he kept searching the mountainside north of the road. He gathered Ethan and Andy around him and asked everyone to sit tight while he checked the terrain. When he returned, he pulled alongside Ethan, who was yanking on the saddle strings to loosen his saddlebag. "Mister Ethan," Red said, "we'll bed down here tonight." He pointed north where the road took a sharp turn. "There is where we leave the road and the easy part ends." He motioned for the three to come closer.

"Men, listen to me and listen good. Lee Sung, I want you to tell your China-boys what I'm about to say. And make sure they understand, ya hear me, Lee?"

Lee barely nodded, looking back at his men.

"From here on, the trail's a mean bitch. Miners have been killed where we're going. Some fell into steep gullies and that's where they stayed. Lee Sung, when I give an order I want you to repeat it to your men and make 'em understand."

Red reached for his tobacco and cut a hefty hunk and shoved it in his mouth and let saliva soften the wad.

"At first the off-road trail is about eight feet wide, there's room from the edge. But as we go, it narrows down. Soon it'll be barely wide enough for a mule to pass. And it'll have curves where, at times, I won't be able to look back and see if everyone's safe."

A black hunk shot from his mouth as he pointed to the stream a hundred yards away. "See yonder? That's Silver Creek. Looks peaceful, don't it? Just wait! Now it's only a couple hundred feet down from the trail. But as we climb, the valley drops down to where it's three thousand feet to the water down a steep incline covered by thick trees and boulders bigger than houses."

Red eyed Lee Sung. "I tell you this because if anyone goes over the side, it's *adiós*! So I don't want any of your men tying ropes between the mules."

Lee Sung nodded, then turned to translate. The Chinese softly mumbled among themselves.

"Red?" Andy asked. "Wouldn't it be safe trailing along the stream where it's half-level compared to the mountainside?"

"Sure it would," Red laughed, "if'n you want to take the chance of being there forever. Landslides have been known to block it.

"And upstream there's a waterfall where boulders make it impossible to get through leading a mule. But in the early days, that's what the forty-niners did. That is, until they found the Indians' trail. The one we're on."

Red warned them about melting snow that caused dangerous runoffs. "The soft earth gives way, and if a slide hits us, neither man nor mule comes back. That's why, up this far, damned few go pokin' for gold. And Mister Ethan, this includes your mean Diablo. It's said that Indians have another trail, easier than this, but I've never found it. And we ain't gonna go lookin'." Red checked the wind, and spat. "The good news is this: when we get near Devil's Mountain, the grade is downhill. It'll drop us into a level meadow, one of the most beautiful places the Sierra has. There's a trout stream that snakes through the meadow where fish are easy to catch. If it weren't so damned high up, it'd make a great place for a town. Trouble is, in the winter you'd never get out. And oh, there's plenty of game for fresh meat. But look out for wildcats and bears. Like us, they're hungry."

•11•

EARLY MORNING LIGHT reflected off boulders, attracting lizards to warm themselves. The Chinese cook scurried about preparing a hearty breakfast: hoecakes and bacon, greens and rice, and fresh-perked coffee.

During the meal, Red Rock warned them: "From here on, watch every step ya take. The trails are tricky as a soft-headed mare in heat. If the earth cuts loose underneath, quicker'n hell, it can dump your ass over the side."

Ordinarily, Red loved to tease; this morning, nothing was funny. "When I tell ya to walk your animals, don't screw around. Git off your heavies and walk 'em!"

Before they broke camp, the Chinese pushed the wagon to the side of the road. Red ran his thumb along the blade of his sharp hunting knife, then sharpened a blunt pencil. He scribbled a note and attached it to the wagon's front seat.

Andy eased over and read what it said. Laughing, he turned to Ethan and read it aloud. "It says: '*Leave this fuckin' wagon be. If ya steal it, I'll find your thieving ass and when you look, your balls will be hanging from a tree. If'n ya cain't read—find some asshole who can. Signed, Yourn—R. R. Henry.*'"

•12•

WILBUR NEEDED ANOTHER whiskey. On the way to town he met the bartender from the Hangtown saloon who was riding home.

"Wilbur, are the strangers still at the hotel?"

The clerk looked around. "No. They took off about an hour ago. The two white men, a wagonload of Chinese, and old Red Rock leading them."

"Where they going?"

"They didn't say."

"You got a guess?"

"No. Haven't."

"Where you headed?"

"Down to the joint, need a bottle."

"Jump on the back of my horse. Ride up to my cabin and I'll give you good whiskey, cheap." He pointed ahead.

"Okay, let's go."

Wilbur was a well-meaning man. But the years in the mountains and whiskey had taken their toll. Blackie's idea of good whiskey was a joke. But after they had killed a pint, Wilbur's tongue got loose. Part of what he said was true; the rest was whiskey.

"You know, I've got a hunch that wagon's not moving an inch, it'll be right here when we get back."

Red's advice wasn't bull; the trail was steep; the vertical sides were so treacherous that should a man fall, he'd be pulverized by huge boulders wedged in the mountainside.

The eyes of the Chinese widened as they walked quietly, leading their mules.

"Lee, your men seem confident enough. The trail doesn't scare them. How come?" Ethan turned and waited for a reply.

Lee Sung shrugged and smiled. "They've worked the Sierra and they've dug for gold. Recently, they've pounded spikes laying tracks for Charley Crocker's train. Thus, they're not afraid."

The Chinese walked in single file, checking each step they took. Suddenly, a yell echoed in the canyon. The Chinese began waving arms, yelling, excitedly. Two curious coolies leaned over the edge and cautiously gazed down the mountainside.

Red halted the party. He walked back to a short Chinese man who trembled as he stared down the mountain. Red leaned as far as he dared. "Someone's dead pack mule, down 'bout two hundred feet. Goods still tied on his back." Red spat.

"What do you think, Red?" Ethan squinted to see.

"Two things: first, he's dead. And second, whoever owned him was smart enough not to climb down. Mister Ethan, we'll leave it at that. C'mon, we'd better rattle our hocks, it's getting late."

They camped on the steep side of the mountain and the Chinese took tuns standing watch over the animals. During the night, chilling winds blew shooting winddevils from the north, sending icy needles through everyone's bones. When the Big Dipper was directly under the North Star, the winds died.

At dawn's first light, Red Rock allowed time for coffee, nothing more. "Boys, if our luck holds, we'll arrive at the downhill grade by sundown. Get your gear, but don't mount. We'll walk 'em until I'm sure." Red traipsed for his pinto.

Andy had been unusually quiet. Though unmentioned, Ethan knew that Boot had a deathly fear of heights. Looking down the steep sides made his stomach lurch and his ears ring. Andy's philosophy was: Kansans belong on the plains!

Red held his hand up, signaling a halt. "You can mount up. From here on it's downhill and the trail gets safer as we go." He pointed at a plateau ahead of them.

Before the sun disappeared over the mountains, Red indicated they were nearly there. "Look at that mountain to the right. See them white boulders next to the timber trees? That, my good cousins, is the gate to yer damned Diablo mine. Take a good look!" Old Red stared at the riders. "Men, you'll hate me the day I take you to the top. You're gonna find your breath gettin' short. Ya see, you'll be nearly four thousand feet above sea level. Boys, that Diablo bastard is like a lyin', connivin' . . . bitch!" Red stood gazing at the mountain. "I don't like this place. I never have. It gives me pimples—on my face, my ass, and on a spot I ain't gonna say."

He shivered as the cold wind blew through his clothes, causing his morose mood to deepen. The last time he'd climbed this trail, a good friend fell. Red buried him.

"I hope we pass through this trip held in the Lord's hands. Not anyone else's!" He glanced at the reddening sky.

The guide's expression disturbed Ethan. Surely it would take more than an Indian legend to break Red's nerve.

"Red, you worried about this Indian curse?"

"Maybe."

"Does Little Cloud belong to the tribe that owns this land on the Diablo?"

"Hell yes, she's one of 'em. Folks say she's the daughter of the chief."

•13•

AS SIGNS OF life appeared in camp the next morning, Red Rock returned with a large buck flung across his horse. The China boys gathered around rubbing their hands over the deer. He untied his kill, allowing it to slide to the ground.

Two Chinese armed with sharp knives butchered and dressed out the meat. They cut strips for jerky to nourish the party while they climbed the Diablo's steep grade. They sliced the deer's rump for a tasty broth loaded with noodles and greens. Later in the day, everyone enjoyed the feast that left stomachs bulging and brains almost too lazy to think.

At Red Rock's suggestion, they broke out a bottle of sour-mash whiskey and made themselves comfortable around the fire. As the flames warmed them, they talked of other places, times, and of men they had known.

"Red Rock," Andy said. "You mentioned earlier that up here you've got bears."

Red Rock chuckled and carefully put down his drink. "If we don't we've got the biggest most ornery, mean-eyed counterfeits a man's ever seen. Give ya advice, too. If ya come onto a bear this time of year, he'll be the meanest bastard you've ever faced. He'll be wakin' from a long winter's nap and he'll be hungrier than all of us gathered about the fire, combined!

"So starting tonight, we'll keep three campfires going all night. We'll take turns standing guard, and if one sneaks into camp the man on duty will wake everyone." Red raised his hand. "This may help ya if'n you face one. Lord, I say, if ya ain't gonna help me, then please don't help that bear!" Those that understood him, laughed.

"Got more advice, Red?" Ethan asked.

Red Rock leaned back and thought a minute. "Two things: shoot straight and pray you kill him. If'n ya don't, some son-of-a-bitchin' bear is 'bout to enjoy a helluva meal!" He punched Ethan's gut, cackling merrily.

"Have you ever bagged one?"

"Killed a bear? Hell, yes. When you visit my cabin you can count 'em. Have I ever bagged a bear—Jesus!"

"How about the mountain lions?"

"The big cats are here and they're a crafty lot. Most of 'em won't come into camp, but when you're out alone, stay alert. I've known 'em to track a man, or be waiting in a tree fixed to jump him. Had a drinking pal who got his arm mangled by one not far from town. Now that scents of humans and fresh meat are drifting in the wind, after dark we'll hear their cries. So if'n ya sneak off to take a leak, stay in close to the fire. Say, pass the whiskey."

"Are you going in the morning, up Diablo?" Andy looked up at the mountain.

"No." Red took a long pull and sighed.

On his elbows, Ethan stared at the flames that colored his rugged face. "Why not?"

"I want everyone to get accustomed to the altitude. If'n you think this is bull, why, get off your ass and hightail it up the mountain and you'll see what I mean. On top of that mountain it's over six thousand feet high."

Ethan hated wasting a day, but Red was probably right. At six thousand feet, the air was far thinner than at Rancho El Norte. Passing the bottle to Andy, he wished he hadn't thought of the ranch. Sabonda's seductive face danced in the fire, and her raspy voice whispered through the wind.

"Another drink, Ethan?" Andy asked.

"No. Think I'll turn in."

Andy swept his eyes around the fire. "Here we are far from home, high in the mountains in a desolate place we know nothing about, and what do we do? Sit and talk about hungry wildcats dropping from trees. Frankly, gents, tonight when I hav'ta go, I'll just step outside my tent and let 'er fly! I'll be damned if'n I'm gonna lose my cherished love machinery to some hungry cat!"

•14•

THE DAYS AT the El Diablo Mine slipped by in a haze of drudgery. In the horizontal tunnel leading to the vertical shaft, they bent their backs to digging rocks, moving dirt, pushing more rock. They fell into their bedrolls after a hasty supper. Red Rock Henry was on the money. Climbing twice a day up the Diablo's mountain strained lungs and bones, and made enemies out of friends.

The morning was brisk and windy and the men huddled around their breakfast coffee, hands warmed by holding tin cups. As the sun rose higher over the Sierra, they prepared for the day's climb back to the mine.

At the blasting sites, picks slammed until blisters turned hard, and backs cramped from digging shafts deep enough for the charges.

Earlier, Lee Sung had spoken of his idea. "Ethan, this morning I'll dig drain holes and place charges lower down the mountainside away from the mine's entrance. After the first powder charge fires, if I'm right, water should flow out of the mine and down the mountain. If it doesn't flow, my plan has failed."

Now, Lee Sung signaled the Chinese laborers waiting below. When the charge exploded on the mine's west side, water burst out, and they jumped up and cheered. "See mister boss, Chinese very smart!" Lee's pidgin broke the tension and everyone laughed. Where others had failed, Lee Sung had begun to lower the level of water that had flooded the Diablo's caverns.

Atop the mountain, the Chinese worked like demons, ignoring torn hands and snarled muscles. Their singsong patter lightened the day's work. In the late afternoon, a snow flurry followed by rain slowed the progress on the tunnel's entrance.

The next day, Lee Sung said: "Today, I plan to be lowered down the shaft and I want eight strong workers on top to handle the ropes. To make certain the tackle gear attached to overhead beams is secure, Ethan, I'd like you to oversee the work. With the water level lowered, I'll test for gold. I know it's here. The Chinese bring luck, you know!"

Lee Sung proudly shook hands with the American he'd taken as a friend.

Work moved slowly, but Lee Sung worked harder. With the water not at a satisfactory level, he ordered a Chinese worker down to measure. After testing, Lee Sung decided on another powerful blast. This time, he placed the charge lower than the others, setting the fuse while inside the shaft.

If the final blast worked, the cavern would drain and flood the mountainside. Lee Sung was confident the final charge would finish the job.

"Andy," Ethan said, "I'd like you to pick half a dozen Chinese and stay in camp with Red Rock. If anyone comes around you know what to do. Keep a rifle handy everywhere you go. Understand?"

On Sunday, May 25, 1883, Lee Sung was ready. He led the way, carrying a wooden case containing the explosives. When they reached the tunnel, Ethan led his men in to the beam of light directly over the shaft where Lee Sung was to be lowered. He checked the pulleys and tested the rope. Lee Sung looked down into the shaft. "This is my day. You see, my ancestors have planned for this." Lee Sung winked. "The fifth explosion will finish the job, and we'll be able to mine gold as never before."

Hopes were high; the last ore samples the Chinese had carried down the mountain contained heavy traces of gold. In the tunnel, Ethan and eight Chinese stood watching Lee Sung adjust his gear.

Ethan poked him. "What's your lucky number?"

The Chinese bent over, his head on the fifth charge. "Number five!" Both men laughed.

Ethan put his hand on Lee's shoulder. "If you don't feel sure about this at any point, we've got plenty of time. If anything isn't what you think it should be, let's call it off."

Lee smiled. "I'm ready. Remember, the Chinese are lucky!"

"Let me check your harness one more time." Ethan's strong hands moved over the harness. "Feels tight."

The Chinese crew held the rope. On command, they gently eased Lee Sung over the side. The harness creaked as the rope fed through the pulley. As he started down, he said, "Tonight, around the fire, we'll have a whiskey celebration."

Ethan's echo bounced off the rock wall. "You gotta deal!"

The heavy tackle groaned, straining the thick timbers supporting Lee Sung's weight. Overhead, loose dirt sifted between the timbers braced against the tunnel's ceiling.

Lee's face disappeared in the darkness. They heard him talking to himself as the rope played out. Swinging slightly, Lee Sung yanked the rope, signaling them to stop. He put the sticks into position and ignited the twenty-second fuse. He tugged on the rope, the signal to raise him to the ledge six feet above his head, with time enough to hop on the ledge away from the blast. Above him, the Chinese strained and began to raise Lee carefully upward toward the rocky ledge. The engineer had calculated everything correctly except the last few inches. "Just a foot more then hold it there. I'm goi—"

WHOOM! A deafening blast erased his voice, shook the earth, and sent shock waves through the mine's hollow caverns. Thick red clouds mushroomed from below, forcing the Chinese back from the shaft's opening.

Ethan fell backward. On his feet again, terrified, he made his way toward the men who had been feeding the line. It seemed minutes before the noise subsided and dust began settling.

The tunnel walls had split like eggshells, spraying rock over workers who lay on the tunnel floor. Ethan raced to the hole and grabbed Lee Sung's line. He felt Lee Sung's weight, and strained on the rope, shouting Lee's name. Rocks splashed into the murky water at the bottom of the shaft. He waited for Lee's signal, then tugged again. The return signal never came. "Gimme a hand . . . pull!"

No one spoke as the rumbling faded into the cavern's dark hollows. The rope went limp.

•15•

THE SPLASH WAS a chilling sound echoing from the darkness below. The Chinese and Ethan stood staring at the rope hanging loosely in their trembling hands. They gathered it in, disheartened, and examined the frayed ends.

Each man knew that Lee Sung was gone, lost in the Diablo's black waters. The Indians' myth held true.

Ethan grabbed a lantern and motioned to the men. Eager hands fastened the rope around him while he tied a double sheep-shank for his legs, and cinched the rope underneath his arms. He checked pulleys, rubbing his eyes as dirt from the timbers flecked his face. The Chinese carefully lowered the heavier man over the edge.

At the ledge, he signaled to stop. He held the lantern near the ledge; there was no sign of Lee Sung. He called out—nothing but his own echo. He yanked on the rope and continued downward until he was near the gurgling water beneath him.

The lantern's light reflected off the water. Ethan judged the shaft to be fifteen feet across, perhaps more. Lee Sung's notebook floated near a piece of torn shirt.

Ethan hated what he knew; Lee Sung was dead. He reached for the notebook and the floating fabric, then signaled to come up. Squeals of the twisting rope echoed from the shaft's rock wall.

The Chinese pulled him in.

Ethan sat against the rock wall, gasping for air. He held up the notebook and the scrap of cloth. None of the men spoke as they staggered along the narrow tunnel. As though they were being followed, the gum sans looked back. The legend of the Indians' curse crossed Ethan's mind. They continued toward the light.

Near the tunnel's opening, Ethan froze. Beneath his feet he felt the earth lift. It began to roll from side to side while a deep-throated rumble filled the air. Louder and louder earthly moans hammered his head, rock loosened and cracks shimmied down the tunnel's walls. From nowhere, a wind twisted dust before his eyes, but it was the sound that terrified him.

Like dolls, men were thrown bouncing off jagged walls. They tried to protect themselves as boulders struck.

The rumbling ceased, all was quiet.

Suddenly again the tunnel floor bulged upward, throwing Ethan into the bracing timbers. The Chinese who scrambled for the opening panicked. Jabbering, they stumbled into the light.

Once outside, Ethan counted heads. Five were missing. His legs wobbled as he led the Chinese down the mountainside toward camp. The treetops bent downward as though an unseen mallet had slammed against the trunks.

Stumbling down the trail, he heard a rifle shot below. Red Rock's horse bolted into sight carrying an empty saddle. Andy suddenly appeared, running to where Red Rock had stood guard.

Red Rock lay facedown, his Hawkens beside him. "What's happened?" Ethan yelled. "Who shot him?"

Andy turned him over. "Christ, I dunno. It happened so fast. That roaring scared me. Everything went crazy. I couldn't stand up. The ground shook apart. Ma gawd, I dunno—I dunno what happened." On Andy's pale face, sweat ran in dirty rivulets.

Then they heard Red mumbling: "Stupid jackass . . . damned horse bucked and ma old Hawkens misfired. Jesus, Ethan, I'm shot bad." Red's voice had an unnatural quiver. He forced a smile. "Men, ya had her first hooraw with a California high roller, and I tell ya, earthquakes ain't no game ta fool with. They kin' kill ya dead as dirt." He coughed. "She was a hard shaker, one of the worst. Dammit, this hurts. Ethan, help me up, will ya?"

Ethan opened the mountain man's shirt and examined his wound. His lips tightened. "He's bleeding bad, Andy. If we don't get it stopped, he's gone."

They applied a makeshift bandage, stuffing the hole in his stomach.

Andy brushed Red's hair back from his eyes. "Where's Lee Sung?"

Ethan looked at the faces of the Chinese who had gathered beside them. "He's dead; blown to pieces." Ethan's voice trembled and his hands shook.

"How?" Andy's jaw dropped.

"Something went wrong, that's all I can tell you.

Here, this is all I found." He showed him Lee Sung's journal and the piece of shirt.

Andy ran his hands over the cloth and the journal.

"I think the damned charge exploded before he got away. He gave the signal he was near the edge ready to climb on. Then the charge knocked us flat."

Ethan turned back to the wounded guide. Red Rock's face whitened and pain showed in his eyes. Blood had soaked through the bandage. A Chinese brought a pack of leaves and made gestures that he wanted to help. They replaced the bandage. The bleeding slowed. When they were nearly through, the earth began to shake as violently as before. Andy yelled, "I'm scared. This is purely the Devil's no-good work. That mountain's gonna crash down on us. Look at them trees, they're gonna break in half! Ethan, over there—boulders! My God, they're knocking down trees!"

•16•

WITHOUT LEE SUNG, it was difficult giving the Chinese orders.

"Red, we've gotta put you on a horse and head back."

Red Rock tried to smile. "Let's not kid one another." He coughed. "I've set my last horse. Now, gimme a good pump of whiskey."

Red raised his hand toward Ethan. "I haven't told ya, but I've seen Indians, and they're not friendly. Now listen. Forget about me—get yourselves and the Chinese *out of here!*"

Ethan held the whiskey bottle close to Red's lips. He took one drink, smiled, and took another. A pleased expression came over Red's face as the whiskey hit him. "Ethan, Andy, I've stayed drunk and horny, filthy and dirty, most of my life. I don't give a whoop what do-gooders say about whiskey, *it pleasures a man.*" He grinned. "Ah, Ethan, if'n ya please."

Ethan lifted the bottle and held Red Rock's hand firmly.

Red's eyes turned glassy and soon he stared at the white clouds drifting over Diablo's peak.

He weakly slurred his words. "Which way is the wind blowing, Ethan?"

"It's not blowing, Red."

"I feel a cool wind. What'n hell, I was born under a wandering star and always said I never seen . . ." Red's chin sagged on his chest, and holding his hand, Ethan felt his hand go limp.

Red Rock Henry died high in the Sierra Mountains.

Ethan heard an eerie voice whispering through the trees, the old vaquero's words. "*Sí!* She can rip a man's heart."

Ethan looked at the trees. "Andy, damn, it's cold."

•17•

ANDY WALKED ALONG the line of mules making sure packs were tied properly. He helped two Chinese lift Red's body across his horse and secured him tightly.

"We'll get him to Placerville because when I say he shot himself, they won't try to hang us," Ethan said. "Who'n hell will believe a man of his experience would have shot himself?"

Andy touched Red. "Yeah, I know what you mean."

"Remember when we started up, Red said there was no perfect time to go? Well, neither is this, but here we go."

Ethan circled an arm overhead, and yelled, "Follow me."

An hour down the trail, Ethan eased back on the reins and rose from the saddle.

"My God, Andy, look. There's been a landslide!"

•18•

ETHAN SLID DOWN from the saddle, and sank into loose dirt that piled up around his boot leather that had worn thin and was punctured from scraping across the hard-rock terrain.

Several of the Chinese moved to the trail's edge and silently gawked at the trees that had been crushed by tons of rock, mowed down as if they had been twigs. Only parts of torn branches showed through the debris.

Ethan waved to Andy. "Go back there and get those men away from the edge. We don't need mules and bodies dumped in that grave." He felt helpless thinking that either the earthquake, the Indian curse, or plain bad luck had placed him in command of a situation he'd soon as not have.

"Which way do we go?" Andy asked.

"I'll be damned if I know!"

The landslide had begun about three hundred feet

above where they stood, and slid down the mountain-side five hundred yards.

Breaking a new trail over unfamiliar county didn't appeal to Ethan, especially when most of the men behind him couldn't understand English.

Seven good men had died uselessly. The Diablo's Indian legend had taken its revenge and all they had to show, instead of gold, was Red Rock Henry's body hanging dead over his horse, Lee Sung's torn shirt, and a waterlogged notebook.

"Sorry I barked at you. I don't know whether I'm mad, afraid, or too nervous to think," Ethan called back over his shoulder to Andy. "Roll me a cigarette, will ya?"

"Sure, hold on." Andy rolled fast, cupped a match between his hands, and held it for him.

"Ethan inhaled. "Do you know the Chinaman called Cho Ling?"

"The taller fella? That speaks a little English?"

"That's him. Go and get him. I've got an idea."

As he stomped his cigarette into the dirt, he glanced up to see Cho Ling walking in front of Andy.

"Cho Ling, stand over here, next to me."

The Chinese nodded and obeyed.

Slowly and clearly, Ethan asked, "Cho Ling, have-you-ev-fer-worked-in-the-mount-tains?" He swept his hand over the terrain, then placed his large hands on Cho Ling's shoulders, and waited.

The Chinese dropped to his knees, and with his forefinger drew two straight lines, and perpendicular lines between shorter lines connecting them. "Andy, I've got it—he's worked on the railroad laying tracks!"

Cho Ling nodded rapidly.

"Go on, say something else." Andy waggled his hands at them.

"We-need-way-back-down-moun-tain. Un-der-stand?" How-go?"

Cho Ling pointed up the mountain, took a few steps in that direction, and pointed again.

"What's he see?" Andy asked.

"He's heading up toward the spot where the slide began. Look, he's stopped about halfway."

'Why's he kicking at the dirt?"

"Andy, why'n hell don't you ask him? Look, he's coming down."

Out of breath, Cho Ling motioned for the men to follow him. He moved to the edge of the trail and looked down, shaking his head while pointing where the rocks had covered the trees.

"I get it, Ethan, he's saying no to that part of the slide."

Cho Ling ran to the other side of the trail and pointed to where he had been nodding at them.

"He means, start the trail at the top of the slide." Ethan took his arm. "You-mean, make-new-trail-above-trail-not-below?"

"Yessee, yessee—you do—you do!"

"I've got it now. He means it's safer to trail the head of the slide instead of below. Makes sense.

"It's easier to trail over firm ground than lower and fight our way through loose dirt. Also, if another quake hits, that loose stuff would go first."

"But that means we gotta climb straight up through boulders and trees, and with mules to drag, that's a bitch."

"You've got a point, Andy. But I believe that he's seen the railroad men doing the same thing."

Andy shoved back his hat and wiped his forehead.

"All right. But instead of beatin' ourselves to death trying to hike uphill here, why not turn around and go back to camp, where the grade is easier, and make our way back toward the slide? It'll take longer but we won't kill ourselves doing it."

"Not bad, Andy. Not bad!"

"Yessee, yessee," Cho Ling belted out, showing off a gold tooth.

•19•

TOWARD SUNDOWN THEY reached a plateau above the old trail, and Ethan gave the word to make camp. Around the fire, Ethan and Andy sat staring deep in thought, watching flames that cast shadows on men's faces.

Andy rolled a cigarette, took a stick from the fire, held it to his cigarette, and took a long drag. Cho Ling came over and politely bowed, pointing to the ground next to Ethan.

Ethan nodded for Cho Ling to sit. Squatting, he held a torn paper in his hand. The fire illuminated the marks that had been made beside Chinese symbols. Cho Ling held up open palms and shook his head.

"Map—way go." He pointed at the markings. Ethan held the paper closer to the fire's light. The drawings showed trees forming a cross, large boulders with an arrow fish jumping from a stream.

"Come sun—you see." Cho Ling's gold tooth glittered as the flames skipped over his broad face.

"Ethan, he's trying to say while we were on the trail from Placerville to the Diablo mine, one of the Chinese drew a map. See, there's the wagon."

Ethan took a closer look at the markings. Some smart Gum san had used his head as Red Rock guided the party eastward to the Diablo mine.

"Boot, I think you're right. He's trying to tell us to look for these markings and if we can find them it means we're hiking in the right direction."

Cho Ling nodded. "Come sun—look!" He pointed at the crossed trees on the map.

Ethan grabbed the paper. "I think I know this marking. Coming up, Red had pointed to a group of trees that lightning had struck. Several had fallen and formed a charred cross north of the trail.

"These marks are boulders," Andy pointed out. "I think Red called them the eagle's nest. They were above the trail, that would have been south."

"It could be right. If we can see these two markings as they're shown, we're on course." Ethan patted Cho Ling's shoulder.

"Boss, savvy-savvy?" Cho Ling grinned.

Ethan smiled. "Cho Ling, boss, savvy-savvy."

Andy added wood to the fire. "Yes, Topeka, I think we've got a chance. Gawd, but I feel awful about Lee Sung, and old Red."

"Don't think about it. But, uh, how's his body doing?"

"It's gettin' ripe. I don't know how the Chinese can stand so close, but they're guarding him like a family."

"I'm going to hate to tell Eddie Ho about his friend. They acted like brothers."

"It ain't gonna set too well either with Red's Indian, Little Cloud."

Ethan nodded and began rolling a cigarette. "Guess as hired guns this is going to be difficult to explain."

Andy agreed. "I ain't clever, but when I think about it, my brain gets stuck. We had Lee Sung's death, the earth nearly shaking us to death, and Red Rock shooting himself, and that's the only gunplay we had. No strangers tried to do us harm." He poked the fire and gazed at Ethan's smoke rings circling above his head.

"A grown man lacks good sense if he believes in evil curses, devils, things like that. Still, when I saw my horse standing kitty-wampus to the ground, I began to wonder." Andy fumbled for his makings, looked up at the velvet sky, and began to roll.

"You've got a point." Ethan exhaled, watching the rings drift upward with the wind. "I'm not a man who believes in Indian legends. But I've never seen so much happen so damned quick. I can't see how we'll take money for this." He threw his cigarette in the flames.

"I guess that's up to Eddie, whatever he thinks." Both men moved closer to the fire, while the cold Sierra wind sent chills through their heavy coats. In the distance, a wolf began to howl at the velvet sky.

The next morning Ethan awoke with a Chinese tugging his arm, pointing east into the sunrise. Ten Indians on horseback stood on the crest of the hill.

•20•

ANDY SHADED HIS eyes from the sun. "Gawd-a-mighty, now what? Where's ma rifle?"

Both men reached for their rifles and waited for the Indians to move. One brave threw back his head and screamed a wolf's howl, like the one they'd heard the night before. The others shook their fists defiantly at the white men's party. Then, abruptly, they turned and rode behind the mountain.

Andy sighed. "Well, what da ya know? That's one for us!"

Ethan put his Remington back in the left scabbard and checked his Sharps on the right. "Maybe they've got more bad medicine they haven't used."

At noon Ethan halted the party. To the north, above them, fallen trees formed a cross. Andy pointed to the eagle's nest. "Thanks to the Chinese, we're heading in the right direction."

Four days after they left the Diablo, in front of them, a mile away, stood Red Rock's wagon.

Closer, Ethan held up his hand. "Andy, tell me what you see." Andy reined his horse, and shaded his eyes with his hand. "Ma God, it's her!"

Little Cloud stood next to the wagon. Behind her, the sheriff and six armed deputies waited.

When Ethan signaled to halt, Little Cloud spurred her black stallion straight for them. Charging past the Kansans, she pulled up alongside the horse carrying Red's body. She untied the rope and lifted the corpse. She draped it in front of her and headed off the road. She disappeared behind a stand of trees.

"You Ethan Sands?" the sheriff asked.

"I'm Sands."

"Welcome back. Damned glad to see you. We've heard about Red Rock. Too damn bad. But that's probably the way he'd have it. Everyone admired Hard Rock Henry."

"How'd you know?"

"Little Cloud got the news. She said you'd be here today. White men can't beat the red man's telegraph." The sheriff nodded. "By the way, Sands, stay away from Little Cloud. She's sore, thinks the white men broke the Indians' law."

Ethan got off his horse. "Sheriff, you want to hear what happened?"

"We felt the earthquake. In the morning, come to my office and I'll fill out a report. Men, you look like run-over mules. Ride into town and get a hotel. I suggest the Oro King. After you've had a rest, we'll talk."

The sheriff and his men started down the road.

"Did I hear right?" Andy pushed back his hat. "We're not suspects?"

"I'm not going to argue."

•21•

FOLKS IN PLACERVILLE gaped at the lazy train of mules and men that passed along the street. Andy and Ethan wired Eddie Ho, then decided to have a drink, a hot bath, and a good night's sleep in that order.

Walking toward the saloon, they felt as if a lead weight had lifted from their shoulders, and were glad to be back in a town. Three gunshots cracked in front of them. Flinging the saloon's double doors wide, three men burst out and ran up the street. Other men barged out the door and looked in both directions, shouting. The men who had departed first were gone.

The Kansans decided to bypass the troubled saloon and continued toward the hotel. Andy spotted a store where he could buy a bottle. As they started for the door, they heard a commotion behind them.

Two men carried a stretcher on which lay a man, his arms dragging limp, his fingers making tracks in the dirt. Andy stopped. "Ethan, that Indian curse, damn, look! That man on the stretcher—that's Taris McCleary!"

Ethan shoved his way into the crowd to have a closer look. Blood soaked Taris's checkered suit. His face was white, his eyes rolled back. And drenched by whiskey, Taris stunk.

Ethan was speechless. A bearded man shouted, "We're hauling this idiot across the street to the doctor's office." One yelled, "Let's hurry, boys, I've got a good hand working and this damned fool ain't gonna live."

Ethan grabbed an onlooker's arm. "What happened in there?"

"What it was, mister, was asshole crazy! This drunken fool was dancing wildlike on a poker table. Then he unbuttoned his pants. He was about to let go on men's faces at the table. One drew a pistol and shot him once when he sagged, and twice while he kneeled."

The man brushed Ethan's arm aside and walked back inside the saloon.

"Anybody know the man who shot him?" Ethan asked.

"Don't think so," a man said. "We heard three of 'em had arrived in town on the afternoon stage, drunk. Strangers, from San Francisco. Never saw nothing like it."

Ethan and Andy fell in behind the stretcher going to the doctor's office.

Dr. Beno ambled casually from the saloon and climbed the stairs. He closed the office door, took a large, unsteady step, and bent over Taris. "He's *dead*! Whose paying?" The doctor swung his head, checking their faces, while he scratched his head.

No one spoke. The doctor nodded at Ethan. "You act like you know him. That's good enough—you pay!"

Ethan paid.

"Now, if you'll excuse me, I'm missing my usual libation with the ladies. It's time for my sundowner. By the way, the undertaker's two doors down."

After visiting the undertaker's, they walked back toward the hotel. On the way, they stopped at the telegraph office and wired Senator Bautista Ricardo about Taris. They withheld how he had died as well as news of the Diablo and of Red Rock Henry.

In the hotel room, Ethan thought bedside manners were a dollar-cents arrangement. Turning around, he poured two hefty drinks, and carried one to his friend.

Andy threw back his whiskey, stood, put the glass on the dresser, and stared at himself in the mirror. "If I ever meet up with that old man you met, the vaquero on Cuesta Grade, I'm going to have him repeat the advice he told you. Only this time, I'm going to write it down!" He reached and poured another.

Ethan wiped the sweat from his face. "When the senator gets our message, he'll know. Till then, we'll sit tight."

"What'n hell was Taris doing here?"

"God only knows, Andy. But his death will be a shock to those who knew him." His mind raced, thinking about Sabonda and how she'd handle the news of her husband shot to death in a gold-town saloon.

Mechanically, he walked over to the dresser and opened a drawer. "Here, take a towel." He threw it at Andy. "I'm ready for a hot one. Bring the bottle." Ethan headed for the door. "A bath won't hurt."

Whether men died in the Diablo, from gunshots in a saloon, or hanging, Ethan thought, men died knowing death's a long ride.

Part 8

His Gun Belt Lay
Across the Bed

• 1 •

THROWING DUST BEHIND the rear wheels, the Sacramento's morning stage was on time. As he turned into Placerville, the driver reined back, halting the lathered team in front of the Wells Fargo station. The driver jumped off the seat, straightening his hat while he rushed for the coach door. At attention, he leaned back on his heels and smiled. "Senator Ricardo, sir, we have arrived."

The senator, genteel in his light blue fingertip coat, cut square in front, with matching trousers tailored in a comfortable summer material, his elegant fedora, perched on his silvery white hair, completed the outfit of the distinguished gentleman.

Two wedded members of the Miners' Rose and Garden Society dipped their parasols, which allowed a better view of the handsome senator. Pleased, they continued down the street. Without a doubt a polished dignitary had arrived in Placerville.

The Kansans quickened their pace, covering the distance over the boardwalk. They pushed aside the curious who had gathered around, and stood smiling at their friend: Senator Juan Ricardo, former *alcalde* of Monterey, wealthy landowner, a man who would hopefully straighten out the ugly mess that confronted them.

After a vigorous round of handshaking, Juan motioned them aside.

"I'm so pleased to see you both, safe. My personal feelings go out to your friends. Frankly, this entire expedition has been beyond my imagination, terrible. Now, then, where can we talk?"

From his coat pocket, he pulled a handkerchief and wiped dust from his face. While Andy picked up the senator's valise, the trio strolled toward the hotel. Ethan related the gruesome details concerning Taris, Red Rock Henry, and Eddie's friend, Lee Sung.

Ethan reached for his saddlebag and took out Lee Sung's notes. "I found this. It's in Chinese, but before his death, he mentioned finding rich ore and he brought down samples to prove what he'd found. We've got some to show you."

The senator took the journal and held it reverently in his hands, hefting it. "Not much left of a man's life, is it?" He tucked Lee's noes in his valise.

They hurried upstairs to their room. Inside the senator strolled to the window, looked up and down the street, then paced back and forth.

"Before I expound on this delicate subject, I'd like to speak of my son-in-law, Taris." Again, he wiped his face.

"I ask that this conversation remain confidential. For now I prefer his death to remain unknown, especially to his wife. Basically, Taris and my daughter have been at odds." He sighed. "It's been a most unhappy affair. For several years, my daughter has gone through hell. Obviously the heavy drinking had poisoned what remained of the marriage, and now I believe I've learned what caused his drinking. Gentlemen, it's pathetic!"

He paused to look out the window as a wagonload of Chinese rumbled past the hotel.

"When Taris arrived in California, people were highly impressed, including me. I believed he was a man of means. Actually, what funds he had, he'd stolen from his father; they had been earmarked for his older brother in New York, and this tormented him.

"Recently, he confessed to Sabonda. He blamed his guilty conscience on heavy drinking instead of truth. Then shortly after both of you had departed for the Sierra, Taris disappeared. Sabonda and I thought surely he'd returned to Ireland to make amends with his father." The senator gestured at the whiskey bottle on the table. "May I?"

Ethan poured him a drink.

"Now, I come to a delicate matter. Two weeks after Taris disappeared, I learned what had happened. He had booked passage on a ship sailing to Ireland from San Francisco." Juan Ricardo paused and shook his head.

"How Taris came to Placerville is beyond me. He must have jumped ship, joined with scoundrels, and stayed drunk."

The senator sipped his drink. "To protect my daughter from the truth, I've concocted a lie. I'll tell her that he sailed from San Francisco and the vessel arrived at the ship's next port, Panama, without him. The captain reported that he'd been lost at sea, presumably drowned. The captain, a good friend of mine, will issue a report of his disappearance. Ethically unusual, but it can be arranged." Andy stood. "Uh, Senator, you'll please forgive me, but uh, wouldn't it be safer to tell

Sabonda the truth? If she knows he's dead, one way or another, what's the difference?"

The senator pursed his lips. "Spoken like an honest man, and perhaps you're right. My fatherly instincts may have overcome my common sense, but after what she's been through, I'm willing to take the chance." He threw back his whiskey.

"Another?" Andy asked.

"Only half, thanks."

Ethan rubbed his chin. "Sir, Sabonda must face how he died. It's obvious that one lie leads to another and sooner or later she'll know the truth."

Juan shook his head.

"I imagine his death at sea would be less painful to her than what actually happened here. Still, this places a burden on both of you; I've made you coconspirators in the lie, and for that I'm uncomfortable."

"Senator, a great deal of my life I've lived a lie. It wasn't so much killing, it was later, when I began to believe what I was doing was right when it wasn't." Ethan paused. "Man to man, I think you're placing your love for Sabonda, your career, your plans, and your good friends on a short walk to despair. You're promoting a lie on behalf of a desperate man who couldn't face the truth, for the sake of a daughter who can. Now I ask, are you sure you want to do it?"

A sparrow scratched the window glass, left his spotted calling card, and spread his wings. Pensive, the senator sat down, reviewing his thoughts. "Mr. Sands, Mr. Love, you're honorable men. I'm proud to call you friends. Your honesty has cleared my mind. I'll tell her straight out and face what comes. However, Taris will get a decent burial here in Placerville. Whatever scandal there is, we'll live through it."

He shook their hands and thanked them. "I've asked

Eddie Ho to meet us in Sacramento. We'll talk about this Diablo business. But don't worry, we'll take care of you. And I'll appreciate your support when I face Sabonda. Now, is there anything I can do for the families of the deceased?"

"Red Rock didn't have anyone," Ethan replied. "And Lee Sung, well, Eddie must know."

The senator removed a gold watch from his vest pocket. "I'd better leave. I've a great deal to do. I'm to take the afternoon stage for Sacramento—and gentlemen, you're both welcome to join me."

Ethan looked at Andy. "That sounds reasonable to me."

"Damned reasonable!" Andy agreed.

"Senator, we plan to ride south to pay our last respects to William Henry. But we'll make it back in time to catch the stage."

The senator started for the door, but Andy stopped him. "Perhaps, Senator, this is not the time and maybe it's improper, but I'd like to ask."

"Certainly, Andy, what is it?"

Andy squirmed. "Sir, in Sacramento, one evening can we find one of them fancy restaurants where important men eat? Have a few shots and maybe a couple slices of rare beef—you know, a real spread. What d'ya say, Senator?"

He smiled. "Señor Love, it's a wonderful idea. It shall be my honor. Gentlemen, until the stage, *adiós*."

Juan Ricardo tipped his fedora, and left.

As Andy began packing, Ethan looked at himself in the mirror. "What are you staring at?" Andy asked.

Ethan rubbed a hand over his face. "I'm looking at a changed man. Things that once concerned me in Kansas seem unreal. Why, I don't know."

•2•

THE KANSANS FULLY enjoyed Sacramento's hospitality. They discovered why California's forty-niners dug and cheated, sweated and died; why miners climbed mountains, wandered into valleys and disappeared. Why they worked so hard and risked so much. One thought occupied their minds: find it, get rich, then spend it, *in San Francisco*!

San Francisco was a mecca where quick minds and clever hands easily gathered wealth.

When the forty-niners came to San Francisco with pay dirt, it became a riotous city where miners squandered gold in gaming houses and saloons, and murder and robbery were rife. One quarter of the town, the Barbary Coast, was out of control with violence and vice. San Franciscans said the town was burnt down and rebuilt six times during those days when gold flowed from the Sierra.

At a meeting in Sacramento, the senator and Eddie Ho agreed that after Diablo's disheartening days the Kansans deserved to see San Francisco's Elephant.

Eddie explained the popular saying. And after they had seen the richly carpeted hotels, the restaurants with pricy menus beyond imagination, the hard-drinking San Franciscans who enjoyed barrooms and dancing with fetching ladies—they understood what the Elephant meant.

Nob Hill where railroad builders and millionaires shared baroque mansions and toasted silver kings in a fashion not known to the poor who were privy to fist fights on Brannan Street. San Francisco, a city were human beings reacted upon one another in peculiar ways that brought out the worst and the best in those who gambled and fortified themselves to: "Come See The Elephant . . ."

San Francisco swayed the Kansans, who had presumed Kansas City the pinnacle supreme.

•3•

AFTER TWO WEEKS of swift days and lingering, carefree nights, San Francisco's depot was a welcome sight for departure. While rising steam from the observation car dampened their faces, the men shook hands with Eddie Ho. Andy put his arm around Eddie's shoulder. "You tell that sister, Heidi, so long for me."

"Who's Heidi?" Ethan cocked his head.

"Uh, tell ya later, you know how it is."

As the train's wheels began to creak, the Kansans rested against the seat, looking through the window.

"If a man's luck sagged and things went poorly," Andy said, "San Francisco's a place that would cheer the livin' and restore the dead!"

Ethan chuckled. "Country boy, you're making sense. By the way, I didn't know you'd met Eddie's sister. What's Heidi like?"

"Ethan, I've never met a woman like her. She's a

cultured lady, charming, talks soft, too. She's taller than Eddie. She's involved with medicine some way." Andy sighed.

"Yep, I tell ya, after hangin' on that elephant's back like I did, quiet country is gonna seem hard to understand. Fast Draw, it'll be a change."

Ethan leaned back against the seat. Something in Andy's words, the way he said them. His eyes, bright when he said Heidi's name. He wondered what was going on inside Andy's head.

The Kansans returned south as they had come, traveling by train through the San Joaquin Valley to Bakersfield, then by stagecoach west. Ethan had an empty feeling. Everything they'd tried thus far, including their big chance, had failed. But the Diablo was behind them. The real value they'd found was new friends. And Eddie Ho and the senator, cowboys on the ranch, Red and the Placerville gang, the Kansan's considered themselves lucky.

Eddie would raise the money and try again, with an expensive new system of power mining, which had worked in flooded mines like the Diablo.

•4•

WHEN THE STAGE arrived in San Luis Obispo, Ethan recognized a friendly face. Sitting atop his white stallion, Rancho El Norte's head vaquero, Jorge, waved at them.

"Señores! I bring you compliments from my señora." He swept his sombrero low in front of him. "She has sent me to escort you to the Rancho. *Muchachos*, it's good to see you again. But look down the road, there are two friends waiting for you."

Sage and Gussie were down the road tied to an oak tree.

"*Vamanos*. Get your horses and we will ride, *amigos*."

Jorge had brought five vaqueros with a supply wagon to carry the Kansans' belongings to the ranch. He felt foolish when he saw how little they had.

"Gotta dollar says I know what's on your mind," Andy said softly.

"Only a dollar?" After a quiet moment, Ethan said, "Yes, I am looking forward to visiting Sabonda. Boot, does that make you feel better, being right?" Ethan laughed.

"Don't make me feel nuthin' . . . but it sure as hell does you! C'mon, ya wanna gallop?"

They approached a stream flanked by sycamores. Tired, they dismounted and signaled Jorge to pull up. They enjoyed splashing cool water over their faces and skipping flat rocks over pools beside the stream. Drying his face, Ethan said, "Boot, we've had an experience. Some good, some sad. But in spite of things, I've learned something of California."

Andy smiled. "What's next?"

"It's not San Francisco!" Ethan shook his head. "City's not for us. I'll admit, it's an exciting place, a world unto itself, a city full of opportunity. But Andy, you and I, well, we like open spaces and a slower pace. You agree?"

"Sort of."

"Now we've met important men, like the senator and Eddie. The future is here, with them. That evening in Sacramento, when you were busy, Eddie said that if we wanted, he'd put us in charge of a worthwhile business—the biggest cattle operation in the county. Later, he'd work us into the produce business in the San Joaquin. He'd guide us in buying land. We both know how well he understands land. We'd be two smart Kansans if we put our roots right here. California is going to grow."

Andy threw down his cigarette, stomped it, pushed back his hat. "So far, what you're saying makes sense."

"Now here's my next idea, Andy. When we get to Rancho El Norte's road, I'm going to Sabonda's. I've had a restless feeling for that woman since I first laid eyes on her. I liked Taris and I don't mean to be walking on a man's grave. I won't talk him down. But if Sabonda has a feeling for me, I'm going to ask her to marry me."

Andy rolled his eyes. "Ethan, I saw it the first day. Never seen you look at a woman that way. She's fine enough to make you proud."

Ethan slapped Andy's shoulder. "You're going to stand up for me, at the wedding."

"You ain't got no better man!"

"Andy, I've said my piece, so we'd best mount up." They rode south. Jorge and his men followed, close behind.

"Ethan, I've got a little unfinished business, too. Kitty Bean is a sweet young lady and I'll bet she'll mature into a beautiful woman. So I'm thinking of riding down to her ranch to see how she and her ma are getting on."

Ethan chuckled.

"You're going to ask her to marry you?"

"Uh, hold on. I didn't say marry! I've got places to go and things to do."

"If you're not going to marry Kitty, what *is* on your mind?"

Andy fidgeted with the Stetson he'd bought in Sacramento. He took off his hat and made a wide, sweeping gesture over his head. "I'm going back to San Francisco!"

"You're *what*?" Ethan's head swung around.

"Yeah, that's right."

Andy tried to get his words in order. He cleared his throat. "San Francisco charged my blood to a boil. The city fascinates me. Eddie's got ideas. He said I could fit in. I'd like a chance to make something of myself other than herding cows. Ethan, quit staring at me."

"I'm not staring. I'm trying to make sense out of the words you're putting inside my head. You say that Eddie has a job for you?"

"More than a job. He says he'll teach me how to manage a produce depot. Learn the business from the ground up. I know I don't speak right at times, but Ethan, I'm not stupid. I can study. Know what I mean?"

"Sounds to me like your mind is set. I guess you've got to find out for yourself, but I'll miss you, Andy. Though San Francisco's not that far away."

Andy put out his hand. "Look, gun-shooter, this ain't the end of the line for you and me. Just think, when the new train comes, I can be here in a couple of days. You and Sabonda can visit and we'll stay in that fancy Palace Hotel, and she'll turn a few heads in San Francisco. Tell ya, partner, she'll turn mine."

They gently reined their horses and resumed riding south.

When they arrived at El Norte's gate, Andy said, "Look, Fast Draw, be casual, take your time. Slow and gentle, that's the way you catch a spooked horse or a handsome woman."

Ethan threw his head back and laughed.

Andy glanced down the road. "I should get Gussie moving. It'll be dark 'fore I get ta Kitty's place."

They shook hands.

Andy put his hand on the saddle horn. "Ethan, California has changed our lives from what they've been. No one is trying to kill you. So keep yourself healthy, Topeka Sands." He pulled down his hat, let out a Kansas yell, and goaded Gussie into a dust-high gallop.

* * *

While Billy had been on the Rancho El Norte, he had been friendly, behaved himself, and the men that rode with him liked the new hand. He made a point of not wearing his guns, as the pearl-handled Colts would have created attention and provoked men into asking questions. On the ranch the men called him Arnie Briggs.

"Howdy, Arnie, how's it going?" Casey Wills asked.

"Not bad. All things being equal. How's it with you?"

"Oh fine, I guess."

"You don't sound sure, how come?"

"I'm worried."

"About what?"

"I've decided to go home, back to Texas to see my ma, she's dying. I've told the *jefe* and he's willing to hold my job for me if'n I get back before the next cattle drive. But that's not all that's bothering me."

Billy stood and stretched. "What is?"

"Money," Casey said.

"Money? That's nothing new. C'mon, spit it out."

"Maybe you haven't heard, there's going to be a shooting contest Sunday. The men have all chipped in to make first place worthwhile."

"How much is worthwhile?" Billy looked interested.

"Hundred dollars is what I heard."

"This Sunday?"

"Sure thing. I'd sure like to win because if'n I don't I'll not have enough train fare to get back to Texas. Damn, I wanna go home."

"How good are you with a gun?"

"Fair, I guess."

"Where I come from, fair don't cut it. Is this shooting match a contest for the fastest draw or who gets most points for targets? Which is it?"

"Both. I'm not too fast. But I can hit the target. They'll have a target shoot first, followed by a contest for the fastest draw."

Billy glanced down at his holster. "Is that the gun you're going to use?"

"That's the one."

"Can I see it?"

Casey pulled the .45 and handed it to him, butt first.

Billy balanced it in his right hand, then his left. "Follow me over behind the barn. I'd like to see you shoot."

Behind the barn, Casey glanced around. "This looks good. I'll set up a few cans." He walked toward the fence. He returned and stood alongside Billy. "You want me to try a fast draw?"

"No. Just take your time and hit three cans."

Casey aimed and fired. He got the first two and missed the third. He carried out another can.

"Let me have your gun." Billy held out his hand. He took the gun and aimed. Squeezed the trigger. The can jumped off the fence. "This gun shoots to the left, too much to suit me. You have another?"

"Nope. Only one."

"Okay," said Billy. "Now draw and shoot when I signal. I'll put up another can."

Casey waited. Billy took out a red handkerchief.

"When I drop it, draw." He stood back away from Casey.

On signal, Casey's hand dropped and he fired twice. The first shot missed the can.

Billy winced. "You fumbled so on the draw, your hand shook enough to make you miss. Casey, you're right. You're fair. Fair won't win the contest. Take off your belt."

Slowly, Casey unbuckled. "Here ya are."

"Put up three."

Casey obliged.

The gun was in Billy's hand before he heard the shots. Two cans went out of sight. The third can spun high and Billy's pistol was back in the holster before the can hit the ground.

"Ma God, Arnie." Casey stared. "You said it shoots to the left?"

"Too much." Billy glanced around. "I'll make you a deal, pal."

"What kind?"

"You want to win the hundred?"

"Worse as hell I do."

"Come over here."

The cowboy stood by him.

"First, you keep your mouth shut." Billy looked around. "I'll enter the contest if you'll do something for me."

"Why hell, Arnie, you'll win."

"That's the idea. If you do what I ask, fifty's yours."

"What do I have to do?"

"I'll tell you later. But for now, *show up*, Sunday. Ya hear?"

•5•

ETHAN HAD STAYED at Rancho El Norte two weeks. He and Sabonda had taken walks, and danced in the moonlight. Sabonda had sung love songs. They had played with colts, taken long rides together across the ranch. A warm closeness developed such as neither had experienced before. Ethan met Sabonda's friends and they enjoyed being with him.

One evening before dinner, Sabonda invited Ethan to join her for a glass of wine. They had a view of the corral where they watched the vaqueros breaking two-year-olds.

After sipping his wine, he told her how, as a young boy, his father had taught him to shoot a pistol. And of how he wished his mother and father hadn't argued over things he hadn't understood as a child.

Her mind began to wander. She wanted to tell him so

many things, but dared not. Her father's confidential plans would interest Ethan but—what if he thought she was trying to capture his love by offering him a financial reward?

Her father had always wanted a son, especially now when the coalition he had formed was prepared to open the San Joaquin Valley. She knew he wanted someone to take over the thousands of acres owned by the family. If elected to the United States Congress, he would have to spend a great deal of time in Washington.

She wanted to tell Ethan of her feelings about children . . .

"Sabonda, are you listening?" Ethan touched her hand. "Are you all right?"

Embarrassed, she reddened. "Yes, yes, of course, about your father dying so young." He didn't continue. His father was still alive; it was his mother who had deserted him when he was sixteen. Luckily the maid interrupted to announce that dinner was served.

The maid had set the table beautifully with flowers in the center. The spacious dining room appeared twice its size when only two were at a table capable of seating twenty. He wondered how Sabonda would react if she lived in a smaller home that he might someday afford. This hacienda, with all its rooms, furniture, cooks, maids, the richness of everything—she had known this style of living always.

"May I offer you a whiskey?" she said, taking his hand.

"I'd enjoy that."

"Good. I'll have one with you."

"I'll be damned," Ethan said, dabbing a napkin to his mouth.

•6•

IT WAS A beautiful afternoon. The flowers had bloomed and a soft, fresh breeze drifted over the Santa Lucias. For a picnic, Sabonda was taking Ethan to her favorite spot near Concho Creek where a hundred oak trees shaded the green pastures. She had brought her guitar because Ethan loved to hear her play and sing Spanish songs.

It would take an hour's ride to reach the creek.

"Ethan, there's so many things, feelings I've never told anyone. I've been in darkness so long, I want a chance to live in sunshine. I want to be married to a man who loves me, have children."

He listened quietly. Perhaps today was the day to probe deeply inside each other and find out what things they truly shared. Sabonda guided him to a shady rise, the grassy spot she wanted, and after stepping down, she untied her saddlebag and took out a bottle of wine. She arranged the blanket, then walked over to where he still sat on Sage, and took his hand and held it against her cheek.

•7•

STANDING BESIDE THE corral, Jorge ran his finger down a list of names and stopped at one. "*Hola*, Monty," he yelled to his friend, "you seen that hombre with the long yellow hair?"

Monty reined the Appaloosa close to the rail. "Come to think of it, I have. Guess I forgot to tell ya, *jefe*, it was the day after Mr. Sands rode in. That fella Arnie Briggs packed and jumped on his horse. Rode off the ranch like he'd been shot. All he said was to tell you he'd send for his pay. Never knew a drifter to leave without his pay, have you?"

"No. That's all he said?"

"That's it."

"Good riddance. Never trusted him. Something about his eyes and that queer smile of his."

Monty coiled his lariat. "Hold on, boss, there's something else about that hombre."

"Say it."

"Last week in Paso Robles I stopped in the sheriff's office. He showed me the latest Wanted posters. I swear I had seen that hombre's face. His hair was dark, and not as long, but I thought it looked like him. I could have been mistaken."

"What'd the sheriff have to say?"

"He's wanted in Kansas and New Mexico, for robbery and killing a man."

"Kinda strange, Monty, sending a poster to California for a man wanted back in that part of the country."

"Maybe not. According to the sheriff, he was last seen in Santa Barbara, at the mission."

"*Extraño*, very strange indeed."

"How come?" Monty asked.

"The only time I talked with him, he told me that a padre in Santa Barbara said he'd had many visitors from Kansas like him, and had to bury one of them. He didn't say what it was about, but he acted so peculiar. This is when I started to watch this gringo, how his eyes fixed on our señora, and I didn't like what I saw. I want you to ask the vaqueros if he talked with any of them. If he did, come to me pronto."

"Say, boss, how'd you like the shooting he did last Sunday? Won the match hands down. He's fast."

"*Sí*, that's what bothers me." Fermín turned away. "Remember what I said, Monty, pronto."

•8•

"THIS IS OUR finest wine." Sabonda held the bottle up, allowing the sun to show its clarity.

Ethan rested atop Sage, pressing his weight against the saddle bow. She put her hands on his leg and pouting, she glanced up into his bewildered face. Theatrically she tossed her head, swinging her dark, long hair across her back. "Señor Sands, there you sit, on your magnificent horse, pretending I don't attract you. Maybe you're afraid? I see *me* in your eyes; you stare at my lips."

Suddenly she stepped back, took a deep breath, and put her hands on her hips. "Ethan Sands, handsome *caballero, get down off that horse*! Make a liar out of me, that is, *if you can*."

Ethan's jaw dropped. Paralyzed, he stared at her. He didn't feel his boots touch the earth, he barely breathed. She was in his arms.

"My lovely sweet lady, sure as bullets don't cry—I'm gonna try!" He pulled her closer. "I have ne—"

Ten yards in front of him, out of a veil of smoke, stood a solitary man, his back to the sun, silhouetted in his black leather coat. Long blond hair dangled beneath his black sombrero. Billy Largo pointed the .45 directly at Sabonda.

"Okay, Topeka, who's it gonna be—you or her?"

Ethan panicked: his gun belt lay across the bed.

"Sands, I've waited for this day when I'd pump slugs in your gut and watch blood run down your leg. But seeing her, I've changed my mind." He moved closer. "I want you to ache like I did when you cut down my sister. Remember her, the dark-haired girl in the bank with the birthmark on her cheek? I looked at them propped in their coffins, cold, drained white, eyes like lead. So, I want you to have something you'll remember, even when you're dead."

He stuck his barrel underneath the brim of Sabonda's hat. "Damn, she's an inviting hunk of love, a woman who has worn the white flower of a shameless life. And I can tell by them torrid eyes she's got it for you, mister dead man. It's sorrowful you can't share it. But where I'm sending you, woman-killer, there ain't much of nuthin' to share." He shoved his .45 in Ethan's face, the barrel across his cheek. "Cold, isn't it?"

Largo had figured that if he stayed around Rancho El Norte, sooner or later Ethan would return. Casey had been on the lookout for Ethan. And the day he arrived, Billy knew the time to kill him was at hand.

Billy turned toward Sabonda. "Sexy woman, untie the rope on his saddle, and use it to tie his feet and hands. I'll check your work. Now, woman!"

With trembling hands, Sabonda untied the rope.

"Lovely, honey, lovely. Sweetheart, you're a mouthwatering kind of woman that'll tighten a man's flesh. So when you've got him tied, you and I are going to show him everything about the pleasures he's going to miss. Start with his feet. Sands, on your belly!"

Sabonda squatted next to Ethan. She placed the rope around his boots and looped it back to hog-tie his hands. On his belly Ethan had his ear to the ground listening to a rumble that made his heart pound. God, he said to himself, let it be horses.

"Ethan, I love you so much. Hold on," she whispered. "God is with us."

She looked up at Billy, who stood over her snarling, his narrowed eyes shooting beams of hate and vengeance that screwed his face into the devil's calling card.

"Move aside, woman, lemme look. I don't wanna get cheated."

Billy tightened her knots, squeezing the flesh until it wrinkled and turned white.

He leaned next to Ethan's face. "You can watch me take off her clothes, a piece at a time. Don't want you to miss a thing, Topeka. I'm good and steady, and I'll show you how it's done."

Her hand over her mouth, Sabonda backed away. Slowly, Billy moved toward her.

"Now, sweet woman, I want this just right. *Lady, I want it all.*"

•9•

CLAWS OF RAGE gouged Ethan's skin. Checking where Billy was looking, he listened again. The rumbling seemed closer.

"Sands, she's an appetizing woman." He grabbed her silver belt buckle and yanked her close to him.

"Are you getting in the mood, honey? Good! So am I."

Ethan tugged vainly at the ropes: the image of his gun lying on the bed battered his brain. He had to stall Billy, any way he could.

"Largo, shoot me. Leave her alone. She's got nothing to do with how you feel. You're making a dumb mistake—like the one that killed your sister—that's why she's dead."

"What'n hell you mean, *a mistake*?"

"In the bank, she had forgotten the balcony that let me get the drop on her. It was dumb, Billy. Y'all should have never let her pull that robbery. But you, Billy, you can be smart. You can kill me and get rich. It's easy."

"What kinda bull-lies you trying to hang on me?" He pulled out his watch. "Three minutes, Sands. Make 'em count. The lady is making me horny, and this time, *I'm on the balcony*!"

Ethan spoke deliberately. "Sabonda's father has more money than you can steal. He'd give a fortune to keep her alive."

"So?"

"You kidnap us. I'll show you where to hide. Write a ransom note, tie it to my dead body, throw me over Sage, and he'll find the ranch. I'll even tell you how to get the ransom without getting killed. Think about what I've said."

Ethan saw his words scratching inside Billy's head. Billy lifted Sabonda's chin. "I love the way your lips tremble, woman, but your lover has got an interesting thought. We'd have time to really enjoy ourselves."

He snapped his head around. "But I ain't got plans for hanging in California, Sands. Killing you my way is quick, and I'll be gone. I ain't buying."

He took a tug at Ethan's ropes.

"Say, speaking of getting caught, you recall when I rode with Charlie Spoon? You shot Charlie and ended our friendship. So what I'm of a mind to do is, I'm gonna prop you up so you can think about the past while I give ya a taste of the present. Oh, Sands, you're gonna hurt, your guts are gonna crawl."

Desperate, Ethan needed more time.

Ethan's eyes scanned the dust over the hills. Then he winked at Sabonda.

"Trying to tell her something, are ya, Sands?"

"Look at the hills, up there behind you."

Billy's hands touched his .45, as he checked over his shoulder.

Riding over the hill in a wide formation like banditos, with rifle barrels glistening, large sombreros pulled down over their eyes, thirty of Rancho El Norte's Mexican vaqueros came toward them. Jorge was at the head. Ethan had felt the horse's hooves striking the earth.

"Billy, if you feel lucky, get on your horse and make a try. But, you dumb son of a bitch, you're going to die a slow, agonizing death. The Mexicans will bury you in sand up to your chin. Oh, a word from Sabonda and you'll live!"

Ethan stared at the riders. A cloud of dust rose behind them as thirty horses skidded to a stop. Jorge slid down from the snorting palomino while every pair of eyes fixed on Billy. Thirty rifles were raised, aiming directly at his chest. Jorge's spurs jangled as he walked over to Billy. Kicking his gun away, he spat on Billy's face.

"*Hombre, sin duda alguna*—without a doubt, gringo, you're a damned fool." Jorge's barrel touched under Billy's nose, around his cheeks, then jabbed his hat off so it rolled in the dust. "You wear a sombrero, and, *cerdo*, you pig, *that insults me and my vaqueros*." He pulled out a knife and flung it, pinning the sombrero to the ground. Sabonda stepped up close to Billy, so he could feel her breath: "*Adiós!*" she said, in her deep, sultry voice.

Largo, a rope around his neck and hands tied behind his back, walked behind Jorge's palomino. And by not running he had saved himself, only for the pleasure of whatever the Mexicans had in mind.

•10•

ETHAN KISSED SABONDA softly on both cheeks and held her close.

When the trembling stopped, she placed her hands on his shoulders and leaned back. "Who, and what, is Billy Largo?"

"Something evil from my past. Actually, I only met him once. He was related to members of the gang that robbed my bank. During the holdup, I shot his nephew and sister."

"Then what he said was true?"

"Every word." He stroked her hair. "That and other killings is why I left Kansas and came to California. Like you, I've lived in darkness and it's no way to live." He used his handkerchief to wipe her face.

"You didn't wear your gun, why?"

"I took my gun belt off yesterday. Guess I was hasty. But it's worked out for the best."

He thought for a moment. "What will Jorge's vaqueros do to Billy?"

A haunting smile crossed her lips. "I'll not describe what I know. They could kill him, but perhaps not. Largo will never think of rape, or bother either of us again."

Ethan reached for the wine. "Here's to us."

Sage and Sabonda's mare stood with their heads facing in opposite directions. Tails swinging lazily, brushing one another. A serene and gentle sight . . . anywhere one might look.

BESTSELLERS FROM TOR

☐ 51195-6 **BREAKFAST AT WIMBLEDON** $3.99
     Jack Bickham   Canada $4.99

☐ 52497-7 **CRITICAL MASS** $5.99
     David Hagberg   Canada $6.99

☐ 85202-9 **ELVISSEY** $12.95
     Jack Womack   Canada $16.95

☐ 51612-5 **FALLEN IDOLS** $4.99
     Ralph Arnote   Canada $5.99

☐ 51716-4 **THE FOREVER KING** $5.99
     Molly Cochran & Warren Murphy   Canada $6.99

☐ 50743-6 **PEOPLE OF THE RIVER** $5.99
     Michael Gear & Kathleen O'Neal Gear   Canada $6.99

☐ 51198-0 **PREY** $5.99
     Ken Goddard   Canada $6.99

☐ 50735-5 **THE TRIKON DECEPTION** $5.99
     Ben Bova & Bill Pogue   Canada $6.99

Buy them at your local bookstore or use this handy coupon:
Clip and mail this page with your order.

Publishers Book and Audio Mailing Service
P.O. Box 120159, Staten Island, NY 10312-0004

Please send me the book(s) I have checked above. I am enclosing $ _____
(Please add $1.25 for the first book, and $.25 for each additional book to cover postage and handling.
Send check or money order only—no CODs.)

Name _____

Address _____

City _____ State/Zip _____

Please allow six weeks for delivery. Prices subject to change without notice.

WESTERN ADVENTURE FROM TOR

☐	58459-7	THE BAREFOOT BRIGADE *Douglas Jones*	$4.95 Canada $5.95
☐	52303-2	THE GOLDEN SPURS *Western Writers of America*	$4.99 Canada $5.99
☐	51315-0	HELL AND HOT LEAD/GUN RIDER *Norman A. Fox*	$3.50 Canada $4.50
☐	51169-7	HORNE'S LAW *Jory Sherman*	$3.50 Canada $4.50
☐	58875-4	THE MEDICINE HORN *Jory Sherman*	$3.99 Canada $4.99
☐	58329-9	NEW FRONTIERS I *Martin H. Greenberg & Bill Pronzini*	$4.50 Canada $5.50
☐	58331-0	NEW FRONTIERS II *Martin H. Greenberg & Bill Pronzini*	$4.50 Canada $5.50
☐	52461-6	THE SNOWBLIND MOON *John Byrne Cooke*	$5.99 Canada $6.99
☐	58184-9	WHAT LAW THERE WAS *Al Dempsey*	$3.99 Canada $4.99

Buy them at your local bookstore or use this handy coupon:
Clip and mail this page with your order.

Publishers Book and Audio Mailing Service
P.O. Box 120159, Staten Island, NY 10312-0004

Please send me the book(s) I have checked above. I am enclosing $ _____
(Please add $1.25 for the first book, and $.25 for each additional book to cover postage and handling.
Send check or money order only—no CODs.)

Name _____
Address _____
City _____ State/Zip _____
Please allow six weeks for delivery. Prices subject to change without notice.

MORE WESTERN
ADVENTURE FROM TOR

☐ 58457-0 **ELKHORN TAVERN** $4.95
    Douglas Jones Canada $5.95

☐ 58453-8 **GONE THE DREAMS AND DANCING** $3.95
    Douglas Jones Canada $4.95

☐ 52242-7 **HOPALONG CASSIDY** $4.99
    Clarence E. Mulford Canada $5.99

☐ 51359-2 **THE RAINBOW RUNNER** $4.99
    Cunningham Canada $5.99

☐ 58455-4 **ROMAN** $4.95
    Douglas Jones Canada $5.95

☐ 51318-5 **SONG OF WOVOKA** $4.99
    Earl Murray Canada $5.99

☐ 58463-5 **WEEDY ROUGH** $4.95
    Douglas Jones Canada $5.95

☐ 52142-0 **WIND RIVER** $3.99
    Dick Wheeler Canada $4.99

☐ 58989-0 **WOODSMAN** $3.95
    Don Wright Canada $4.95

Buy them at your local bookstore or use this handy coupon:
Clip and mail this page with your order.

Publishers Book and Audio Mailing Service
P.O. Box 120159, Staten Island, NY 10312-0004

Please send me the book(s) I have checked above. I am enclosing $ _____
(Please add $1.25 for the first book, and $.25 for each additional book to cover postage and handling.
Send check or money order only—no CODs.)

Name _____

Address _____

City _____ State/Zip _____

Please allow six weeks for delivery. Prices subject to change without notice.

WESTERN DOUBLES

☐	50529-8	AVALANCHE/THE KIDNAPPING OF ROSETA UVALDO	Grey	$3.50 Canada $4.50
☐	50547-6	FRONTIER FURY/WHITE MAN'S ROAD	Henry	$3.50 Canada $4.50
☐	51617-6	KIDNAPPING OF COLLIE THE YOUNGER/ OUTLAWS FROM PALOUSE	Grey	$3.50 Canada $4.50
☐	50542-5	LONE WOLF OF DRYGULCH TRAIL/ MORE PRECIOUS THAN GOLD	Drago	$3.50 Canada $4.50
☐	50544-1	THE LONGRIDERS/THE HARD ONE	Prescott	$3.50 Canada $4.50
☐	50540-9	LOOK BEHIND EVERY HILL/ THE BIG TROUBLE	Frazee	$3.50 Canada $4.50
☐	50536-0	PROSPECTOR'S GOLD/CANYON WALLS	Grey	$3.50 Canada $4.50
☐	50532-8	RED BLIZZARD/THE OLDEST MAIDEN LADY IN NEW MEXICO	Fisher	$3.50 Canada $4.50
☐	50526-3	THE RIDERS OF CARNE COVE/THE LAST COWMAN OF LOST SQUAW VALLEY	Overholser	$3.50 Canada $4.50
☐	50534-4	THAT BLOODY BOZEMAN TRAIL/ STAGECOACH WEST!	Bonham	$3.50 Canada $4.50
☐	51316-9	WILD WAYMIRE/GUN THIS MAN DOWN	Patten	$3.50 Canada $4.50

Buy them at your local bookstore or use this handy coupon:
Clip and mail this page with your order.

Publishers Book and Audio Mailing Service
P.O. Box 120159, Staten Island, NY 10312-0004

Please send me the book(s) I have checked above. I am enclosing $ _____
(Please add $1.25 for the first book, and $.25 for each additional book to cover postage and handling.
Send check or money order only—no CODs.)

Name _____
Address _____
City _____ State/Zip _____
Please allow six weeks for delivery. Prices subject to change without notice.